Two Feeders, No Waiting

by Ron Ostlund

PublishAmerica
Baltimore

© 2009 by Ron Ostlund.
All rights reserved. No part of this book may be reproduced, stored in a retrieval system or transmitted in any form or by any means without the prior written permission of the publishers, except by a reviewer who may quote brief passages in a review to be printed in a newspaper, magazine or journal.

First printing

All characters in this book are fictitious, and any resemblance to real persons, living or dead, is coincidental.

PublishAmerica has allowed this work to remain exactly as the author intended, verbatim, without editorial input.

ISBN: 1-60836-243-4
PUBLISHED BY PUBLISHAMERICA, LLLP
www.publishamerica.com
Baltimore

Printed in the United States of America

In loving memory of Whitey, an albino squirrel and long time resident of the front lawn at the Nelson Gallery, whose idyllic life was cut short when he thought *Guard With Weapon Drawn* was part of an outdoor exhibit.

List of Stories

Can't We All Just Get Along? 9
    Part 1: Sylvia 9
    Part 2: Getting to Know You 21

The Mighty Squirrelitzer 35

50 Ways to Lose Your Squirrels 51
    Part 1: Faux Seeds 51
    Part 2: Conquering Mr. Fling-Um 62
    Part 3: The Best De-Fence 73

Little Sherman 91

Turning Pro 107

Incident at Big Rock 127

The Seed-O-Rama Show 143

Where There Are No Seeds the Squirrels Perish 165

Playing Chess with the Man 185

Two Feeders, No Waiting 205

SquirrelFest 229
    Part 1: When the Acorn Is Ripe 229
    Part 2: It Will Fall from the Tree 242

Can't We All Just Get Along?

De Boom. Boom. De Boom.

"Can't you hear it?" She looked into a cloudless sky and ruled out thunder as the cause for the noise. She'd seen no flash so she knew it wasn't the report from an explosion.

Roscoe put on his bathrobe and joined her. "It sounds like it's coming from over there, by the Clearing." She put a paw on her forehead to shade her eyes.

De Boom. Boom. Boom. De Boom.

Roscoe heard it this time and as Chairman of the Committee for the Protection of Neighborhood Resources he knew he needed to find out what was going on. He was half way down his tree when Penny Sue called out he was still wearing his bathrobe.

He didn't hear her, his thoughts were focused on what was causing the noise.

He was forced to slow down when he reached the path to the Clearing. It was crowded with strangers carrying pennants and banners that read, *"Watch Out For The Marching Cougars,"* and, *"Pardon Our Band Attitude!"* They all seemed to be in a hurry to get to the Clearing.

He stepped in line and moved with the crowd until it turned left and took the path to the field next to the school playground.

He saw Edgar, standing on the platform outside the meeting room, welcoming the visitors and giving directions.

He could see members of the Committee collecting seeds and stamping a purple **P** on the back of the paws of those who'd **P**aid.

Roscoe climbed the steps and stood next to Edgar. "What's going on? When I checked last night there was nothing on today's schedule that would account for this. And, unless there was a meeting while I was gone, I don't remember voting on anything that would bring visitors to the Community."

Edgar smiled and waved to someone in the crowd. "It's the marching band competition Roscoe. And no, it was not approved by the Committee but you were gone, Seed Man had moved, and…" Edgar shrugged like the answer was obvious.

"And?" What was obvious to Edgar remained hidden from Roscoe.

"And I thought, why wait until you come back? Why not be proactive? Why not…" he patted his back pocket, removed a crumpled sheet of paper, and said, "read this." He handed the paper to Roscoe.

**"Think Your Marching Band Can't Be Beat?
Prove It At The Community Of Abner Parade Ground.
Saturday at high noon.
There's only one sheriff in this town and
The Marching Demons of Abner
are going to shoot you down."**

"I put the part in about the sheriff because of the high noon reference." Edgar pointed proudly to the bottom of the page.

"I made the connection Edgar." Roscoe got it okay, but he also got that Edgar should have known better then to do something like this on his own. He was a former Chairman of the Committee and knew when someone got a harebrained idea and struck out on his own it always ended in disaster.

"How much?" Roscoe asked.

"I'm sorry?" Edgar scratched his head, not sure if Roscoe was asking how much he was charging the spectators or how many marching bands had signed up.

"Seeds. Profit. How much have you made?"

"Well, it's a little early to know exactly…"

"Generally? Approximately? Make a guess?"

Edgar put a paw under his chin as if in deep thought. "Well, there's advertising costs of course. And renting the field. Insurance and having a member of the safety team present in case there's an accident." Edgar looked at Roscoe as he added up the amount required for putting on a marching band competition.

"How about clean up? Crowds that size leave a lot of trash behind."

"Clean up?" It was a new thought for Edgar.

"See, that's why it's better for a Committee to work on a project this size. Someone would have thought about cleaning up when the competition is over and built that into the fee."

They stood on the platform and watched the last of the spectators hurry toward the parade field.

De Boom. Boom. Boom. De Boom.

"They're about to start," Edgar pulled away and started down the steps, "I'd better get out there."

Roscoe put a paw to his ear, the noise of the marching bands was so loud he couldn't hear what he was saying.

Edgar pointed to himself, then the parade field, and made walking motions with his fingers.

Roscoe saw Lloyd, the owner of *The Squirrel's Nest*, wearing ear muffs, walk across the Clearing with a pot of walnut tea and a plate full of nut cake to sell to the visitors.

Roscoe shook his head and mumbled, "That's another thing Edgar hadn't thought of," when he saw members of the Community walking around with their paws pressed against their ears. He knew someone would be blamed for the noise coming from the parade field and he was sure it wouldn't be Edgar.

Later in the day Darin and Roscoe stood at one end of the conference table while the rest of the Committee sat around the other three sides.

"Look," Roscoe explained, "I know we're a little short of seeds but it's way too early to panic. Our experience with the marching bands this morning can't be…" He stopped when the door to the meeting room opened and Webster, the librarian, entered. He was followed by a small group of strangers.

"And this is the meeting room where all of the important business of the Community is conducted," he spoke quietly as he walked backwards and urged the group to keep up. He turned and was surprised to see the room was in use. Rather than apologize and leave, he whispered, "We're in luck, a Committee meeting is in progress. Let's move closer and see if we can hear what's being discussed." The group he was leading edged closer to the table.

"Webster, could I see you outside for a minute?" Roscoe tucked a paw under Webster's elbow and hurried him out of the room. As they were leaving he heard Darin introduce himself to one of the visitors.

TWO FEEDERS, NO WAITING

"What's going on?" Roscoe stood on the platform at the top of the steps with his face inches from Webster's.

"Seeds?" is all Webster could say after being hustled out of the room by an obviously upset Roscoe. "It's about seeds." He held up a small bag that Roscoe was sure couldn't contain more than a half a dozen seeds.

"I don't get it. Why does everyone think we're about to starve?" Roscoe shook his head. "I'll be the first to admit our reserve supply is lower than usual but we don't gain that much by leading tours or hosting marching band competitions."

Webster looked at the ground. It dawned on him the small amount he'd received for leading the tour would barely cover the cost of the advertisement he'd placed in *The Abner Echo,* the local newspaper. What little was left over would have absolutely no impact on the food shortage facing the Community.

"I thought it would…" His words trailed off, he couldn't think of anything else to say.

"Look, I'm sure you meant well, but the next time you get an idea like this run it past the Committee will you?" He patted Webster's shoulder letting him know everything was okay between them.

When they returned to the meeting room Darin was letting each of the guests take a turn sitting at the Chairman's desk.

Webster got the groups attention and announced they would be going to the library now. As they were leaving the Committee members waved and thanked them for stopping by.

Marvin pushed his way past the visitors, spotted Roscoe, and hurried across the room. He spoke quietly so only Roscoe could hear. "Our seed worries are over my friend." He looked over his shoulder to make sure no one was listening.

Roscoe shook his head and told Marvin. "If this is another crazy scheme like the last group that was in here…"

"I'm talking about a feeder tube full of seeds Roscoe. I'm talking about a feeder pole smack dab in the middle of a yard." He stepped back and smiled, "And, last but not least, I'm talking about a 100%, slam dunk, bona fide replacement for Seed Man."

While Roscoe and Marvin were talking some on the Committee were discussing the possibility of having guests stop by the meeting more often. One of them suggested having a, *Get To Know your Committee Night* but all conversation stopped when they heard Marvin mention Seed Man's name.

Roscoe pointed to an empty chair at the conference table. "Have a seat Marvin and tell them what you just told me."

It was supposed to be a secret trip by the Committee to investigate Marvin's report of a new source of seeds. They left the meeting room, said "Have a good day," to one another and acted like they were going to their nests for a nap but, when they regrouped around Roscoe's tree, half the Community was waiting for them.

Roscoe shot a look at Marvin and asked, "Who did you tell?"

"Only Webster. That's it." Marvin was embarrassed to see so many from the Community gathered there. He scratched his head and mumbled, "I may have said something to Jules," and followed that with, "possibly Sparky. But that's it, honest."

"Well what's done is..." Roscoe started to move on but stopped when he heard Marvin mumble, "I think I mentioned it to Edgar."

Roscoe sighed. He should have known better than to try to keep a secret from the Community. He'd hoped the Committee would be able to check out the feeder, and make sure it was safe before letting the rest of the Community know about it. From now on, he decided, if he wanted to keep something a secret, he'd stand on the platform outside the meeting room and tell everyone in the Clearing, "We're going on a scouting trip to check out a new source of seeds. Feel free to join us." He was sure if he did, they would ignore him and go on about their business. He'd learned from bitter experience that secrets and Community members were a lethal combination.

As the search committee was preparing to leave, Penny Sue asked if it would be okay if a few members of the Women's Auxiliary joined them.

When Roscoe grudgingly said he guessed it was okay, she and several of her friends said they thought it would be fun to turn the outing into a picnic. He tried to explain this was not that kind of outing, that it was a difficult and dangerous trip through hostile territory to check out what would probably turn out to be a false alarm.

But, before he could say anything, they were gone, preparing the things they would need for the picnic. Someone suggested they should do this every year to celebrate the day Marvin discovered the new feeder.

"We could call it *FeederFest*. It will be like *SquirrelFest* but without floats," someone said enthusiastically. Immediately he was bombarded with questions about why he was leaving out floats and if he thought the Committee would declare it an official holiday so they could take time off from work and get paid for it.

A half an hour later Penny Sue said everything was ready and they all followed Marvin along the path that leads to the Big Rock, the monument that marked the boundary between their Community and the Community of Ben. They looked longingly as they walked past Seed Man's vacant house and remembered the good times they'd had there.

Finally, Marvin held up a paw, indicating they should stop. Several in back making the case for why floats should be included in *FeederFest*, missed his signal, and plowed into the back of those in front of them. An argument started over who's fault it was and got so loud Roscoe had to run back and tell them to quiet down.

When he returned, Marvin pointed to a large backyard, lined on three sides by a chain-link fence. In the middle of the yard was a pole and on the pole was an arm that held two feeder tubes.

"Let's check it out," Marvin whispered.

Roscoe couldn't hear what he said. The noise of the crowd behind him grew as they asked one another if that was the yard Marvin had been talking about or if it was the one next to it. Several had trouble seeing and tried to move closer but were stopped by those in front of them. Angry words were exchanged and a scuffle broke out as those in back fought to improve their position.

Marvin and Roscoe had only taken a few steps toward the fence when they heard someone say, "Hey! Hey! Hey! Where do you think you're

Community check it out. If he's wrong, we'll leave. If however he's right, we're willing to negotiate." He lifted both paws, shrugged, and asked, "Fair enough?"

"Yea, I hear what you're saying but we can't make that kind of decision on our own." Melvin thought if he stalled long enough they'd lose interest and leave. "We've got to talk this over with our Chairman."

"No problem," Roscoe told him, "as you can see, we anticipated something like this so we brought our lunch. Take as much time as you need, we have all afternoon."

"Great." Gus said without much enthusiasm.

As he and Melvin walked away Roscoe heard them say, "Can you believe the little pip squeak with the glasses had the nerve to say I don't speak right?"

Gus chuckled, shook his head, and told him, "You sound good to me."

Penny Sue and Roscoe we're visiting with friends after finishing off the last of the nut cake she'd brought when Marvin tapped him on the shoulder, pointed toward the evergreen, and said, "Looks like we've got company." Standing near it was a new person. In back of him he saw Melvin and Gus, and behind them was an entire Community.

The new person walked confidently toward them. "Russell, I'm Chairman Max and the boys here tell me we have a little problem."

"It's Roscoe Max, Chairman Roscoe of the Community of Abner." Roscoe moved away from the others and stood in front of Max.

Max chuckled. He knew his name was Roscoe but he thought he'd see how he'd respond if he called him something else.

"Chairman huh? They elect them kind of young in your Community don't they?" Max circled Roscoe, sizing him up. "So, why don't you and your merry band of picnickers pack up your stuff and leave?" Roscoe saw Max make a quick glance toward the feeder and then back to him.

"And why don't you pay back all the seeds you've eaten from the feeder tube on **our** side of the pole?" Roscoe crossed his arms defiantly over his chest.

TWO FEEDERS, NO WAITING

"You didn't know the feeder was here," Max leaned forward and thumped Roscoe's chest with his paw, "so we don't owe you nothing."

Roscoe brushed his paw away and did some chest thumping of his own. "But **you** knew one of the tubes was on our side. You knew the boundary between our Community is over there. Even a casual glance will show one of the feeder tubes is on our side of the line." He was not going to be pushed around by Max or anyone else with the fate of his Community hanging in the balance.

Max glanced at the feeder. When he turned back to Roscoe his demeanor had changed. He was no longer a bully protecting his territory but an embarrassed Committee Chairman looking for words to describe what he wanted to say. "The thing is," he spoke so softly Roscoe had to lean forward to hear him, "we have a problem."

"You mean you have a problem don't you?" Roscoe shot back.

Max seemed nervous. "No Chairman Roscoe, I mean we…" He didn't get to finish what he was going to say. A blast from the back of the house tore a chunk out of a tree limb above their heads. The group from Abner scattered while Melvin and Gus dove beneath the evergreen.

Roscoe ducked and ran for shelter behind the Big Rock. Max was a step behind him. When they were safely hidden behind the rock Max said, "It's a bird feeder Roscoe, and the guy wants to keep it that way. Birds only. No squirrels allowed. Got it? We haven't made it into his yard, let alone take seeds from the feeder."

"That's it? A fence and a human with a shotgun?" Roscoe laughed thinking Max couldn't be serious. "Is that all that's keeping you from going to the feeder?" Roscoe stayed low as he made his way back to the fence.

"Did I mention Sylvia?" Max asked as he followed close behind.

"Sylvia? Is that the human's wife?"

Max shook his head no.

"Let's see then with a name like Sylvia I'm picturing a cute little puppy or maybe a kitten." Roscoe looked at Max and chuckled. "Don't tell me big bad Gus is afraid of a little…"

While Roscoe was talking, Max reached above his head and shook the fence. At the sound of one chain rubbing against another, a small door at the back of the house flew open and the largest cat Roscoe had ever seen raced across the yard and slammed into the fence, inches from where he was standing. It's dark green eyes were dilated and trained on him. He could hear a low growl coming from deep inside the creature's enormous chest. He watched as she reached through an opening in the fence and tore away chunks of grass with her huge paw and sharp claws.

Roscoe smiled confidently when he looked over and saw Sparky making sketches in his notebook. "Chairman Max," he said as he turned to face him, "today is your lucky day."

Part 2: Getting to Know You

"So, how is this going to work?" Roscoe stood at the conference table along with the other members of the Committee.

On top of the table, was a scale model of the yard of the one they now called Bird Man because of his preference for birds at his feeder.

Sparky stood next to Roscoe holding a wooden pointer. Roscoe had invited Marvin, Jules, and Webster to join the Committee as they worked on what they voted to call, *Operation Big Cat*.

"Well," Sparky said as he reached across the table and aimed the pointer at the fence. "It looks like Sylvia didn't know we were there until Chairman Max shook the fence. So, I guess step one is to get over the fence without touching it."

"How about the shotgun?" Roscoe loved thinking about problems like this as much as Sparky enjoyed solving them. They were the perfect blend of two different ways to look at a situation. Sparky used the detached, scientific approach while Roscoe relied on intuition and raw emotion. It was obvious Max and his followers lacked the brain power the Community of Abner had in abundance.

"He has to leave the house sometime, so we place a look out here," he pointed to a place in the yard next to Bird Man's house. "When he leaves, whoever is stationed there let's us know he's gone."

"Are you thinking about doing this during the day or at night?" Darin asked as he walked around the table trying to get a better look at where the scout would hide.

"We couldn't see his signal at night and can't risk making any noise," Sparky shrugged. "If I had more time I suppose I could work something out electronically but…" He stood for a moment thinking about various ways to transmit an electronic signal.

"Sparks?" Roscoe said quietly.

"What? Oh, sorry." He shook his head trying to get back to his answer to the Sylvia problem. "With our current seed situation we don't have time for anything too complicated, so our first attempt should be during the day." He looked around the table and the Committee members nodded that's what they were thinking.

"How do we get over the fence without touching it? None of us can jump that high." Webster had squatted down and was looking at the model. "Is it really that tall? The fence I mean. I don't remember…"

"According to my notes, yes it's that tall, plus or minus an inch or two." Sparky opened his notebook and flipped to the page he was looking for. "Six feet six inches is what I wrote down. But that's approximate, I couldn't get close enough for an exact measurement." He closed his notebook and put it on the table. "We need to clear the top of the fence by at least six inches and that means a minimum height of seven feet."

Everyone looked at their neighbor, amazed at the thought of going over something that high without actually touching it. They could easily clear a three foot barrier but that was a long way from the kind of jump required to make it over Bird Man's fence.

While they were thinking about the fence, Sparky pulled a piece of paper from his back pack and pinned it to the wall. It showed a board balanced on top of a log. Arrows with notes beside them identified which was the board and which was the log.

"My first approach was to have two of you clasp your paws together and throw a third person over the fence but after a few attempts it proved too hard to control. You have to consider the strength of the throwers and the weight of the one being thrown."

He shrugged and looked around the table before saying, "I discarded that idea."

The members of the Committee sat back in their chairs overwhelmed by the knowledge that solving a problem like jumping over a seven foot fence was going to be a lot harder than they thought.

Roscoe smiled. He'd worked with Sparky long enough to know his style of problem solving; think of a solution, experiment, and then discard that idea for a better one. He knew it would take awhile to work through the options but when he finished, the answer would be worth waiting for.

Sparky walked them through two other ideas he'd discarded. One involved a pole and vaulting over the fence. The second required a slingshot and a willing volunteer. He'd rejected the first because of the danger of the pole falling on the fence and alerting Sylvia. The second, although effective, would take too long to set up. "So right now I'm leaning toward a catapult."

Someone laughed thinking he was joking.

One of the Committee members whispered to his neighbor if they decided to go that route they should call it the *Sylviaput*. The one he was talking to chuckled quietly.

Sparky either didn't hear the remark or chose to ignore it. "It's quick to set up and take down and easy to calculate the trajectory of the one going over the fence." He smiled and pinned a second piece of paper next to the first one. It showed the same catapult drawn on the first sheet but this time there was a stick figure on each end. He explained about force and the advantage of the fulcrum but most of what he said was wasted on the Committee because none of them had the technical background to understand what he was talking about. Down one side of the page he'd listed what he'd identified as Jumper 1 and Jumper 2 and the height and weight of each Committee member had been carefully tabulated. Next to the word *Conclusion* he'd written Roscoe's name and beside it his weight was listed as one pound three ounces.

"I figured you'd want to be the first one over the fence." He looked at Roscoe and raised an eye brow.

Roscoe nodded he agreed.

"Now that we have identified Jumper 1, we turn our attention to Jumper 2." Sparky studied the faces of those around him. "By adjusting the length of the board, almost anyone can get him over the fence."

Suddenly everyone was talking, making the case for why they should be Jumper 2. It didn't take long for them to figure out this was the glamour job with the maximum amount of glory and the minimum amount of risk.

Sparky waited for them to quiet down before continuing. "Once Roscoe is over the fence, he will nail the cat door shut, and with Sylvia out of the picture, we can help ourselves to as many seeds as we want. Since the cat can't get out and Bird Man is gone, climbing the fence is no longer a problem, so we can go over and back as often as we like."

The quiet that followed his solution to the, getting over the fence problem, was broken by enthusiastic applause from the Committee. Several shouted, "Bravo," and seemed relieved they weren't the one selected to go over the fence. "I thought you were joking when you mentioned the catapult but you know, it just might work." Darin said as he stepped back and took another look at the model.

"Okay, quiet down, we're not finished." Roscoe tapped the table with his paw to get their attention.

"Oh, right," Sparky was lost in thought, working on an alternate solution if the catapult idea didn't work out. "We'll need two volunteers to carry the board and another one to carry the log."

He looked in the disappointed faces of the Committee members. They wanted to be the one to send Roscoe over the fence, no one wanted to do the grunt work of getting the equipment there and back.

After what seemed like hours of wrangling, assignments were made, teams were organized to bring the seeds back to the storage bin, and a time was set to leave for Bird Man's yard.

Since Marvin was the one who found the feeder he was picked to be the lookout, watching from the edge of the yard for Bird Man to leave. He would go first, ahead of the others, so he'd have plenty of time to get in position.

The next morning the *Operation Big Cat* team gathered in the Clearing. Sparky was looking at two boards, trying to decide which one to use. He favored the longer one but it would be more difficult to maneuver around the sharp turns in the path to Bird Man's. He chose the shorter one but wished he could try them both before it was time to leave.

Roscoe is more of a big picture thinker and figured they could work out the details once they got to Bird Man's yard, no one knew how long they would have to wait before they got the signal from Marvin to move the equipment in place.

Marvin went over the signals to make sure he had them right; arm down meant Bird Man was there, arm up said he was gone. The team formed a circle around him, put their paws in the center, and hollered, "Seeds." They cheered as he took off for the hiding place.

Penny Sue insisted Roscoe take something to eat so she packed his lunch.

What was supposed to be a quiet departure for the *Operation Big Cat* team ended up being a noisy farewell since almost everyone in the Community had come to the Clearing to see them off.

When they finally left, an argument broke out about which was the best path to take. Roscoe settled the matter by saying they would follow the same route they took the day before since they were familiar with it. An uneasy quiet followed because several were upset the route they suggested hadn't been chosen.

When they got to the area near Bird Man's, Roscoe checked to make sure Marvin was in place. He was and he quickly lowered his arm indicating Bird Man was home.

The launch team placed the board on top of the log in an open space behind the Big Rock. Jules was given the job of keeping an eye on Marvin in case the situation with Bird Man changed.

Sparky touched Roscoe's shoulder and motioned for him to step on the end of the board. He'd been stretching, trying to loosen up before his trip over the fence. The one chosen to be Jumper 2 leapt in the air and landed on the board sending Roscoe high in the air. He came down in almost the exact place he'd been when he was warming up. He gave Sparky a questioning look but he was too busy writing in his notebook to see it. As far as Sparky was concerned, this was part of the process; you try something, consider the results, make adjustments, and try again. He slid the log closer to Roscoe, made a few quick measurements and, satisfied things looked right, motioned for them to try again.

This time Roscoe almost landed on top of the second jumper who'd done his part and was slapping paws as he walked past the other members of the launch team.

As he got to his feet Roscoe saw Gus and Melvin standing by the evergreen, pointing and laughing at them. He was about to go over and ask what they thought was so funny but stopped when Jules ran into the practice area. "He's gone. Bird Man, I mean, not Marvin. He's still there but, ah, the signal, arm raised. Bird Man. Gone." He was out of breath and excited that things were moving along so quickly. He looked at Roscoe hoping he hadn't left anything out.

"It's too soon. We're not ready." Sparky was concerned he hadn't had a chance to finalize the details of the catapult.

"We have to go now Sparky, we may not have another chance for a while." Roscoe was standing next to Sparky who was shaking his head no, they needed more time to get it right. "What if it doesn't work? What if you go to far? What if you hit the top of the fence on the way over? Sylvia will be on you before you know what's happened."

"It's launch time Sparky, give it your best shot." Roscoe motioned for the launch team to move the equipment closer to the fence.

Sparky slid the board in position, stepped off the distance to the fence, then moved the board forward an inch.

While he was writing the exact distance the catapult was from the fence, he heard a thud as Jumper 2 hit the board sending Roscoe sailing over his head and into the yard.

The launch team started to cheer but stopped when Jules told them to pipe down. It wouldn't do any good to get Roscoe over the fence if his teammates caused Sylvia to come out to see what was going on.

Roscoe ran across the yard as fast as he could. Since he hadn't had a chance to practice running while carrying a hammer and nails he discovered it was harder than he thought it would be. He felt a nail slip from his paw but he didn't have time to go back and look for it. He got to the cat door and with one blow drove in a nail, securing the door to the frame. He immediately heard Sylvia, realizing something was wrong, throw herself against the door, trying to get out and protect her yard.

Roscoe drove another nail in the door preventing any chance of the cat getting loose. He could hear her claws tearing at the thin piece of plywood that separated them.

With Sylvia temporarily confined and Bird Man out for the afternoon Roscoe went directly to the feeder. He climbed the pole and hung upside down from the feeder tube ready to taste the seeds to see if their hard work had been worth it. He'd just taken a bite out of a seed when he heard the cat door break in pieces. He watched with dread as Sylvia ran into the yard like a bull released into a ring, looking from side to side, ready to destroy whoever had tried to imprison her. She stopped in the middle of the yard and sniffed the air. She cocked her head to one side, listening for the slightest sound that would tell her where the intruder was. Then, as if something floating in the air tipped her off, she slowly turned her head and looked at Roscoe.

He was paralyzed with fear, hanging helplessly from the top arm of the feeder pole, unable to move.

Her growl was so ferocious members of the launch team, safely behind the fence, huddled together for comfort. Sylvia flew to the pole and leaped up, grabbing it half way to the top. She climbed to a place inches from Roscoe, pulled back an enormous paw, and prepared to strike when she heard a tap on the kitchen window.

She looked and saw the barrel of a rifle being pushed beneath the half open window. There was little doubt who the rifle was aimed at.

If cats could smile, Roscoe later explained to Sparky, Sylvia did as she slowly backed down the pole and sat obediently at the bottom, waiting for what was left of his wounded body to fall to the ground.

Roscoe was sure this was it, he'd tempted fate one too many times. He glanced quickly to the side of the yard and saw Marvin with his paws pressed against his head and a look of anguish on his face for the mistake he'd made. He'd seen a car pull out of the driveway and hadn't thought to check to see who was behind the wheel. He mouthed the words, "I'm so sorry."

The launch team pressed against the fence, helpless to do anything to save their Chairman. Sparky was trying to get one of them to jump on the board and send him into the yard but he couldn't pull them away from the horrible scene playing out in front of them.

Roscoe looked back at the window and saw Bird Man adjust his aim and began to squeeze the trigger. His last thought was of Penny Sue and he wondered how she would take the news.

He closed his eyes and waited.

Nothing happened.

He opened his eyes and saw movement on the perch on the other side of the feeder tube. He looked closer and saw a golden finch tugging on a seed caught in the opening, oblivious to the scene unfolding around her.

Bird man lowered his rifle and yelled for Sylvia to get away from the feeder. Sylvia's eyes flicked from Roscoe to the finch then back to Roscoe. He'd been a challenge, something for her to play with, but the finch would be a welcome change from her normal diet of dried food and water.

Her tail swished from side to side as she crouched, preparing to climb the pole before the bird flew away. She was about to leap when Bird Man grabbed her by the scruff of her neck and lifted her off the ground. He placed his face close to hers and said angrily, "Sylvia! You know better than that." His voice softened as he cradled her in his arm and carried her back to the garage, "Ms Finch is our guest."

Roscoe discovered he was shaking from the strain of hanging upside down and the tension of the moment. He heard Jules screaming for him to get down, to run for it while he had a chance.

He shifted his position and the moment he did the finch flew off in surprise, she'd been so focused on removing the seed she hadn't noticed him next to her.

He shot a quick glance at the kitchen window. To his relief he saw it was closed and Sylvia's face pressed against one of the panes. He moved to a sitting position on top of the feeder and told himself what he was about to do was completely insane under the present circumstance. Bird Man could return to the window or send Sylvia back in the yard now that the finch was gone.

But he couldn't help himself. He lay down on top of the feeder arm, propped his head on his paw, and finished eating the seed he'd pulled from the feeder tube.

He heard Sylvia howl in frustration and smack the window with her paw. She knew exactly what was going on, he was taunting her.

That's enough, he told himself as he jumped off the feeder and hustled across the yard.

A relieved launch team cheered as he got closer; he'd looked danger in the eye and walked away unscathed.

Melvin and Gus left the evergreen, anxious to go back and tell Chairman Max what they'd seen.

Roscoe climbed the fence and dropped into the arms of a relieved Sparky. They fell to the ground laughing and slapping each other on the back.

"Well?" someone asked. "How were the seeds?"

Roscoe smiled and licked his lips, "A bold flavor with a hint of safflower oil."

The launch team cheered and fought for the chance to be the first one over the fence.

Sparky was all business and asked Roscoe if he'd gone too high? That could be adjusted he explained as he wrote in his notebook. Had he gone too far into the yard? Roscoe's safety was his first concern but with that no longer an issue there were some technical details he needed to work out.

His questions were interrupted by a blast from the back of the house and he jumped as the ground near him erupted, sending dirt and grass in the air.

"Let's get out of here guys," Roscoe hollered over the nervous chatter of the Committee members. "We've got some serious thinking to do."

No one argued about which path to take and they didn't stop running until they reached the Clearing. They were out of breath from their dash from Bird Man's and exhausted from the anxious moments when Roscoe's life hung in the balance.

"I don't think we need to mention this to anybody." They all knew what Roscoe actually meant was the shouldn't say anything about his experience at the feeder to Penny Sue.

He glanced over and saw Jules, lagging behind and looking anxiously over his shoulder, down the path they'd just taken. He took a few steps towards Bird Man's and appeared to be considering returning to his yard.

Roscoe left the others and asked what was going on.

"It's Marvin," he mumbled, afraid if he said too much he'd be distracted and miss seeing him.

"What about him?" Roscoe asked.

"He didn't come back with the rest of us." Jules stood on his toes hoping to see his friend walking toward him and waving he was okay. "I'm worried."

Roscoe thought for a moment before saying, "Let's find out what's holding him up." They cautiously worked their way back down the path.

They slowed as they got closer to Bird Man's yard. A quick glance in the direction of the evergreen told them Melvin and Gus hadn't returned to their post. They were probably back with their Community, telling the story of Roscoe's failed attempt to outsmart Sylvia.

They crept behind the Big Rock thinking it would give them protection as they checked the corners of the yard for Marvin. Once in position they stood, trying to find something that told them he was waiting for things to calm down before leaving his hiding place.

What they saw was Sylvia, lying at the base of the feeder. They guessed she was hoping a bird or better yet a squirrel, would make another attempt to get seeds but this time she'd be ready for them.

Her tail flipped contentedly from one side to the other.

They heard Marvin's voice coming from somewhere near her.

Roscoe used paw signals to tell Jules they should move closer to the fence. He feared the worst. In his mind he could see Marvin pinned beneath Sylvia's giant paw as she toyed with him, waiting for the right moment to deliver the fatal blow and put him out of his misery.

They stayed low and followed the fence line to a place where they could get a better look at what was going on.

They weren't prepared for what they saw. Marvin was laying with his back against Sylvia's stomach, tossing a seed in the air and letting it land in his open mouth. Sylvia had a dreamy look on her face and her head was resting on her front paws while she stared fondly at Marvin.

Between bites of seed they heard him say, "That's what made it so bad. He was my best friend and I let him down. I almost got him killed."

Roscoe heard Sylvia purr, it sounded like she was saying, "Yes, I understand. I know how you feel. Keep talking you'll feel better."

"We went to seed school together and have known each other forever. He almost went the way of all squirrels because I failed to see who was driving the car…" Marvin couldn't finish. He was overcome by the thought of what his mistake had almost cost the Community. "I mean it wasn't just Roscoe I let down, it was the whole team."

"Psst," Roscoe tried to get Marvin's attention but Sylvia saw him first. She looked confused, not sure if she should stand and attack or stay where she was.

Aware something had changed, Marvin looked over Sylvia's stomach and saw them. "Hey guys, sorry for taking so long getting back but I was just telling Sylvia about…well, you probably heard."

Roscoe didn't think it was a good idea to get any closer to the fence. "What's going on Marvin. I don't…"

"Oh, you mean Sylvia?" Marvin stood and patted the cat on the stomach. She rolled over on her side hoping the stomach pat would turn into a chest rub. "I was so upset at my mistake, and I'm really sorry about that Roscoe. I guess I was nervous and when I saw the car leave, I assumed…" He stopped and tried to think of what to say next. "Oh yeah, she told me you were okay. She saw you leave." He shrugged, that was it in a nutshell.

"What I meant is, what's going on with her?" Roscoe made a gesture with his head toward Sylvia.

"Well, I thought you were a goner. She was half way up the feeder. Then Bird Man was at the window with his gun. I heard an explosion and, I don't know, I guess I passed out or fainted. When I came to, everyone was gone except her," he patted Sylvia again and she purred. "She was licking her paws so, naturally, I thought you had, well, you know…" Marvin shrugged.

"So I climbed over the fence, ran across the yard, and told her to take me too since it had been my fault in the first place." Marvin hung his head, he knew he would remember the moment for the rest of his life.

"She didn't know what to do," he turned toward Sylvia, "did you girl?" Sylvia shook her head no. "I fell to my knees and told her to go ahead, finish me off, I couldn't go on living with the thought of what I'd done to my best friend. Then," Marvin seemed embarrassed to go on, "she started to cry. I'm telling you, I couldn't believe it when I saw a tear drop from those beautiful green eyes. She opened her paws and," he blushed and looked at the ground, "gave me a hug." He laughed when he saw the look on their faces, "Believe me guys, I was as surprised as you are."

"So, we can use the feeder, she has no problem with that?" Roscoe was still not sure everything was on the up and up.

Marvin looked at Sylvia who nodded. "Sure, that's fine with her."

"But what about the other guys, Melvin and Gus? How come all they had to do was touch the fence and she practically tore them apart?"

"I think, and this is just a guess on my part because we haven't talked about it, but I don't think they tried to get to know her." Marvin joined Roscoe and Jules as they made their way to the fence. Sylvia walked behind them.

"Do you think we should tell them about this?" Marvin nodded in the direction of the evergreen.

Roscoe thought for a moment before saying, "Let's wait. This kind of knowledge could come in handy."

Roscoe and Jules waited for Marvin to climb the fence and join them. They saw he and Sylvia facing each other. "It was great meeting you Sylvia," Marvin said softly and received a satisfied purr from her. "I'll be back to see you tomorrow I promise."

Then he was over the fence and standing next to Roscoe. Sylvia walked slowly back to the garage, turning occasionally to check on the progress of her new friend.

"Who would have thought?" Roscoe said as they walked along the path to the Clearing.

"Apparently not Melvin and Gus." Marvin said it so casually his friends almost missed it.

They laughed, threw their arms around each other and headed home, anxious to tell the Community about the surprising developments in Bird Man's yard.

The Mighty Squirrelitzer

from the new feeder until the safety team could block the way with a series of orange cones.

It wasn't long before he heard Marvin and Sparky coming up the path. Marvin was talking excitedly about his discovery while Sparky was writing everything down in his notebook.

Marvin pointed in Roscoe's direction and they came over and stood beside him. Sparky removed a pair of binoculars from his backpack to get a better look at the device in the yard.

"It says *Shower Of Seeds* on the end of the disc." He moved to a different spot and looked again. "I think it's safe but to make sure, why don't you go out and pull on the ring so we can see what happens?" He patted Marvin on the arm and pointed at the device.

Marvin looked surprised. "Why me? I'm the one who found it. Why can't one of you do it? Or someone on the Committee?"

"Because I have to take notes on what happens when you pull on the ring and I can't be in two places at the same time. Roscoe is Chairman of the Committee and shouldn't be put in dangerous situations." He made a show of looking around the yard before finishing with, "I don't see anyone from the Committee out here, do you?"

"So you're saying it's dangerous?" Marvin looked worried and bounced nervously from one foot to the other.

"That was a poor choice of words on my part." Sparky couldn't understand why Marvin wouldn't be curious about the device in the yard.

"But it was the first thing that came to mind wasn't it?" Marvin glanced at the yard, at Roscoe, and finally back at Sparky. "You said Roscoe shouldn't be put, and I quote, 'in a dangerous situation.' I was standing right here when you said it."

"Okay, okay, it's no big deal. I'll go and you can fill out the preliminary inquiry sheet." Sparky handed Marvin his notebook and took a step toward the fence.

"What's, Initial Observa..." Marvin tried to sound it out but the word, observation, was new to him.

"Just make a few comments about the time of day, the weather, you know, that kind of thing. And It might be a good idea to describe the approximate size and shape of the device. I usually draw a sketch at the bottom of the page to remind me what it looks like when I get back to the lab." After straightening Marvin out on what to put on the inquiry sheet, Sparky turned back to the fence.

"Does cloudy have one d or two?" Marvin asked then shrugged and handed the notebook back to Sparky. "Never mind, I'd rather face a dangerous situation than try to fill this thing out, it's too much like being back in seed school."

Marvin entered the yard and cautiously approached the *Shower Of Seeds*. He looked back at Roscoe who gave a thumbs up sign hoping to show support for what he was about to do.

Sparky gave a shooing motion with his paws telling him he should get on with it.

He hesitantly grabbed the ring and pulled. He looked around, and thought he heard the sound of rain falling on grass. He held out his paw, palm up, but didn't feel anything.

He pulled the handle a second time, stood quietly, and heard it again. He looked down and was surprised to see seeds on the grass around his feet. "You don't have to be a genius like Sparky to figure this one out," he mumbled as he picked up a seed and bit into it.

He waited a moment, and let the burst of flavor at the center of the seed linger in his mouth. He heard something bounce off the ground near him and when he looked up he saw Roscoe gesture for him to come back and join them. He grabbed a few more seeds before returning to the fence.

"So that's where it gets it's name." Sparky said quietly as he finished his sketch of the new feeder. "There's no pole to climb, no hanging upside down, nothing. You just pull the handle and out come the seeds. It must be new to the market because I haven't seen anything in my catalog collection about it."

"What are we waiting for? The *Shower Of Seeds* awaits." Marvin was anxious to get back and pick up more seeds before the rest of the Community showed up. Sparky was too busy writing in his notebook to answer.

He was surprised when Roscoe grabbed his shoulder and shook his head no.

"Before you go back in the yard Marvin, ask yourself this question. Why would someone like Bird Man who has shown nothing but hostility towards us, suddenly install something like that?" He pointed to the *Shower Of Seeds*.

"See, that's your problem Roscoe. Since you've become Chairman you don't just do stuff anymore. Now you have to think about it and try to figure out what's behind everything. Maybe he had a change of heart. Did you think of that? Maybe he likes us now." Marvin pulled Roscoe's paw from his shoulder and walked away mumbling, "You've changed Roscoe, and not in a good way."

"Hey Marvin take it easy. You can't just think about yourself when you're Chairman, you have to…" Roscoe stopped when he realized Marvin was too far away to hear.

He was baffled by Marvin's outburst and asked Sparky, "Have I really changed that much?" He hated to think he'd upset one of his best friends. But a lot had gone on in his life in a short period of time; he'd been elected Chairman of the Committee For the Protection of Neighborhood Resources and just recently been joined with Penny Sue.

Sparky looked up from his notebook. "Yeah, you've changed but we all have. There's nothing wrong with change Roscoe, we can't be kids forever."

"I don't know, he was pretty upset when he left." Roscoe picked up one of the seeds Marvin had thrown on the ground and studied it.

"He'll get over it," Sparky said confidently. "I wouldn't worry about it if I were you." Roscoe wasn't sure how much he should trust the advice of someone with no social skills and who prefers the solitude of his lab to the party atmosphere of the bowling alley.

The next morning Roscoe sat at his desk in the meeting room trying to get his notes from last nights Committee meeting in order but his heart wasn't in it. He woke up several times during the night wondering if maybe he'd become too serious; he didn't seem to laugh as much as he used to.

Norvell opened the door. "Oh good you're here. Marvin told me to tell you that Bird Man has done it again." He started to close the door but stopped when Roscoe asked, "Did he say what it was?"

Norvell thought for a moment. "Not really. He just told me to tell you what I, ah, told you he told me to…" He scratched his head and gave Roscoe an odd look as he tried to remember what Marvin told him to say.

"Why didn't he come himself? He knows my door is always open." It bothered Roscoe that Marvin would send a stranger with a message he could have just as easily delivered himself.

His question was met with a shrug before Norvell closed the door.

Roscoe stopped by the lab and got Sparky before going to Bird Man's yard. When they arrived, Marvin was leaning against the fence waiting for them. He didn't say anything but gestured with a nod they should look at the feeder.

They did and were surprised to see the *Shower Of Seeds* was gone and had been replaced by a pole several feet high with metal rods coming out of the top at an odd angle. Stuck on each rod was an ear of corn.

"Well I never thought I'd see one of those." Sparky was smiling. "*A Corn Tree Club*, I have a picture of one in an old catalog, they're practically antiques."

"How does it work?" Roscoe asked and heard Marvin suppress a laugh because he thought the answer was obvious.

"Ears of corn are screwed to the rods so they won't come off, at least that's the theory. It looks innocent enough but when you grab one, the whole thing spins around. If you hold on to the corn too long it will throw you clear across the yard. The human who built them didn't think we were smart enough to figure out how to unscrew the corn from the rod. They assumed we'd grab an ear of corn and run off."

They heard Marvin chewing on something and when they looked, he held up an ear of corn he'd taken from the *Corn Tree Club*.

"You better put it back Marvin, at least until Sparky is able to make a thorough study of the situation." Roscoe hated to say anything because he knew he'd come off sounding like a stick in the mud but he had to do it for the good of the Community. He was sure as soon as word got out there was corn at Bird Man's the place would be swarming with Community members.

"Tell Roscoe to forget about it." Marvin tossed a half eaten ear of corn in their direction and walked away.

"Don't worry Roscoe, I've done some research. Marvin's right on this one, it's perfectly safe." Sparky picked up his back pack, anxious to get back to his lab and finish the experiment he'd been working on.

"What about the rod Marvin removed the corn from?" Roscoe inspected it to see if it had any sharp edges that could hurt anyone. "Maybe we should put out a couple of orange cones just in case." He tapped his foot as he considered the safest course of action.

"Do what you think best Roscoe but I doubt if it will be out here long. The way things are going, Bird Man will replace it with something new before anyone knows it's out here."

"I guess it's all right then. I was just thinking of the little ones, you know, cutting their paws on the sharp edges." He looked at Sparky for reassurance.

"Gotcha," Sparky said and started back to the lab.

Roscoe was sure Bird Man was up to something and it bothered him that he couldn't figure out what it was. For two days in a row he'd introduced a new, novel seed dispenser. Not that it was all bad, they now had an abundant supply of food in the emergency storage bin. It just seemed odd, he hadn't seen anything like this before. He couldn't remember Seed Man changing anything at his feeder.

The next morning Roscoe was sitting on the edge of his bed trying to wake up when he heard someone climbing his tree. He hurriedly slipped on his robe and walked to the edge of his nest to see who would be coming by this early.

It was Marvin and he was out of breath. Whatever had driven him to see Roscoe had been urgent enough to overcome the ill feelings he'd shown over the past few days.

"Bird Man's. Quick." He paused to catch his breath. "I'll get Sparky. Meet you there. You're not going to..." Roscoe missed the last part because Marvin had almost reached the bottom of his tree before he finished what he was saying.

TWO FEEDERS, NO WAITING

They stood by the fence, staring at the latest addition to Bird Man's feeder collection. The *Corn Tree Club* was gone and a new one had taken its place.

"What is it?" Marvin asked.

They were looking at a plastic tube that ran parallel to the ground and was just wide enough for someone their size to crawl through. Three boxes were spaced evenly along the tube. After the first box the tube looped up and made a complete circle before connecting to the second box. After the second box, the tube dipped down, ran underground for a few feet, then shot up at a steep angle and turned to connect to the third box.

A feeder tube, filled with seeds, hung inches from the last box.

"It's called *The Mighty Squirrelitzer*. I found some literature on it in the trash dump at the back of the yard." Sparky took a step closer. "The entrance is higher than I pictured."

"What does it do?" Roscoe was still feeling the effects of a sleepless night and his thinking wasn't up to speed yet.

"**It** doesn't do anything Roscoe, **you** do." Sparky hadn't taken his eyes off the device since he arrived. "You enter through the tube up there." He pointed to the end of the tube above their heads.

"How?" To Marvin it appeared to be too high for them to reach.

"Good question Marvin, I'll get back to that in a minute." Sparky moved forward and stood under the first box. "When you reach the first box you are confronted with two circles. Push the right one and you continue to the second box. But, if you pick the wrong one..."

"What?" Marvin asked anxiously. "What happens if you pick the wrong one?

Sparky shrugged. "It depends on which model he bought." He thought for a moment. "The point is, you have to make it through each of the boxes before you get the seeds."

Marvin ran the length of the *Squirrelitzer*. "Why can't you just go straight to the feeder tube?"

"Because they located it so you can only reach it from the last box. It's a great design. They obviously gave it a lot of thought." The fact that it was impossible for anyone to bypass the system and get the seeds didn't seem to bother Sparky, he admired the craftsmanship.

"What do you think we should do?" Roscoe wasn't sure if he should call for the safety team or go ahead and try to figure out how it worked.

"We'll send Marvin through, then you can decide what to do." Sparky crouched down and studied the place where the tube went beneath the ground.

"I knew it," Marvin exclaimed and threw his paws in the air. "Every time there's a hint of danger I'm always the guinea pig." He paced angrily in front of them. "You never choose Jules or Webster. Oh no, it's always, let Marvin do it."

Roscoe and Sparky stood quietly while Marvin continued to vent his frustration. Finally he wore down and said with a note of resignation, "Okay, how do I get up there."

"Way to go," Roscoe gave him an encouraging pat on the back. "Here's what I was thinking."

Roscoe explained his plan and soon Sparky was on all fours with Roscoe standing on his back. Marvin stepped on Sparky, climbed on Roscoe's shoulders, reached up, grabbed hold of the tube, and pulled himself up.

He cautiously crawled through the tube until he reached the first box. There were two circles in front of him just as Sparky had described it. He tried to turn and go back and ask which one he should choose but the tube was too tight; he was sure Sparky would say it was designed well.

"Okay," he told himself, "It's up to me." He faced the two circles and tried to decide which one to pick. "Normally I would choose the one on the left, but they probably figured everyone would so I'm picking the one on the right." He lifted a paw in the air, ready to push the circle on the right, but stopped. "What if they figured I would choose the opposite of what I normally would? But, they may have thought I would..." Marvin told himself not to over think the problem, that he should stay with his first thought.

He pushed the circle on the left and immediately the bottom of the box fell away, sending him hurtling to the ground. He was taken by surprise and the normally agile Marvin landed badly. When he finally got up Roscoe noticed he was having trouble putting weight on his foot.

They watched in amazement as the spring hinge on the bottom of the box slowly slipped back in place. No one moved until they heard a click as the floor locked in place.

"I should have picked the one on the right," he reported and watched Sparky write his first choice in his notebook.

"Okay we know how to get through the first box, let's move on to the second one." Sparky looked at Marvin and pointed to the entrance to the tube.

Marvin waited thinking Roscoe would step up and take his turn exploring the new device. He was still a little woozy from being dropped out of the first box.

"Well, get moving, we haven't got all day." Sparky pushed Marvin toward the entrance.

"We? You keep saying we and I'm the one doing all the work," he grumbled as he limped toward the opening.

"I have to record your choices. We can't afford for Roscoe to go, he has a Community to run. So…" Sparky raised his eyebrows suggesting any fair-minded person would come to the same conclusion he had.

"Okay. Okay." Marvin climbed on Roscoe's shoulders and pulled himself into the tube. He made it to the first box, pushed the circle on the right, and watched with relief as the disc blocking the entrance to the second tube slide to one side.

He scampered around the loop between the first and second box. He didn't know if it was his imagination or if the tube was getting smaller the further along he went.

He entered the second box and once again found he was looking at two circles. He told himself not to think about it too much, he had a 50-50 chance of picking the right one. He tried to remember which one he picked at the first box but being trapped in a narrow tube with no way to escape was starting to get to him. He finally remembered his last choice was the disc on the right so he touched the circle on the left with his paw. He saw the lid of the box slowly move to one side and tried to imagine what was coming next.

Before he could come to a conclusion he was rising rapidly in the air. His natural compass was thrown off and he was trying to turn around to see where he was going when he slammed into the trunk of a tree. Pain shot through his back and for just a moment he lost all feeling in his legs.

"Left or right?" Sparky stood above him with his pencil poised above his notebook. He didn't ask if he was hurt or needed medical attention. It slowly dawned on Marvin he was part of a scientific study and Sparky's only interest was in gathering data.

"Right. I mean the one on the left." Marvin shook his head trying to get the two images of Sparky to become one. "I picked the one on the left."

Marvin knew it was useless to protest, they'd come up with an answer for whatever he said. He put his paws up, cutting off any further discussion and hobbled over to the opening.

"Up you go. We've got the combination for the first two out of the way, there's only one more to go." Sparky and Roscoe helped him reach the entrance to the tube.

He took a deep, calming breath before climbing in. He panicked for a moment when he couldn't remember his first pick, then it came to him. He hit the circle on the right and continued down the tube to the second box. He chose the right disc on the next one and relaxed as it slid to the side revealing the entrance to the third tube.

It was so small he could barely crawl through it. He crept along, fighting the anxiety that came from being in an enclosed space that offered no way to turn around and go back. Before he knew it he was underground and starting the steep climb to the third and final box. The surface of the tube was slick and he had to fight for every inch as he moved forward. When he got to the final box he rested a moment. He could imagine Sparky asking Roscoe what was taking him so long. The only thing that kept him going was the thought of the tube of seeds waiting on the other side of the door. He cleared his mind of distracting thoughts and focused on the problem in front of him. Would the creators of *The Mighty Squirrelitzer* select a combination of right, right, left or right, right, right? The first one felt right to him so pushed the circle on the left.

For a moment nothing happened. The box didn't move but neither did the door to the tube of seeds open. He thought there must be a malfunction of some kind and was considering backing down the tube when the box began to shake. It was subtle at first, just a light, tickling sensation in his feet. Then it got so bad he had to press his paws against the sides of the box to keep from bouncing all over the place.

The shaking stopped and when things returned to normal he thought that hadn't been so bad. He started to reach for the disc on the right but stopped when he felt the box began to turn. It picked up speed, eventually he was spinning so fast the two circles in front of him became one. To Marvin's relief, the spinning finally slowed and eventually stopped. Then the floor slid away and he tried to grab the sides of the box to keep from falling but the walls were slick and there was nothing to grab hold of. He realized it was hopeless, stopped struggling, fell from the box, and landed on the ground upside down.

He rolled over and clung to the grass, trying to stop things around him from spinning. He thought he might be sick. He was on his paws and knees, rocking from side to side, waiting for the dizziness to end when he caught sight of Sparky's feet.

"What was your last selection? I hope you didn't choose the one on the left." There was an odd tone in his voice that Marvin took to mean, "Only a fool would have picked that one."

Marvin rolled on his side hoping to ease the pain in his hip and cover the embarrassment of having made three wrong choices in a row.

"Okay then, it looks like the combination is right, right, right. Up and at-um Marvin, the reward for all of your hard work awaits."

The last thing on Marvin's mind was food. He pulled himself to his feet, staggered to the opening, and climbed in. He had no trouble making it through the boxes now that he knew the combination. He was relieved when he saw the disc at the entrance to the third box move to one side revealing the feeder tube.

He nibbled on a few seeds but his stomach was still churning from his experience in the third box and he discovered he'd lost his appetite. He was still groggy from being spun around and his shoulder and leg ached from the falls he'd taken. His back still hurt from when he hit the tree. He put the seed he'd been eating back in the tube and carefully lowered himself to the ground.

"Good work Marvin, you did it." He heard Roscoe say but all he could think of was at last, the whole *Squirrelitzer* experience was finally over.

Sparky nodded he agreed with Roscoe; that was about as much praise he would get from Sparky. To him, it was an exercise in logic and, as far as he was concerned, Marvin had made three wrong choices.

"So, what do we do now?" Marvin asked.

"We wait," Sparky said and walked away.

"For what?" When Marvin didn't get an answer from Sparky he looked at Roscoe. "What are we waiting for?"

Roscoe could only shrug because he had no idea what Sparky was talking about.

Jules kicked at a stick with his foot. Sparky told him to hang around Bird Man's yard and let him know the minute anything happened. So far, he'd talked with Sylvia, walked around the Big Rock a dozen times, and was now entertaining himself by kicking a stick into the fence. "This is a great way to spend an afternoon," he grumbled.

He walked over to the Big Rock and stood with his back against it so he could keep the yard clearly in view. When his legs got tired he slid into a sitting position, he could see the feeder just as well from there he reasoned.

He sat up and looked around, aware he'd dozed off. When he sat down it was quiet in Bird Man's yard but now there were at least a dozen humans on his deck. The lawn chairs were arranged to provide an unobstructed view of *The Mighty Squirrelitzer*. He saw Bird Man serving drinks to his guests who were talking amiably with one another in quiet voices.

Jules took off for Sparky's lab to let him know what was going on.

Sparky sent him to get Roscoe and Marvin and tell them to get to Bird Man's as fast as they could.

Soon, they were huddled together in the shadow of the Big Rock. When they showed up, all conversation on the deck stopped, and the humans tip toed to the lawn chairs and quietly sat down. They heard Bird Man say, "Quiet now we don't want to scare them. You're going to love this."

"You're on Marvin, it's your show," Sparky had one paw on Marvin's shoulder. "You paid the price discovering the secret code that gets you through the boxes to the seeds. You've earned the right to be the first one through."

Marvin wasn't sure he wanted to have any part of this, the memory of spinning around in the last box was still fresh in his mind. "What if he changed something? What if instead of right, right, right it's something else? What if I…"

He stopped talking when Sparky squeezed his shoulder. "Calm down Marvin, I've had Jules out here keeping an eye on things and no one has come near the feeder. Right Jules?"

Jules hesitated, not sure if he should tell them he'd dozed off while on duty. He nodded yes, he'd been there the whole time which was technically true. He didn't feel this was the moment to mention he'd been asleep for part of it.

"Go slowly. Repeat the code to yourself and if that doesn't work just look at this." Sparky slipped a rubber band around his right wrist. "You'll be fine." He patted Marvin's shoulder and got in position to help him reach the entrance to the tube.

They heard Bird Man whisper to his guests, "Creative little guys aren't they? See, they're helping the skinny one get to the opening. I put it higher off the ground so they couldn't…hold on, he's in the tube."

His guests studied the diagram he'd prepared for them with a description of what they could expect when the squirrel entered each box. "Drop," was written above the first one. "Toss," was by the second, and "Shake, rattle, and roll," was printed next to the third.

Marvin crawled down the tube and faced the first circle. He hoped Jules was telling the truth about keeping his eye on things while he was gone. "Well, I'll know in a second," he said out loud, closed his eyes, and pushed the circle on the right.

The disc slid slowly to one side and he breathed a sigh of relief.

Moving through boxes two and three was as easy as getting past the first one. He had to fight to keep from laughing when the last circle slid away and he saw the tube full of seeds in front of him.

He gave a quick glance toward the deck. The humans were standing and looking at him. He heard Bird Man say, "It's a fluke I'm telling you. The possibility of his getting them all right is about a million to one."

Their attention swung back to *The Mighty Squirrelitzer* when they saw Sparky standing on Roscoe's shoulders, reaching for the opening.

Sparky is not the kind to draw attention to himself. Normally it's the opposite; he goes to great lengths to keep from being noticed. But, maybe it was because Bird Man had invited his friends over to watch members of the Community of Abner make fools of themselves. Or maybe it was because the makers of *The Mighty Squirrelitzer* thought they'd designed the perfect anti-squirrel device and they'd figured out how to get through it in only three tries. Whatever his motivation, he stood above the entrance to the first tube and waved to the humans on the deck. Then he flipped around and entered the tube, backwards.

A gasp came from those on the deck as they watched him move from box to box, only slowing down long enough to wait for the doors to open. When he appeared at the last box he grabbed the feeder tube, hung by one arm for a moment, and dropped triumphantly to the ground.

He ran back to Roscoe with a broad smile on his face.

"What was that all about?" Roscoe asked, half laughing.

"I have no idea." Sparky giggled and tried to talk at the same time, "I couldn't help myself."

They glanced over to the deck in time to see the last guest walk dejectedly through the kitchen door. They could hear Bird Man say, "I have burgers planned for later. And more drinks…" His shoulders dropped as the last guest pulled the door to the kitchen closed, leaving him on the deck, alone.

He stood helplessly as he watched the squirrels celebrate beneath *The Mighty Squirritzer* then he drew back his arm and threw the tongs he was going to use to turn the hamburgers at them.

It fell harmlessly a few feet from Roscoe. He looked at Sparky and without saying a word picked up the tongs, carried them over the fence, and back to the Clearing.

"Hey guys," Marvin hollered through cheeks filled with seeds, "I think I'll go through *The Mighty Squirrelitzer* again?"

Roscoe and Sparky couldn't hear him, they were laughing too hard.

50 Ways to Lose
Your Squirrels

Part 1: Faux Seeds

"What do you call that?" Edgar plopped a seed down in front of Roscoe. There had been no, "Good morning." Or, "Sorry if I'm interrupting anything." He just climbed over the edge of Roscoe's nest, walked over to him, and shoved the seed in his face.

Penny Sue had been up for some time, cleaning and straightening their nest, but until the moment Edgar arrived, Roscoe had been sound asleep. A Committee meeting that should have been over in minutes had run late into the night and ended with no decision on this year's seed school budget.

"I don't, I mean, I…" Roscoe was having trouble adjusting to Edgar barging into his nest. He was also fighting the growing feeling of resentment that Edgar or anyone in the Community felt it was perfectly okay to enter his nest whenever they felt like it.

"Couldn't this wait until…" Roscoe said through a yawn.

"No Roscoe, it can't wait. I'm simply asking what you call that." Edgar pointed to the seed he'd placed on Roscoe's pillow. "It's not the most difficult question in the world."

Roscoe shook his head and tried to figure why Edgar was so upset. "I realize I'm not as knowledgeable about some things as you are Edgar, but even to my untrained, inexperienced eye, I'd say it's a seed."

"Hah to that," Edgar shot back, barely allowing Roscoe time to finish. "That shows how much you know about what's going on around here."

His aggressive behavior caused Penny Sue to say, "Grandpa, take it easy."

"This isn't personal Penny Sue, it's business. Roscoe knows that." Edgar raised his paws letting her know as far as he was concerned no foul had been committed. He turned back to Roscoe and said, "Try it Mr. Chairman." It sounded more like a demand than a request.

Roscoe started to say it was a little early for him to be eating but realized Edgar wouldn't leave until he got what he wanted. He picked up the seed, took a bite, and immediately ran to the edge of his nest and spit it out.

"My point exactly," Edgar grumbled as he walked over to Roscoe who was still picking the remains of the seed from his mouth. "Sawdust?" Roscoe managed to say, "It's filled with sawdust? Who'd pull a trick like that?"

Biting into the fake seed and ending up with a with a mouth full of sawdust coupled with Edgar barging into his nest without being invited had pushed Roscoe past the limits of his usual easy going manner.

"Look Edgar, I just woke up, okay? So I have no idea what's going on. I'll need a little time to gather some information but I'll look into it and get back to you. How do you know it isn't someone's idea of a practical joke?"

"Does Bird Man strike you as a practical joker?" Edgar folded his arms across his chest and glared at Roscoe. "Need I mention the hot and spicy seeds he put in the feeder a few weeks ago? Or covering the openings of the feeder tube with see through tape? His intentions are pretty obvious to me, he wants us out of his yard, it doesn't take a committee to figure that out."

Roscoe decided someone needed to be the grownup in the conversation so he asked, "Would you mind starting at the beginning and bringing me up to speed? At the moment I have no idea what you're talking about."

They stood facing each other, neither wanting to be the first to back down. Finally Edgar's shoulders dropped and he walked to the edge of the nest.

"It all started this morning." He went on to explain that he'd had trouble sleeping and finally, at daybreak, he'd gone to the feeder. That's when he discovered the tube on the Abner side of the feeder had been filled with fake seeds. He'd followed the procedure spelled out in the *Big Book of Important Things* and notified Lester the head of the safety team who immediately put an orange cone at the base of he feeder letting everyone in the Community know there was a problem.

Then he'd come to Roscoe to file a formal complaint.

Roscoe was sure when the rule was written Abner assumed the Chairman would be in his office when he received the complaint and not in his bedroom.

Edgar produced another seed and they studied it. With a chance to take a closer look Roscoe noticed printing on one side. He paced back and forth trying to decide what to do. Finally he said, "Take this to the library and have Webster look at it," he handed the seed back to Edgar. "I'll get Marvin to talk to Sylvia, maybe she knows what's going on."

"My thoughts exactly," Edgar said quickly. Although, if the truth were known, he hadn't a thought in his head. He'd been so upset since he found the fake seeds he hadn't begun to think about what to do about it.

Roscoe found Marvin in the Clearing and after a brief description of the problem he said he'd be more than happy to spend time with his friend Sylvia.

When they reached the yard they were relieved to see the cat door was open indicating Bird Man was gone. Marvin climbed the fence and was half way across the yard when Sylvia flew out of the cat door and knocked him to the ground. He was about to ask if she wasn't playing a little rough when she rammed him again, sending him rolling across the grass. Her paw struck the ground inches from his face. When she was so close he could smell cat food on her breath she whispered, "He's on to us. Take this and go."

She handed him a scrap of paper and let out a yowl. She gave him a head start to the fence before she got to her feet and ran after him. Marvin heard her paw slap the fence beneath him as he rolled over the top. "Sorry," she whispered before letting out another howl, reached through the fence, and raked the ground near his foot with her paw.

Before starting back to the Clearing, they saw Bird Man standing near the door of the garage, holding Sylvia in his arms and saying, "Good girl Sylv. We won't see bad old Mr. Squirrel in our yard for awhile."

When they reached the Clearing they stopped running and sat down on the bench next to the Statue of Abner to catch their breath. "What was that all about?" Roscoe was puzzled, Sylvia hadn't behaved like that since the first day they met her. "I thought she was your friend."

"She said Bird Man figured out what was going on so she was faking it, making it look like she was doing her job. If it had been for real I wouldn't be sitting with you now."

They sat quietly thinking of the impact not being able to go to the feeder would have on the Community. Fortunately, because of Sylvia letting them know when Bird Man was gone, they'd been able to fill the bin they kept for emergencies.

"Oh," Marvin said as he remembered the piece of paper she'd given him. "She gave me this before telling me to run to the fence."

Roscoe took the paper and opened it. The writing was terrible but what, he wondered to himself, do you expect from a cat? He wouldn't dare say anything like that now that Marvin had become friends with Sylvia. The best he could make out after reading the note several times was, "boK *50 Way 2 loosen Yur Squirlz.*"

He had no idea what it meant.

"Let's go over to the library and see what Webster has learned from the writing on the fake seed." They hurried across the Clearing and entered the library.

Webster looked up but Roscoe wasn't sure if he saw him or not. He has a way of blanking everything out when he's working on a library problem. Roscoe saw Sparky at a table in the reference section and motioned for him to come over and join them.

Webster blinked and looked surprised to see his friends standing at his desk. "Oh, sorry, I was just..." He shrugged not sure how to explain what he'd been thinking about. "It's the classic librarian dilemma," he told them as a way to explain why he hadn't seen them come in. "Where do you put a book written by an author who's name starts with Mc?" He stopped talking when he noticed they weren't interested.

"What did you find out about the seed Edgar brought over?" Roscoe saw the seed laying on top of the reference table next to an open book and a magnifying glass.

"Seed? Oh, you mean…" Webster picked up the seed and handed it to Roscoe along with a magnifying glass. "It says, *Faux Seed,*" on one side. Webster nodded as he spoke like they understood what he was talking about.

"What kind of seed?" Roscoe asked.

"Faux. It means synthetic or artificial. Not the real thing" He turned the book so Roscoe could read the definition for himself. "And there's definitely sawdust inside or something like it."

"Where'd you get that?" Sparky took the capsule from Roscoe and pressed it between his fingers, testing it's strength.

Roscoe told him the story of how he got the seed and showed Webster the note Sylvia had given Marvin. He gave him a moment to study it before asking, "What do you think?"

"I'd say Bird Man has some serious squirrel issues. Is that a 50?" Webster pointed to the note. "I had no idea there were that many ways of getting rid of us."

Roscoe scratched his head. "How'd you come up with that?"

"Well Roscoe I see a lot of really bad writing on applications for library cards so I'm used to figuring things like this out." He pointed to a place in the middle of the note. "If you change loosen to lose you get, 50 Ways to Lose Your Squirrels. My guess is the faux seed is one of them."

"To me, the question is what are we going to do about it? The Community can't last long with seeds like that." Roscoe put both paws on top of the check out desk and looked at the others hoping one of them could come up with an answer.

They stood quietly for a moment, not sure what could be done to get things back to normal at Bird Man's. They had to admit since discovering the feeder in his yard nothing had been normal. The first time they came near his fence he shot at them with his gun. Then he tried to scare them away by sending Sylvia out to get rid of them. He changed feeders every day to keep them off balance. And now this, putting seeds in the feeder tube that were filled with sawdust.

"Let's turn the tables on him. Go on the offensive." Marvin smiled at being able to remember one of Coach Bobby's sayings. Coach Bobby had accumulated an impressive number of wins when he coached the Find the Nut team at seed school. His philosophy was simple; attack, move forward, and never, never back up.

"Like?" Roscoe gestured for Marvin to provide a few details for his, turn the tables idea.

"Beats me," Marvin looked embarrassed, he couldn't think of a way to take the offensive when dealing with faux seeds.

"Termites." A voice from somewhere among the book shelves got their attention. Buford, a helper in Sparky's lab when he's not attending seed school, took a cautious step toward them.

"What do termites have to do with anything?" Roscoe didn't see the connection between the faux seeds and termites unless he was saying he'd discovered termites in the library and had nothing to do with the problem they were discussing.

Buford cleared his throat and pushed his glasses back in place. "Well, we ah, just studied about them last semester, that's all. It was just a, ah…" He took a deep breath before continuing. "Oh yeah, they build a trail on the foundation of a house from the ground to where the wood begins so they can go in and out and not be exposed to the sun. Of the house I mean. The termites. Going…" He looked at them, hopeful they got the basic idea of what he was trying to say.

They didn't.

Even Sparky, considered by the Community to be its brightest member, didn't make the connection.

"Well, see, I thought, you could like, open some of the seeds, mix the sawdust in some gooey stuff, and stick it to his wall. You know, make it look like he had them. Termites I mean."

Sparky listened for a moment then slowly nodded his head. He saw where Buford was going with his idea. "And Bird Man thinks…"

"Right. So he has to get a…" Buford and Sparky were finishing each others sentences and moving on to the next one, leaving Roscoe and Marvin to wonder what they were talking about.

"Hold it." Roscoe threw his paws in the air, he couldn't take it any longer. "Would you two slow down? I have no idea what you're talking about. Could you at least use complete sentences and bring it down to my level?" Roscoe wished he could think like they did but he knew that's all it was, a wish.

"Guys," he called after them but it was too late, the entrance to their world had just closed for the day. They left the library continuing their unique way of conversing, one starting a sentence and the other finishing it. Roscoe was sure they'd eventually end up at the lab searching for the perfect glue to hold the sawdust together.

"I think bok is actually book." Webster's comments brought Roscoe's attention back to the note Sylvia had given Webster. "And the rest is something she copied, see a few of the words are spelled correctly." He pulled a book from the shelf behind him, laid it on the reference desk, and opened it to a place he'd marked. He ran his paw down the page and stopped where, at sometime in the past, he'd made a small check mark.

"There it is," he turned the book so Roscoe could see. "It's published by Hassle Free Press. Listen to this. 'A do it your self manual on a variety of clever ways to get rid of backyard pests.'"

He looked at Roscoe and they were both shocked. They'd never thought of themselves as backyard pests, they'd seen themselves as lovable woodland creatures.

The next morning Sparky and Buford were back in the library discussing the best way to apply the substance they'd mixed in the lab. They'd sent Marvin ahead to see if he could make contact with Sylvia and find out what was going on with Bird Man.

Marvin stepped off the path when he saw Sylvia resting with her back against the fence. He hid behind the Big Rock and looked around for something to throw to get her attention.

After two unsuccessful tries, she finally rolled over and saw him. She stood and began patrolling the fence, occasionally smacking it angrily with her paw. Between each show of force she was able to convey to Marvin that Bird Man was not home but that his neighbor was the one who told him what had been going on in the yard when he was gone. He meant it as a joke, pointing out how clever the local squirrels were, but Bird Man failed to see the humor in it.

Marvin looked over and saw the neighbor sitting on his deck, drinking a cup of coffee and reading the newspaper. Bird Man was gone but the neighbor was so close he couldn't see any way to get to the house to apply the mixture of sawdust and glue without being seen.

When Roscoe, Buford, and Sparky finally got there Marvin filled them in on what was going on. Buford noticed the yard next to Bird Man's wasn't fenced so he proposed a bold plan. Marvin would go down the side of the fence in the neighbor's yard and Sylvia would act like she was stalking him, waiting patiently for him to make the mistake of climbing over the fence. That would provide a diversion to distract the neighbor from what was really going on.

The plan worked to perfection and the neighbor bought it. From time to time he would drop his newspaper enough to look over the top of it. He watched with interest as Sylvia crept along the fence staying far enough back to keep her prey from getting suspicious. He was fascinated by what was going on and was sure he was watching a scene that had been played out since the dawn of time. He made up his mind to tell Bird Man that Sylvia had been alert and on the job, keeping his yard free of squirrels. He soon lost interest in what they were doing and turned back to his newspaper.

When Sparky and Buford reached the point where the neighbor could no longer see them, they climbed the fence and began applying the sawdust mixture to the exposed part of the foundation. When they were finished they looked at what they'd done and smiled. To the casual observer it looked exactly like termites had come out of the ground and gone directly to the joists supporting the house.

They picked up their equipment and climbed back over the fence. They saw the neighbor was busy working a puzzle in the newspaper so they took their time getting back to the others waiting for them behind the Big Rock.

"How are we going to get Bird Man to discover the termite trail?" Roscoe asked.

"We're covered on that, Roscoe." Marvin pointed to the back of the

TWO FEEDERS, NO WAITING

house where Sylvia was stretched out next to the fake termite trail. "She said she thought she could get his attention when he comes out to put seeds in the feeder."

Marvin smiled at the resourceful Sylvia. He'd worried that she may have gone back to her old, hostile ways when she knocked him over but it looked like he'd been hasty in his judgment. Without her help, they wouldn't have been able to pull the fake termite trail trick on her owner.

"I don't think we all need to be out here, it may be awhile before Bird Man returns." The four friends formed a circle with their heads almost touching like a huddle before the start of a Find The Nut game. "Sparky why don't you and Buford take the first watch? If he's not back by the middle of the afternoon, Marvin and I will take your place. I'll have Lester organize the safety team to work in shifts if he's not back before dark."

They agreed to go along with his plan and as Roscoe and Marvin were leaving they could here Sparky and Buford discussing the material they'd mixed with the sawdust. Sparky wondered if it would have been better to mix two parts sawdust to one part glue and Buford argued that would make it too thick.

It wasn't long before a breathless Buford was knocking on the meeting room door and announcing that Bird Man was back. He told them things were moving along faster than expected and they'd better step on it if they wanted to see the whole thing.

They'd just arrived at the Big Rock when Bird Man opened the door to the garage and stepped into the yard. They watched with interest as he motioned for Sylvia to come inside. She looked at him for a moment and then, as if she was upset about something, turned away.

He called her again and waited by the door for her to come to inside. When she didn't move he became concerned. "What is it girl?" He asked almost begging for a response. He walked over and crouched down next to her. "What's the problem Sylv?"

The team huddled behind the Big Rock were too far away to hear what else was said but they got enough from the tone of his voice that he was concerned he'd done something to upset her. They watched him bend to pick her up. When she was a foot off the ground he stopped.

He put her down and, staying in a bent over position, walked the few feet to the foundation of his house. He got down on all fours and studied the trail that started below the ground and disappeared beneath the pale blue vinyl siding.

He stood up and scratched his head. It looked like he was trying to remember if the trail had been there yesterday.

He reached in his pocket and pulled out a small, rectangular object Sparky identified as a cellular phone. He punched in some numbers, talked for a moment and hung up. He went back to Sylvia and gently picked her up. Before they entered the garage she lifted her head and winked to her friends watching anxiously by the Big Rock.

"Yes!" they heard Marvin say as he punched the air with his paw, and shouted, "You go girl."

With the technical part of the problem out of the way, Sparky and Buford lost interest and turned the backyard vigil over to Marvin and Roscoe.

Marvin had just asked Roscoe if he thought there would ever be a time when he could invite Sylvia to meet the rest of the Community when they heard tires squeal and watched a purple truck screech to a stop in front of Bird Man's house. A plastic model of a termite clung to the roof of his truck and they could hear the music of, *The Flight of the Bumble Bee*, coming from a speaker mounted in the creatures mouth.

They watched in surprise as their old nemesis Uniform Man followed Bird Man into the backyard and over to the termite trail on the foundation wall.

Bird Man's neighbor put his newspaper down and moved to the edge of his deck to get a better look at what was going on. He was sure if his neighbor stopped the termites from attacking his house, his wooden deck would be the next target on their agenda.

Uniform Man pulled a container from his termite inspection kit. He scraped some of the termite trail from the wall and dropped it in the plastic tube. He snapped the lid shut, shook it for several seconds, and held it up to the light so Bird Man could see the results. Then they were both on their hands and knees studying the trail. Uniform Man rubbed the trail with the back of his hand and gestured for Bird Man to do what he'd done.

They talked as Bird Man led him to the feeder and removed a faux seed. Uniform Man bit off the end and watched with interest as the sawdust ran out. He stood motionless for a moment while he processed this new piece of information. The fake termite trail and the seeds filled with sawdust added up to only one thing as far as he was concerned; squirrels.

Suddenly Uniform Man spun around and scanned the back yard. Roscoe grabbed Marvin and pull him behind the Big Rock just as his gaze reached them.

He pointed in their direction and said something to Bird Man who shook his head yes. He made a sweeping motion with his hand as he described how the squirrels climbed his fence and came to the feeder. Uniform Man put a hand on his shoulder and slowly shook his head. Roscoe guessed he was telling him termites were the least of his problems.

Bird Man pulled money from his billfold and handed it to Uniform Man as they crossed the yard and moved to the garage. As he was about to step through the door, Uniform Man stopped and gave the yard one last look. His eyes came to rest on the Big Rock and stayed there for what Roscoe felt was an eternity.

Finally he broke off his gaze and followed Bird Man inside.

Marvin and Roscoe whooped and high pawed each other. The first round in *The Battle at Bird Man's* was over and they'd won.

It would have gone down as a complete victory if it hadn't been for the appearance of Uniform Man. But they'd dealt with him before and it wasn't like they were keeping score but so far they were undefeated.

They gave one last look at the what remained of the faux termite trail before heading back to the Clearing.

Marvin couldn't wait to tell everyone what had gone on at the feeder and the role his friend Sylvia had played in pulling it off.

Part 2: Conquering Mr. Fling-Um

The joy of turning the tables on Bird Man and making the faux termite trail from the sawdust in the seeds he'd put in the feeder didn't last long. Roscoe was so sure real seeds would replace the imitation ones he'd stationed Buford by the Big Rock with instructions to let him know the moment Bird Man stepped in his backyard.

But, instead of rushing into the Committee meeting room and announcing things at the feeder were back to normal, Buford walked in, helping his brother Norman to the wooden bench beneath the small window.

"What's going on?" Roscoe left his desk and stood next to Buford.

"I wish I could tell you Roscoe." Norman answered thinking Roscoe was talking to him. He was still a little dizzy from his experience at the feeder. "Buford told me everything was okay so I climbed the pole and the next thing I knew I was upside down in the middle of the yard. Sylvia helped me get back to the fence and, well," he shrugged, "that's all I remember."

Roscoe looked at Buford hoping he could add a few more details but he shook his head and said he was visiting with someone when he heard Norman scream.

"Get Sparky," Roscoe told Buford, "Norman and I will head back to Bird Man's and meet you there. Maybe we can figure this out."

Norman got a funny look on his face, he wasn't sure he wanted to go anywhere near the feeder.

TWO FEEDERS, NO WAITING

It took Buford and Sparky a while to join them; Sparky was in the middle of an experiment when Buford stopped by the lab and they both got involved and lost track of time.

When they finally reached the fence, Roscoe explained the problem while Sparky moved to get a better look at the strange object on top of the feeder pole.

"Does anything look familiar?" Roscoe was anxious for any piece of information that would help solve the latest feeder problem.

"There's a name or something on top but I can't make it out." Without taking his eyes off the feeder Sparky said, "Buford, run back to the lab and get my…"

"It says *Mr. Fling-Um*. It was the last thing I saw it before I, well, you know." Norman interrupted, thinking he'd save Buford a trip to the lab. He shuddered as he remembered what happened after reading the name on the feeder.

"Okay, you're right." Sparky squinted and now that he knew what to look for he was able to read it. "Norman, go back to the feeder and see if you can repeat what happened, it could have been a fluke."

Norman took a step sideways, hid behind his brother, and shook his head no. He didn't want to be out here in the first place and he definitely wanted nothing to do with *Mr. Fling-Um*.

"Come on Norman this is important," Buford urged him on.

"For the Community," Roscoe added.

"And the quest for scientific data." Sparky used what he thought was the most persuasive argument.

"Couldn't you get someone else? I mean, I've already…" Norman stood with his back against the Big Rock, trembling with fear while the others formed a half circle around him.

"Sure, we could," Buford answered, "but we'd have to go back to the Clearing…"

"…who knows how long it would take to talk someone into coming out here." They were at it again; Buford starting a sentence and Sparky finishing it. "Then we'd have to go through a long explanation of how it works and what they were supposed to do."

"By then Bird Man will be back and we've lost a golden opportunity to figure out what's going on." Roscoe wrapped it up and turned to Norman.

Norman looked around, hoping someone from the Community who hadn't heard what happened to him had decided to come to the feeder for a mid-morning snack. He whimpered quietly when he didn't to see anyone.

After taking a moment to pull himself together he nodded okay and walked to the fence.

He took his time crossing the yard, delaying as long as possible the climb up the pole. He made it to the top, reached for the ring that circled the feeder tube and ended up like before, flat on his back in the middle of the yard.

He remembered turning over several times while he was in the air and seeing Bird Man's neighbor laughing and pounding the top of the picnic table with his hand.

With the neighbor on his deck, Sylvia could only watch from the garage. She couldn't afford to help Norman up and risk getting another bad report.

Norman got to his feet and staggered to the fence. Somehow he made it over and dropped to knees. He remained like that for a few minutes before things stopped spinning. While he waited, he massaged his shoulder hoping the ache he felt was just a bruise and not something more serious.

"Well, what do you think?" He asked when he was able to stand without holding on to the fence.

Roscoe looked at Sparky anxious to hear what he had to say.

Sparky pulled on his chin whiskers and scratched his nearly bald head before saying, "This may take awhile."

Roscoe and Norman walked back to the Clearing in silence while Buford stayed behind with Sparky and discussed possible solutions to the *Mr. Filing-Um* problem.

Roscoe called an emergency meeting of the Committee for the Protection of Neighborhood Resources. It was exactly the kind of problem they were facing that caused the founders of the Community to form the Committee in the first place.

When they were finally assembled, he explained why he had called them together and asked Norman to share his experience at the feeder.

When he finished, Darin, the senior member of the Committee asked, "What do you expect us to do about it?"

Roscoe was relieved when the meeting room door opened and he saw Sparky and Buford slip in. Before Sparky could sit down, Roscoe asked him to come forward and answer Darin's question.

Sparky pushed his glasses in place with the back of his paw and immediately started on the technical aspects of his plan. He'd just finished a lengthy description of calculating the effects of centrifugal force on a spinning object when he saw Roscoe shake his head no and motion with his paw to dumb things down so the Committee could understand him. He nodded he'd try, cleared his throat, and continued, "I'll need several volunteers and the first thing I'll do is weigh them. Then they'll go out to the feeder and get thrown from *Mr. Fling-Um*, like Norman was. When they land, I'll measure how far they are from the pole. The combination of weight and distance will give me an idea of the kind of force I'm dealing with."

"Let me make sure I've got this straight." Ferrel gave Sparky a funny look as he placed his elbows on the conference table. "You want us to grab the ring around this feeder thing, get thrown from here to kingdom come, then lay in Bird Man's yard unprotected until you run out and measure how far we are from the feeder pole? Is that the basic idea?" As usual he'd become the spokesman for the rest of the Committee.

Sparky thought about his question for a moment and then nodded yes, that summed it up pretty well.

"And this will tell you what?" Ferrel got up from the conference table and moved closer to Sparky.

"Well, if this *Mr. Fling-Um* device can throw someone that weighs a pound a specific distance, then I can extrapolate the…" He saw Roscoe running his paws across his neck, signaling that he was getting too technical again. "Oh, ah, what I mean is, I can figure out how strong it is and what it's going to take to shut it down." He shrugged, the answer seemed obvious to him.

Ferrel scratched his head. "I'd say as far as the first part goes, the getting flung from *Mr. Fling-Um* part, a little experience would be a definite plus, wouldn't you?" He looked at the Committee members and watched them nod their heads they agreed that having experience in this sort of thing would be a definite plus.

Sparky started to say as far a getting information was concerned it wouldn't make any difference one way or the other but Ferrel cut him off. "As a matter of fact, my guess is, a younger squirrel after going through this horrible ordeal might not have as many aches and pains the next morning as some of the rest of us." He chuckled when he said it and the Committee members laughed with him.

Sparky was not good at trying to explain the importance of gathering accurate data to those who'd gone no further than *Introduction To Science, Level 1* at seed school. What he was talking about was doing the grunt work required before coming to a conclusion. You set up an experiment, run it, record the data, and see where it leads. For him weight and distance were the big items and what happened to those involved in the experiment, well, if it wasn't something you could measure he really didn't see the point in talking about it.

"Take me for example." Ferrel continued sharing his thoughts, "If I so much as miss a limb when I'm climbing a tree and have to spin around and grab another one, my shoulder will ache for a week. It's hard to imagine what would it would be like if I were hurled through space and landed topsy-turvy in that human's yard. And, if that's not enough, there's the cat, what's her name?" He snapped his fingers and someone on the Committee whispered, "Sylvia." Ferrel shuddered before saying, "That's the one. Just thinking about what she's capable of doing while I'm out cold from being thrown from the feeder gives me the creeps." He made a show of dabbing an imaginary handkerchief against his forehead.

Roscoe stepped forward and gestured for Sparky to sit down. He'd explained what he thought was a workable plan, it was a Committee matter now. "What are you saying Ferrel?"

"Oh, I think it's pretty obvious what I'm saying Roscoe. Not that I mean to suggest you're a little too close to your buddy Sparky to see the flaws in his plan or maybe it's just that you're too close to the problem to see the obvious answer." He waved a paw letting everyone know he was moving on to a new subject. "Be that as it may, what I hear Sparky saying is we need someone with experience in the area of what did he call it? theoretical experimentation."

Roscoe started to interrupt and say Sparky had said just the opposite, that he was the one who said it, but before he could, Ferrel pressed on. "And, it would be better if this volunteer," he made little quote marks with his paws when he said volunteer, "was young and athletic."

"Which leads to what?" Roscoe made a gesture that Ferrel should finish what he was trying to say.

"Him," he pointed across the room to Norman.

A look of panic swept across Norman's face. He had a feeling if he hung around after Sparky finished something like this might happen.

"Now just a minute Ferrel, you heard him earlier, he's pretty shook up by the whole…"

"Mr. Chairman," Ferrel interrupted again, "you stated earlier that this is considered an official Committee meeting. So, I move that Norman be our permanent volunteer in this and any future experiments to determine the strength of any potentially dangerous device regardless of its configuration. And, that he should continue in that capacity until Sparky determines he has gathered enough information to come to a reasonable conclusion concerning the proper approach to solving this and any future problems."

Before Roscoe could object some one seconded the motion and a vote was called for.

Ferrel's motion passed five to one and the meeting was quickly adjourned with the Committee members congratulating one another on their ability to act quickly and decisively to head off a potential Community crises.

Norman stood by the window and watched the Committee members walk down the path to their safe, non-threatening nests. He brushed a tear from his cheek with his paw.

"Looks like you're it Norman." Roscoe spoke but Norman didn't turn around.

He shook his head yes, it looked that way to him too.

Roscoe knew his word was good and if Manny was the only one willing to take on *Mr. Fling-Um*, he'd be the last one to stand in his way.

"I understand there's a fence," he said in a husky voice.

Roscoe nodded yes there was a fence to climb.

"I'll need help. Me and fences don't…"

"We'll take care of that part Manny." Roscoe was overjoyed that someone had the courage to come forward, especially someone Manny's size. "When are you thinking about going out there?" Roscoe needed to know how much time he had to get a crew together to lift the fence high enough for him to crawl under.

Manny looked surprised at the question. "Now!" After saying it, he turned and slowly waddled up the path to Bird Man's yard.

"I can't possibly be ready before the first thing in…" Roscoe stopped, he knew there were no words strong enough to hold him back once he made up his mind.

He had no trouble finding volunteers to lift the fence. Some who'd been watching felt embarrassed that someone on the fringe of the Community like Manny had the courage to come forward when they'd been afraid to.

By the time Manny got there, the fence lifting team was in place and had worked out a way to get it high enough for him to squeeze under. As he slid beneath the fence those holding it up offered words of encouragement, although if truth were told, they had doubts he could pull it off.

When Bird Man's neighbor looked over the top of his newspaper and saw him ambling across the yard he jumped out of his chair, hurried inside, and closed the sliding glass door in case the giant squirrel changed directions and decided to come after him.

Sylvia was sunning herself near the back of the house but when she saw Manny crawl under the fence, she ran inside the garage and closed the cat door behind her.

Bird Man was walking past the kitchen window and glanced out to see what kind of birds had been attracted to the squirrel free feeder. He rubbed his eyes and leaned over the sink to get a closer look when he saw Manny leaning against the feeder pole, catching his breath from the walk across the yard.

TWO FEEDERS, NO WAITING

He tapped on the window and made a shooing motion with his fingers as Manny started up the pole.

When he got close to the top, he reached out with a paw and grabbed the ring that circled the feeder tube.

His weight caused the ring to turn, pulling him away from the pole. He took hold of the ring with his other paw and let go of the pole with his feet. His total weight was now supported entirely by the thin plastic ring around the device.

Mr. Fling-Um made a few jerky attempts to turn, trying in vain to gain enough momentum to throw him from the feeder. His weight proved to be too much and a corner of the ring pulled away from the feeder tube and before long the ring with Manny still clinging to it fell to the ground.

Pieces of *Mr. Fling-Um* were scattered around the base of the feeder as Manny slowly rolled over, grabbed hold of the pole, and pulled himself to his feet.

"You shouldn't have done that to Normy." He said and shook his fist in the direction of Bird Man's house. He was too far away to be heard and, if he had, it would have sounded to Bird Man like a series of squeaks and clicks. He rested for a moment, gathering enough strength to make the trip back to the fence.

Bird Man watched in disbelief. The handbook that came with *Mr. Fling-Um* said it would, "Outsmart the cleverest back yard pest and beat them at their own game." In addition it said the owner would, "Enjoy hours of amusement as these mischievous creatures are flung to the far corners of your yard."

When he saw pieces of *Mr. Fling-Um* and a tube full of seeds scattered over the ground, he tossed the handbook in the trash.

Manny was greeted with cheers as he wriggled under the fence.

Roscoe was waiting for him by the Big Rock and thanked him on behalf of the Community for what he'd done. He finished by saying, "There is no way to put a price tag on what you have accomplished."

Manny thought for a moment before grunting he could think of one.

Soon members of the Community were walking behind Manny as he slowly made his way back to the Clearing.

They each carried a small bag of seeds they'd picked from the grass around the broken feeder.

According to Manny's instructions half of the seeds were to go to Norman and the other half were to be delivered to his nest.

Roscoe felt it was a small price to pay for the sacrifice they'd made for the Community.

Part 3: The Best De-Fence

Manny's fame for saving the Community from *Mr. Fling-Um* lasted two days, because that's about how long most of the residents of Abner can remember things. Of course, Manny's attitude didn't help. He told those who thought they were doing him a favor by delivering seeds to his nest to, "Put 'um down and keep going."

He was not one who encouraged visitors.

Talk about *Mr. Fling-Um* stopped completely the day they carried Loren to the Clearing on a stretcher.

Things had been running smoothly since the encounter with *Mr. Fling-Um*. Bird Man finally started putting regular tasting seeds in what the Community called, "The Abner Side," of the feeder. It was really a technicality since the Community of Max was still reluctant to use their side, unwilling to accept Sylvia's change of heart as genuine.

Looking back, Roscoe could see he let his guard down too soon, he should have known Bird Man wouldn't give up that easily.

When they brought Loren to the Clearing they decided to leave him there because the aroma of something burning still clung to his fur. One of the Committee members commented, "If we bring him inside it will take a month to get the smell out of the meeting room." Loren's paws were blistered and even though it had been a while since he'd experienced whatever happened, he was lying on his back with his eyes open, staring intently at the blue sky but seeing nothing.

He'd gone to the feeder on his own so no one actually saw what happened. They found him in pretty much the condition he was in now.

Before long he began to moan.

Finally, he sat up and introduced himself to those gathered around him, which was confusing since most of them had known him all his life. It was obvious to the most casual observer something was out of whack.

Two members of the safety team ran over, wrapped him in a blanket, and encouraged him to lay back down.

Roscoe called a meeting of the Committee for the Protection of Neighborhood Resources but he wasn't sure how much good they could do since they knew nothing about what happened to Loren. When Sid the trauma counselor mentioned something about the feeder, Loren looked at him like he was trying to remember what happened and when he finally did, he started to cry.

Roscoe knew not having any factual information about the incident wouldn't slow the members of the Committee down. In the past they'd argued for hours with a lot less to go on than they had on what happened to Loren.

So far, they'd been meeting for over an hour. Sid had explained in detail that Loren was suffering from what was known in the counseling profession as PTFD or, *"Post traumatic feeder disorder."* Ferrel on the other hand was sure he'd been scared silly by a, "Creature from outside our solar system, probably some kind of alien life form. Gee whiz, isn't it obvious?" He'd argued, "Just look at his paws, you don't get a burn like that around here."

Their discussion came to a halt when Jules stuck his head in the meeting room and hollered, "You guys better come outside, it looks like we've got another one." After making the announcement he started to leave but spun around like he'd remembered something important. "This time we've got ourselves a witness."

The Committee couldn't decide if they should stay inside and continue arguing about what caused Loren's condition or go outside and find out what actually happened. They were still trying to make up their minds when Roscoe excused himself and left the room.

He could see another body lying next to Loren, who'd finally relaxed and fallen asleep. Traces of a smile played at the corners of his mouth. The new victim however, looked exactly like Loren had when they'd brought him to the Clearing.

"Who is it?" Roscoe asked someone at the back of the small crowd that had formed around the latest victim. There seemed to be less interest in this one than when they brought Loren in. The newness of a Community member being carried to the Clearing on a stretcher had worn off and Roscoe heard someone comment as they walked away, "You see someone like that once and you've seen them all."

Some visiting in the Clearing didn't even look up when they carried the second victim in, they just continued talking and moved up wind.

"Your not going to like this," the person next to Roscoe said grimly.

"It's not Penny Sue is it?" He couldn't make out the features of whoever was lying there but from the person's comment he'd assumed the worst.

"Penny Sue? Oh no, no nothing like that. If that's what you're thinking though, maybe this isn't so bad." He nodded and kept his eyes fixed on the bundle on the ground.

"Right I guess I just...who is it?" Roscoe asked as he moved toward the victim.

"It might be best if you stay back Roscoe, I mean this one smells real bad." One of the members of the safety team told him as she placed an orange cone next to the lifeless body.

Roscoe stopped when he caught the profile of his friend Marvin. His eyes were open but had a vacant look. His lips moved like he was chewing seeds or silently reciting a poem. Both his paws were wrapped in bandages the Women's Auxiliary had torn and wound in balls to be used by the safety team for occasions like this.

"Do you think he'll be okay?" Roscoe asked one of those who brought him in.

"I'm sure he will, but it's going to be awhile before he's able to pick seeds from a feeder on his own, his paws are burnt pretty bad."

Sympathy for his friend gradually turned to anger as it slowly dawned on Roscoe this was the work of Bird Man. Both victims had been at the feeder when whatever happened put them in their current condition.

Until now he'd seen Bird Man's gimmicks at the feeder as a mind game, coming up with clever ways to challenge the members of Abner. This time though he'd crossed the line in his attempt to keep them away from the feeder.

It looked to Roscoe like Bird Man had removed the gloves of decency and taken his tactics in a new, more dangerous direction. If Roscoe had anything to say about it, he'd show him he'd made a big mistake taking on the Community of Abner and putting its members at risk.

"Get Sparky," Roscoe called to Darin who, seeing the look of determination on his face, took off across the Clearing for Sparky's lab without asking why.

He turned to Norman who was kneeling next to Marvin, patting him on the shoulder, and telling him he was going to be okay. "Norman, I want you to go to Bird Man's yard and see if Sylvia can tell us anything about what's going on." He started to ask where the witness was but stopped. "Oh, tell her Marvin's going to be okay. I'm sure she's worried sick, they're friends you know."

When Norman got close to Bird Man's yard, Sylvia ran to the fence and studied his face for some sign of Marvin's condition. She was sure she'd never see him again. She'd been the one who pulled him from the feeder pole, dragged him to the fence, and waited anxiously for someone from the Community to come out for a snack.

After learning he was going to be okay she looked relieved and volunteered, "We talked for awhile and he didn't seem to be in a hurry. Then he put his paws on the pole and started shaking. I could smell something burning and his eyes got a funny look. So I knocked him down and carried him to the ah…" She stopped, her sobs could be heard across the yard. Bird Man's neighbor looked up from his newspaper trying to determine where the noise was coming from.

"Take it easy Sylvia, he's going to be okay. You saved his life." Norman tried to think of an important question to ask, because he knew he'd be interrogated by Roscoe when he got back to the Clearing, but he couldn't come up with one.

"I don't know if it will help but I saw my master hook some string to the feeder pole early this morning. It may be nothing I just thought…"

TWO FEEDERS, NO WAITING

She stopped talking when she realized the neighbor had put his newspaper down and moved to the edge of his deck to see what was going on at the back of the yard.

"Sorry Norman but I've got to..." Her words turned into a hiss as she arched her back and smacked the fence above his head.

As he was running back to the Clearing he heard her say, "Tell Marvin I'm sorry. I should have..." She stopped, unable to say more, overcome with emotion as she pictured her friend, lying unconscious beside the feeder pole.

"Strings?" Sparky looked up from his place at the conference table. "She actually used the word strings?"

He and Roscoe had been discussing the feeder problem when Norman entered the meeting room and told them what Sylvia said.

Roscoe had put out the word that no one was to go near the feeder until they could figure out what was going on. He had Lester place an orange cone by the fence, warning anyone who hadn't heard what happened to stay out of the yard. Then, he ordered Darin to open the bin where the emergency seed supply is kept. It wasn't a long term solution but, if they took it easy, it would last for the rest of the week.

"That just doesn't make sense. Let's go out and take a look." Sparky got up from his chair and hurried out of the room. Roscoe gestured for Norman to come with them.

Norman hesitated. He knew if he went and some experiment needed to be done he'd be the one doing it, but he was curious about what was happening at the feeder so he decided to tag along.

"Well, I can tell you one thing right off the bat, they aren't strings," Sparky studied the feeder through his binoculars. "They're wires just as I thought."

"And that means?" Roscoe didn't see where he was going with this, wires or strings sounded the same to him.

"Well, it could mean a lot of things but it probably means electricity," Sparky answered confidently. "That would explain the blistered paws and signs of shock." He had a tendency to mumble when he spoke because his lips weren't capable of keeping up with his brain as it evaluated data and zipped through alternative solutions to the problem. "The thing I need to know now is, if it's on all the time or only when we show up."

He pulled the binoculars back up and studied the feeder again. He was about to put them down when he saw a bird leave the branch of a nearby tree and land on the perch of the feeder tube. It pulled a seed through the opening and flew away.

Sparky smiled and mumbled, "Well, that answers that question." He told Norman to, "Run over and touch the feeder pole. Bird Man's gone and his neighbor is not on his deck so the coast is clear."

Norman gave Roscoe a look that pleaded for him to step in and point out how dangerous it was. There were already two bodies stretched out in the Clearing and he had no desire to become the third.

"I think you'll be okay," Sparky added to encourage him.

"You think?" Norman looked at Sparky then back at Roscoe. "Is that the best you can do? You think I'll be okay? You saw what Loren and Marvin looked like and I'm supposed to feel good about this because you **think** I'll be okay? Is think the best you've got?"

"I'm almost positive nothing's going to happen. I'm 99% sure" That was as far as Sparky could go, he was too much of a scientist to say anything was 100% sure until he ran a few tests.

Norman muttered to himself as he walked to the fence. "He's almost positive and I'm supposed to feel good about it?"

Sylvia got out of her bed in the garage and pushed the cat door open when she heard Norman climb over the fence. She gave a quick glance at the deck and when she saw the neighbor wasn't there, she joined him when he was half way to the feeder.

"Didn't you see the orange cone?" Sylvia knew Roscoe had put the feeder off limits to everyone in the Community.

"It's Sparky. He wants me to touch the feeder pole." He shook his head as he said it; he couldn't believe he was actually going to do it.

Sylvia left him and was going back to the garage when she saw Roscoe wave for her to come over to the fence.

They watched Norman turn and look their way, hoping the wave was meant for him and he'd received an eleventh hour pardon. Instead, he saw Sparky gesture with his paws he should go ahead and get it over with.

Norman closed his eyes, reached out, and touched the pole with the tip of his finger.

Nothing happened.

He grabbed the pole with both with both paws and was relieved when it felt like it did all the other times he'd come to the feeder.

He looked at Sparky hoping he'd see some sign that said he'd done enough. Instead, he saw him put one paw over the other, telling him he should climb to the top of the pole.

Norman shrugged, resigned to seeing the experiment through to the end.

He started climbing, thinking as long I've looked danger in the eye I might as well be rewarded for it.

Sparky made a note on his pad then asked Sylvia if she could go inside and look for a small black box. "I'm guessing it's close to the kitchen window."

She nodded okay, crossed the yard, and disappeared through the cat door.

Roscoe was about to say things were working out pretty well when he saw the neighbor open the sliding glass door and step out on his deck. He set a glass of ice tea on a small table and started back inside to get a magazine but stopped when he saw Norman hanging upside down, picking seeds from the feeder tube.

He looked at the cat door expecting to see some action from Sylvia. About the time he'd made up his mind to go back inside and leave a message on Bird Man's answering machine Sylvia shot out of the garage and chased Norman to the fence. She stayed a few inches behind him, apologizing as she ran. He leaped for the bar at the top of the fence and barely cleared it when she grabbed for him.

She howled and tore at the fence with her paw. When she did, she threw a crumpled scrap of paper through an opening that landed at Norman's feet.

He picked it up and ran to catch Roscoe and Sparky who were moving quickly down the path to the lab.

Once there, Sparky went to a large piece of cardboard nailed to the wall. He made a rough sketch of the feeder pole, the feeder, and the back of Bird Man's house. Then he added wires that ran from the window to the feeder. He stepped back and studied what he'd drawn, checking to make sure he'd left nothing out.

While Sparky was at the board, Norman flattened the scrap of paper Sylvia had thrown at him and compared it to what Sparky had drawn.

"She gave me this before I left." Norman lifted the paper so Roscoe and Sparky could see. They'd missed seeing her do it because they'd started back to the lab before she chased him out of the yard. They knew something had changed to make Sylvia act the way she had and assumed Bird Man had returned home.

"What's a pull?" Norman was looking at the sketch and didn't understand some of the notes Sylvia had written. A shaky line lead away from the word **pULl** and an arrow at the end of the line pointed to the feeder.

"I think she means pole," Roscoe explained. "And here, where she's written, **stRrmgs**, she probably means strings but Sparky says they're not really strings but wires."

"How about the, **fFo** and **No** she's written near this box by the window?" Roscoe looked over Norman's shoulder and couldn't figure it out either.

While they were trying to solve the notation problem, Sparky had focused on the way she'd drawn the wires. She showed one looped around the feeder pole while the other disappeared in the ground. She'd written near the end of the wire, "**somThiNks boRRoweD there**."

Sparky smiled. As soon as he saw the note he knew exactly what was going on. He was sure she meant buried, not borrowed and, if that was the case, he immediately came up with two ways to beat Bird Man at his own game.

One was subtle, he would never know what was going on.

The other was spectacular.

In his hurry to make a few corrections to his drawing Sparky accidentally knocked Sylvia's sketch off the table. He picked it up, threw it back, and turned to add a final detail to the drawing.

TWO FEEDERS, NO WAITING

"Off and On," Norman said excitedly. "It says off and on."

Sparky gave him a look that asked, "What are you talking about?"

Norman pointed to the paper. When Sparky threw it on the table it landed upside down. What appeared on the sketch as **fFo** and **No**, turned out to be **oFf** and **oN** when seen backwards.

That was the last piece of the puzzle Sparky needed to complete the picture and confirm his plans. He looked at Roscoe, smiled his crooked smile, and raised his eyebrows a couple of times.

Then he started talking so quickly Roscoe had no way of keeping up. "Bird Man controls the flow of electricity to the feeder by this switch." He pointed to the box he'd drawn by the kitchen window. "It's usually off. That's why you didn't get shocked when you touched the pole." He looked at Norman and nodded. "That makes sense doesn't it? You don't know who might wander into your yard and accidentally touch the feeder pole. Or maybe one of his precious birds would get fried if it was on when he left the house."

He drew a big circle around the base of the feeder. "So, he turns the switch to on when he sees one of us crossing the yard and bingo, we get shocked. But, what we're interested in is not what's attached to the pole but right here." He drew a circle around the place where the second wire stopped just past the feeder pole.

Roscoe and Norman looked at each other and mouthed the words, "We are?" They knew better than question what he meant and break his train of thought by asking what he would consider to be meaningless questions. He preferred to work alone, sometimes staying in his lab for days if he was trying to solve a particularly difficult problem. When he finished he'd come to the Clearing with dark circles under his eyes and so thin he looked like he'd gone on a hunger strike.

"On the sketch, where she says the wires go to, 'somethink borrowed there,' she was closer to the truth than she thought. The wire connects to a rod or nail or what is technically referred to as a ground; without it, nothing works. No shock. No buzz. Zilch. Zero. Absolutely, positively, nothing."

Sparky stepped away from the board and smiled before asking, "So guys, what do you want? The old element of surprise or the ever popular, kaboom?"

Roscoe had never seen Sparky like this. He was normally cool and unemotional as he analyzed every part of whatever problem he was working on. When he finished he'd explain the results in a detached, almost disinterested way. At that point the excitement of discovery was over and the rest, he would explain with a shrug, was just working out the details.

But now, he was hopping from one foot to the other, giggling like a kid who just discovered seed school was closed for a snow day and mumbling, "Oh boy, this is going to be good."

He stopped and it was like he'd just noticed there were others present. He looked at Roscoe, raised his paws and said, "What?"

"You lost us buddy. We have no idea what you're talking about." Roscoe had learned from working with Sparky on other projects that the best approach was to say what was on his mind and not try to sugar coat it or act like he understood when he didn't.

"Oh, right I see." Sparky stopped dancing around and went to the board. "Plan A, we remove the ground and replace it with a nonconductor like a piece of wood or something like that. He looked at them, eyes wide, expecting a nod of recognition. When he didn't get it he continued. "Anyway, he turns on the switch but nothing happens. The problem with that approach is he'll probably figure out what we've done and fix it. Then we're back to square one. See what I mean?"

Norman and Roscoe shook their heads yes but weren't any closer to understanding what he was talking about than when they started. It didn't make any difference because Sparky kept going like there had been no question mark at the end of his sentence.

"**BUT**, plan B, and this is a solution you're going to love, will bring the little black box to its knees. Not literally, it's just a box it doesn't have knees." It was hard for them to follow what he was saying. He kept laughing and smacking the top of the table with his paw. From Roscoe's perspective he was getting sillier with each passing moment, saying things like the black box not having knees.

"So, we attach another wire here," he made a black dot where the wire went into the ground, "and we runs it to de-fence, like a datta," He'd slipped into some kind of strange accent. "And presto, chango, shazam, **kaboom**. Boys," he was laughing so hard he could hardly talk, 'we've got ourselves a blackout."

Roscoe and Norman didn't know what to say because they'd been lost since they entered the lab. They weren't sure if he said he'd found a way to back something out or knock someone out but it didn't make any difference because neither one made sense to them.

"Sparky, are you okay?" His conduct was beginning to worry Roscoe.

"No Roscoe, McBoscoe, I'm not *okay*. I'm so far beyond *okay* I can't see it in my rear view mirror. If *okay* is a nut, I'm a tree. If…"

Roscoe hated to interrupt but he wasn't sure how long he'd keep going. "I'm just, concerned about you, that's all."

Sparky reached over and patted Roscoe on the head. "And don't think it's not appreciated my friend. No harm no foul." He giggled as he said it. "I'm going to get some wire, why don't you tell everyone to meet by the Big Rock at sundown? This is really going to be something Roscoe," he mumbled as he walked away. He stopped and pointed a finger at them. "I will personally guarantee you will never see anything like this again." He continued to the back of his lab and Roscoe could hear him say, "Oh boy, I can hardly wait."

The message started out as, "Meet at the Big Rock tonight for something you'll never see again in your lifetime." But, by the time it made it to the last member of the Community, it had changed to, "We're going to have a fight with another Community so bring some big rocks."

It was no wonder then that several members of the Community chose to stay in their nests and that Dirk and his gang of rough necks from the dump were the first ones to show up.

When Roscoe explained why they were there, Dirks group was divided on whether to hang around and watch the fireworks or go back to the dump and play cards. For them, watching fireworks was several steps down from fighting another Community.

The crowd that had gathered at the Big Rock was getting restless and

Roscoe had to ask them to quiet down. Finally Sparky showed up and had Buford hold the drawing he'd made of Bird Man's yard so everyone could see it. He asked Roscoe to point to various places on the paper as he explained why he'd invited them here.

"Bird Man has a box called a transformer by the kitchen window." Roscoe pointed to the black box by the window on the drawing.

"It's called a transformer because it changes or transforms AC current to…" His attempt to explain the details of the inner workings of the transformer was met by yawns and the sight of several closing their eyes and dozing off. In general, the members of the Community were not that interested in the technical side of things. To them something either worked or it didn't, that was good enough for them. And, if it didn't, they knew Sparky could fix it.

"When birds use the feeder the transformer is turned off and everything is okay." A murmur swept through the crowd wondering why they'd been asked to come to the Big Rock way past their bedtime just to hear it was okay for the birds to use the feeder. They didn't have to come all the way out here to hear what they could have read in *The Abner Echo*.

Besides, a light rain was falling and it was starting to get cold.

"But," Sparky had to raise his voice to be heard above the grumbling, "when anyone from the Community comes to the feeder, he turns the transformer on and, well, you saw what happened to Loren and Marvin." The crowd quieted down. They had indeed seen what happened and couldn't help but wonder what it would have been like if they'd been the one who touched the pole.

"Earlier this afternoon when Bird Man was gone Buford and I, actually Buford did most of the work, changed a few things around." Sparky stopped, he wanted them to know what they'd done but knew if he got too deep into the details he'd lose them. He would have loved to have explained to them all that went into deciding whether to replace the object Bird Man used with a non-conducting ground or to run the wire to the fence but he knew it would be lost on them. "He took one of the wires," Roscoe pointed to the wires coming from the black box on the drawing, "and hooked it to the fence here."

TWO FEEDERS, NO WAITING

Roscoe tapped the end of the pointer on the black dot that represented where the wire connected to the fence.

The crowd was silent.

Most of them weren't very good at reading maps and were still trying to find out where, on the sketch, the Big Rock was located. Those who managed to grasp some of the reason for changing the connection from the pole to the fence didn't see what difference it would make.

Finally, someone said, "Isn't that something? And you say Buford did that?"

Sparky turned to Roscoe, pleading for him to take over. After all, it was his idea to let the crowd know what was going on in the first place.

Roscoe nodded and stepped away from the drawing. "You're going to have to stay away from the fence a while longer. The Committee order not to go to the feeder is still in effect. Tonight you will see…" Roscoe stopped when he saw everyone in the crowd swing their eyes away from him to the back of Bird Man's house. Most in the crowd had only heard of Sylvia, so when they saw her walk through the cat door and stretch, they gasped and stepped back.

"Forget about the transformer thing Roscoe, I'll take my chances with the feeder pole rather than that cat any day." Someone spoke from the back.

Efforts on Roscoe's part to explain that she was their friend were lost as many of them gathered their things and headed back to the Clearing; they'd seen enough. They wondered if that was the point of the whole exercise, to scare them half out of their minds.

"Please wait, you're going to miss the fireworks." A handful stopped at the mention of fireworks and came back, but most of them kept going.

"The reason Sylvia, that's the cat's name, went back inside and closed the cat door is to let us know Bird Man has come home." Roscoe pointed to the garage as he spoke.

The crowd nodded but couldn't see what difference it made. They asked one another if they'd ever seen anything as scary looking as the cat before? They stopped talking and thoughts of Sylvia vanished when they saw Norman climb the fence and begin the long walk to the feeder.

He'd only taken a few steps in the yard when the porch light came on, flooding the back of the house with light. Rather than run back to the fence after being caught in the yard, Norman stood on his back feet and waved in the direction of the kitchen window. Community members could hear him saying, "Thank you. Thank you very much." He locked his paws behind his back, bent at the waist, and began moving toward the feeder like an ice skater, sliding from one foot to the other, as he sailed effortlessly across a frozen pond. Occasionally he'd throw in a spin or a twirl.

Bird Man looked out of his kitchen window, it was obvious to those by the Big Rock that he was reaching for the thing Sparky called the black box. He was so absorbed in watching Norman approach the feeder he didn't notice a change had taken place in the wires that ran from the window to the feeder pole.

When Norman was close to the feeder Bird Man moved the transformer to the window sill and placed his thumb on the switch.

Norman stood beside the pole thinking it was all about trusting Sparky now. If he had any lingering doubts about his technical skills, he should turn and run back to the safety of the fence, he'd had his fifteen seconds of fame. But, he knew Sparky was careful in his work and if he said nothing would happen when he touched the pole that was good enough for him.

He reached out and the moment his paw touched the pole he heard a click as Bird Man slid the switch on the transformer from the off position to on.

Instantly a shower of sparks erupted from the place on the chain link fence where Buford had hooked the other end of the wire.

Norman could hear members of the Community say, "Oh." Then they heard a pop from inside Bird Man's house and watched in amazement as all the lights went out.

The crowd applauded and stepped closer for a better look.

There was another explosion in front of Bird Man's house and sparks from a box mounted on a pole high in the air rained down on his sidewalk and driveway.

Before the crowd huddled near the fence could react to the exploding transformer, the houses on either side of street grew dark and those inside rushed out to see what was going on. For the first time in his life Norman saw the backyard and the street in front of Bird Man's house grow dark. It was, he thought, what it must have looked like when Abner, the founder of the Community first came here and claimed it as their new home.

His attention was brought back to the moment by the sound of the crowd chanting Sparky's name. He could see through the smoke slowly rising from the yard members of the Committee trying to lift Sparky on their shoulders while he kept backing away and saying, "It was nothing. Really. That's okay. No thanks." He looked at Roscoe, pleading for him to do something.

"The ban has been lifted and the seeds are on the house." Roscoe removed the orange cone from in front of the fence and bowed as the members of the Community who'd remained for the show forgot about Sparky, scrambled over the fence, and raced to the feeder.

"But not on Bird Man's house," Sparky hollered after them.

"Why not his house?" Roscoe asked, knowing the answer.

"No lights," Sparky said trying to look serious.

Roscoe heard sirens in the distance and saw Bird Man and his neighbors standing in the street, pointing to the fire shooting out of the transformer above their heads.

He wondered what other Communities did when faced with situations like this and didn't have someone like Sparky to bail them out.

He turned to say something but discovered Sparky had gone. There was no reason for him to hang around, the problem of the electrified feeder pole had been solved and all that remained were details.

Little Sherman

Penny Sue climbed in their nest, her face flushed from the effort. She was breathing quickly, not from exertion but excitement. The thing that told Roscoe something special was going on was the wide smile on her face. Not that she's a sour puss, she smiles a lot, but there was something different about her.

She walked to a place directly in front of him and stopped, blocking the light he needed to read his book.

"What's going on?" he asked.

"Guess who's going to pay us a visit?" Her smile remained in place.

"Penny I couldn't guess…"

"Little Sherman," she said before he had a chance to finish.

"Little Sherman?" Roscoe tried to think of where he'd heard the name but couldn't come up with anything. "I'm not sure if I know…"

"Lois and Elliot's son Sherman. That's what they call him, Little Sherman. He's only three months old." Roscoe wondered about the sound in her voice. There was something different and it bothered him that he couldn't figure out what it was. She seemed more alive and enthusiastic than when she left earlier for the monthly Women's Auxiliary meeting.

"Lois and Elliot have a baby?" Roscoe knew he'd been busy but took pride in keeping up with what was going on in the Community but it looked like he'd missed this one. His job as Chairman of the Committee for the Protection of Neighborhood Resources had taken every minute of every day for months and he saw no relief in sight. First, Seed Man moved away taking his feeder with him. Then there was the experience with Bird Man that practically cost him his life.

This had been his first day off in weeks. He had no meetings and no appointments scheduled. He'd planned on finishing the book he'd checked out of the library that was almost overdue. Friend or not, if he was late getting the book back he knew he'd get an earful from Webster.

After that, he was seriously considering taking a nap.

"Well I guess we better see what we need to do to get things ready for the little tyke." He hoped his voice sounded more enthusiastic about the visit than he felt. He was still shook up from the Bird Man experience. He hadn't slept well the last two nights, waking up just before Bird Man pulled the trigger of the shotgun that was aimed at his head.

"There won't be time for that," Penny Sue said a little too quickly as far as he was concerned.

"Why? When are they coming? This afternoon? Tomorrow morning?" Roscoe hoped it was in the morning, he needed rest and plenty of it.

"Actually, now," Penny Sue walked to the side of the nest, leaned out, and waved to someone on the ground.

In seconds Lois, Elliott, and a toddler Roscoe guessed was Little Sherman, climbed in his nest.

"This is so sweet of you," Lois said. "We'll only be gone for the day and unless there's some traveling snafu, we should be back before dark." She was talking to Penny Sue but looking at Roscoe, she was having second thoughts about leaving her son with him.

"Take all the time you need, we'll be fine." Penny Sue took Sherman's paw and walked over to Roscoe. "Sherman, say hello to Uncle Roscoe."

Little Sherman stood in front of Roscoe and stared at the floor of the nest. He finally looked up and said, "**HiRoscoenicetomeetcha.**"

Roscoe looked at Penny Sue and shrugged, he hadn't understood a thing the kid said. "Did you get any of that?" He scratched his head and wondered if he was developing a hearing problem.

"Well of course silly. He said Hi and that it was nice to meet you or something along those lines. Isn't he cute?" Penny Sue attempted a pat on Sherman's head but he ducked and avoided her paw.

Lois and Elliot hugged their son, told him they'd be back soon, and that he was to be good for Aunt Penny and Uncle Roscoe.

"Are you sure that's what he said? I didn't catch any of it." Roscoe felt uncomfortable, Little Sherman hadn't taken his eyes off him as his parents hugged him and said goodbye.

"Roscoe with someone this young, you can't just listen with your ears," she put a paw to her ear then moved it over her heart, "you have to listen here too." She patted her chest.

She stood quietly for a moment and looked fondly at Little Sherman and then, in a sudden change of mood announced, "Well, I guess it's time for me to go."

"Go?" Roscoe looked at her, shocked she was thinking of leaving him alone with Sherman.

"Oh, didn't I tell you? The Women's League is having lunch after the morning meeting." She spoke quickly as she brushed the fur around her face. "I just came by to drop Sherman off and pick up the five seed casserole I made." She smiled at Sherman and then told Roscoe, "I'll be at the Senior Center if you need me."

"But Penny Sue, you can't just…" Roscoe stopped. There was no reason to continue, she was already half way to the Clearing.

He watched the path for a moment, hoping she'd caught the note of panic in his voice and turned back. When he saw her follow the curve that leads to the Clearing, his heart sank.

He turned and discovered Sherman had followed him to the edge of the nest.

"**Whatwegotodonow?**" He asked.

Roscoe had no idea what he said or what he was supposed to do with a three month old for who knew how long.

"I've got a great idea, why don't we sit down and read this nice book about…" Roscoe stopped when he saw Sherman shake his head no and get an angry look on his face.

"**Noreadbookweplay.**" He folded his arms across his tiny chest and stared at Roscoe.

"After we read, we can go…"

"**Wego?**" Sherman sprang in the air, twisting in the same motion so he was facing the entrance to the nest and, before Roscoe could react, he was over the side.

"Sherman wait," Roscoe called as he hurried across the nest and looked over the edge.

Halfway down the tree he saw Sherman hanging from a small branch. He looked up at Roscoe and without a trace of fear said, **"Menoclimbdownsogoodyet."** His small arms were stretched out to their full length and his toes pointed toward the ground twenty feet beneath him.

"Okay. Okay. Don't panic. Take it easy." Roscoe tried to keep his voice calm as he crawled past Sherman. "Hold on, I'll figure something out," he said with more confidence than he felt. When he reached the ground he looked up at Sherman's trembling body and knew he couldn't hang on much longer.

He started to tell him to let go of the branch but before he could, he heard a snap and watched in horror as the limb gave way. Sherman fell into his arms, knocking him down, and sending them both rolling across the grass.

Sherman struggled to get out loose. **"Again. Wedoagain."**

"I don't think so little buddy, once is enough for today." Roscoe helped him up but kept Sherman's paw gripped tightly in his.

"Wedonow?" Sherman looked up and asked.

"Well I thought we could go to the Clearing and…" Roscoe stopped and shook his head. Was he beginning to understand what the kid said?

Sherman yanked his paw from Roscoe's and took off down the path to the Clearing. Roscoe decided he would leave the word "go" out of any further conversation he had with Sherman.

Roscoe jogged to keep up, not that Sherman was that fast a runner, he was all over the place. He'd go forward several feet, then lurch to one side, or drop to the ground if a leg wasn't in the right position to hold him when his foot came down.

As they approached the Clearing, Roscoe hollered for his friend Marvin to grab Sherman and hold him until he could catch up.

It took Marvin a moment to figure out what he said. When he finally did, it was too late, as Sherman ducked under his outstretched arms.

TWO FEEDERS, NO WAITING

Marvin took off after him, knowing a busy street was not far from the Clearing.

Sherman was tiring. He ran with his head down as the bouncing and falling got worse. But he kept going, unaware he'd left the boundaries of the Community of Abner and entered the world of humans.

At the last moment Marvin leaped forward and grabbed his foot. He heard a squeal and held on as Sherman rolled over and tried to jerk his foot free.

"**Letgofoot.Letgofoot.**" He hollered but Marvin had no idea what he was saying.

Roscoe finally caught up with them as they struggled on the ground. He marveled that someone as small as Sherman could put up such a fight.

"Okay little guy, recess is over, let's go back to the nest and take a nap. What do you say?" Roscoe stood on one side of him with Marvin on the other, each holding a paw.

"**Nonap.**" He protested as they approached the Clearing. "**Menotakenap.**"

Marvin chuckled. "I used to be the same way when I was his age, I hated naps. There was just too much to do to spend a second in bed." He thought for a moment. "Now I can't wait for my lunch break."

They laughed as Sherman struggled to break free.

"**Nonap.PleaseRoscoenonap,**" he continued pleading as they walked past the statue of Abner. Community members, standing around visiting, looked at them and smiled, they'd seen Little Sherman act like this before.

They were at the base of Roscoe's tree when Marvin said, "I guess you can take it from here." There was a moment when he released his grip and Roscoe turned preparing to carry him to his nest. Sherman felt the change, pulled his paw away, and broke free.

Roscoe watched hopelessly as he scampered down the path to the Big Rock that separates their Community from the Community of Ben. Crossing the border between Communities is not what concerned him, relations between them were good. Youngsters from Ben out on their own for the first time often made a wrong turn and ended up in the Clearing.

What did concern him was that the Big Rock was directly across from Bird Man's yard.

Marvin and Roscoe picked up the pace as they ran after him.

They watched Sherman bounce along, occasionally falling in the grass on the side of the path. "Please go straight," Roscoe whispered, it was almost a prayer.

The two grownups were closing the distance that separated them from Sherman. "Go to the Big Rock," Roscoe yelled and waved his arms.

Sherman slowed for a moment, something caught his attention. Roscoe hoped he'd heard him and for the first time since he'd been in his care, decided to do as he was told.

As they got closer, Roscoe heard it too. Music was coming from the back of Bird Man's house and along with it he could hear the low hum of human voices. Bird Man was entertaining guests in his yard.

Sherman did the unthinkable, he veered left, and headed straight for Bird Man's yard.

"Don't worry Roscoe," a breathless Marvin tried to encourage his friend. "He'll never make it over the fence, he's too small and not strong enough to climb something so…"

Marvin stopped talking and watched in amazement as Sherman slipped under the fence and continued in a full sprint toward the back of the house.

"Nutcake.Memelnutcake," they heard him say as he gasped for breath.

The humans spread around the yard were busy talking and laughing, they didn't see the small splash of color running toward them.

But the dog one of them brought did.

He blinked and squinted, trying to bring into focus what was traveling toward him in such an odd way; bouncing from side to side, taking one step back, before lowering his head and moving unsteadily forward.

He whimpered. He stood. He wagged his tail. At last there was something at the party that was interesting. He took a hesitant first step forward and then broke into a full sprint toward the object, going through some inner geometry that predicted exactly where their two bodies would collide.

TWO FEEDERS, NO WAITING

Because of the distance that separated them, Marvin and Roscoe could only look on in horror, powerless to save Little Sherman. The fence separated them and the dog was too close.

Roscoe's mind reeled. What will I tell Lois? He remembered the look of doubt on her face when she realized he would be taking care of her son. How could he possibly explain his inability to keep a three month old out of trouble? And what would Penny Sue think? His head hurt from worry and his heart ached.

He looked up when he heard a bang and saw a white flash fly out of the cat door at the back of the garage. It was Sylvia, one time enemy of the Community of Abner but because of Marvin, she was now their friend. She quickly maneuvered through the forest of legs that were between her and Little Sherman.

The dog was focused on the ball of fur coming toward him. He was about to make a mid-course adjustment as he tried to keep up with the stops and starts of the approaching object. When they were only a few feet apart and the dog had opened his mouth preparing to bite down, Sylvia plowed into him.

He rolled over and yelped in surprise. He'd been blind sided, so focused on the object in front of him he'd been unaware there was anything remotely close.

Sylvia didn't stop after the collision. She swerved to one side, picked Sherman up with her teeth, and ran straight to the fence. She placed a bewildered Sherman on the ground, his heart beating from exertion and frightened by the huge white cat standing over him.

"I think this belongs to one of you?" Sylvia said and chuckled.

Sherman didn't protest when Roscoe reached under the fence and clamped a paw on his shoulder.

"I'm baby sitting Sylvia," Roscoe told her. "I can't thank you..."

Sylvia cut him off with, "No problem." She was not big on sentimentality. "Are they watching?" She jerked her head in the direction of the house.

Roscoe nodded yes and she instantly smacked the fence and howled.

Roscoe picked a bewildered Sherman up and ran toward the path to the Clearing.

He'd just made the turn at the Big Rock when he heard Bird Man tell Sylvia, "Now you go back and apologize to Fifee." Even though he was scolding her it was impossible for him to keep the pride from his voice. He pointed to the fence and explained to the guests, "It's the squirrels. She hates them."

Marvin looked at Roscoe and said, "Fifee? Boy, they sure give their pets strange names."

Finally Roscoe climbed in his nest. As soon he stepped inside, he felt Sherman go limp and knew he'd fallen asleep, exhausted from his afternoon play. Roscoe sat down, unwilling to let go of his paw, afraid if he did they'd be off on another adventure.

He felt a tug on his arm and opened his eyes expecting to see Penny Sue back from her meeting. Instead, he found he was looking into the concerned face of Edgar.

"We need to talk," he said in a serious tone.

"I don't think this is the best ti..." Roscoe stopped when he felt Sherman squirm at the sound of Edgar's voice. It took a moment before he settled down and was sleeping soundly again.

"Perhaps not for you Roscoe but there are things that need to be said." Edgar spoke in a whisper. It was obvious he'd rehearsed his speech and was anxious to deliver it regardless of the situation.

Roscoe gave up, he knew there was no chance of getting him to wait until later.

"It won't be long before I go the way of all squirrels. I'm sure you're aware of that." Edgar was having trouble with the way whispering made things sound. It removed the emotional highs and lows he'd planned to throw in at crucial moments in his speech.

"Edgar that's so far down the path I wouldn't..." Roscoe stopped as Edgar raised a paw, cutting him off. Edgar thought for a moment, trying to remember where he was before he was interrupted.

"Oh yes," he said, "the way of all squirrels. Anyway, I'd hoped by this time, how shall I put I?, the family circle would remain unbroken." He raised his eyebrows, asking with the gesture if Roscoe understood what he meant. "Continued," he added in case Roscoe didn't get it. "Carried on."

"Edgar, Penny Sue and I have talked about this and when we're ready we'll..."

"Have I shared my personal experience with you Roscoe?" Edgar continued like he hadn't heard him.

Roscoe started to say yes, a number of times, but Edgar didn't give him a chance.

"Edna and I thought exactly as you two are thinking; take some time to get to know each other, establish ourselves in the Community, build our first nest and, when everything is perfect, think about having children."

Edgar smiled and nodded knowingly before asking, "Sound familiar?" He shook his head, suggesting the folly of that kind of thinking. "Then we had Edgar Jr., he's named after me you know."

Edgar stared somewhere above the rim of the nest, a light mist covered his eyes. "Then Edna discovered she couldn't, well, you know, have any, ah...that was it for us. We had Edgar Jr. of course but what if we'd waited a little longer to have him? Why, we might have missed the joy of parenthood. And of course there would have been no Penny Sue." He finished with a rise in his voice like he wanted Roscoe to consider what his life would be like without Penny Sue.

He looked at Roscoe through tear filled eyes. "Do you understand what I'm saying?" he whispered.

"Yes sir, I do." Roscoe replied. He could have argued the case for waiting but he knew he would be wasting his breath, they'd been through this a number of times. He also knew if the conversation continued their voices would get louder and Sherman's nap would be cut short.

"Good. Glad to hear it. Couldn't be better. I think it's important to talk about these things from time to time." Edgar turned and left the nest.

Roscoe sat back in his chair, suddenly aware that his arm had gone to sleep where Sherman's head pressed against it.

Edgar's head popped over the side of the nest. "Did I mention there's a Committee meeting in fifteen minutes?" He waited to make sure Roscoe heard him, waved goodbye, and was gone.

Roscoe figured he must have dozed because he vaguely remembered hearing more scratches on the tree trunk and waking up mad at the thought that Edgar was returning with another argument for parenthood.

"Edgar," he said, "I've got the picture okay? Were just not…" He opened his eyes and realized Penny Sue was back, standing next to his chair.

"What's this about Edgar?" She gave him a curious look.

He had to blink the sleep from his eyes because both his arms were still wrapped around Sherman.

"Well, your grandfather didn't think we were moving along fast enough in the, ah, child production department." He blushed when he saw Lois and Elliot standing behind her, apparently finished with whatever business they'd planned to do and were back to pick up Little Sherman.

They smiled at the sight of Roscoe, sitting in his favorite chair with their son resting safely in his arms.

Penny Sue took Sherman from Roscoe and in the process woke him up.

"Mommy and Daddy are here now Little Sherman," his parents leaned forward and spoke softly, allowing him time to wake up from his nap. Lois held out her arms and said, "We're going home now snookums."

Sherman twisted in Penny Sue's arms and reached for Roscoe.

"MestaywifRoscoehefun."

He jumped from her arms and grabbed Roscoe's leg.

"No, Sherman, it's time to go home. And," Roscoe gave a quick look at Penny Sue, "I have to go to a meeting."

"Roscoe," Penny Sue was astonished, "you understood him."

"Yeah well, I guess I do. Kind of." Roscoe felt his face flush.

They listened to Sherman scream as he was carried down their tree.

"NooomestaywifRoscoe."

"Sounds like you made quite an impression on the little guy." Penny Sue took his paw.

"Well, we had a little trouble at first but after that, yeah, I guess we did okay." Roscoe wondered if he should say anything about the close call at Bird Man's. He decided it could wait. "You know, it may sound silly but I think I'm going to miss him."

There was a long pause and Roscoe started to say he'd better get going but stopped when he heard Penny Sue say, "Roscoe."

It wasn't her saying his name that stopped him, it was the way she said it. She hadn't said his name like that since they were dating.

"Yes," Roscoe gulped, not sure what was coming next.

"I talked to Doc the other day." Penny Sue walked around the nest straightening things.

"Talked? Like, Hi Doc how are you doing? Or…"

"More like, I made an appointment and we talked." She closed the book he'd been reading and put it on the table next to his chair.

"Talked?" Roscoe tried to swallow but couldn't, his throat was suddenly dry. "Is there a problem? Are you okay?" Roscoe was uncomfortable with the thought that he'd been so busy doing Committee work he hadn't noticed she wasn't feeling well.

"Oh no, nothing like that. I'm fine." He could tell there was something she wanted to say but hadn't worked out exactly how to say it. She seemed to be debating if this was the right time.

"Meeting's about to start Roscoe," someone hollered from below their tree. "Better get a move on."

Then it was quiet.

Roscoe gulped. "Is there…"

"We're expecting." She decided not to beat around the bush and just come out and say it. She knew if she didn't he'd leave for the meeting and who knew when she'd have a chance to tell him.

"I'm sorry. We're what?" Roscoe stood with one foot on the edge of the nest, not sure he'd heard her right.

"Expecting." Penny Sue glowed.

"Are you sure? You don't look…" Then it hit him and he rushed back across the nest. "Here, sit down. Can I get you something? A cup of water? It's a little drafty maybe I should get your sweater or shawl?"

"I'm fine." She giggled and pushed him away. "I'm just two weeks along but according to Doc, she changed her voice to sound like the gruff old doctor who'd served Abner faithfully for so many years. "One week, one month what difference does it make? You either are or your not."

"We're pregnant," Roscoe said quietly. Then he thought of being

Committee Chairman and the demand it made on his time. "I'll see if they can find another Chairman. I don't need to be gone so much. With all the meetings and Annual Conference coming up…"

"Don't be silly, you love your work as Chairman. And, you're good at it. I'll just have someone to take care of while you're away." She smiled. She'd had a few days to get used to the idea, but this was all new to him.

Roscoe heard the door to the meeting room bang shut, someone was sending a message. "Probably Ferrell," he said. "I better go or he'll try to take over. I can hear him now, telling the Committee how important it is for the Chairman to be there on time."

They both laughed. He walked over and put his arms around her.

"Congratulations," he said softly.

"You too," she whispered.

"Hello. Mr. Chairman. Any brain cells firing inside that head of yours?" To emphasize the point, Ferrel leaned across the table and tapped Roscoe's head.

"Huh?" Roscoe looked up and tried desperately to remember what they'd been discussing.

The meeting had been going for over an hour and other than remembering it had something to do with SquirrelFest coming up in a few months, he had no idea what, if anything, they'd been discussing. From the time Penny Sue told him they were expecting he felt he'd been wandering around in a fog. One minute terrified of the responsibility of raising a child in these difficult times and the next unable to wait to have someone like Little Sherman to tuck in bed at night.

"Well, which way are you going to vote Roscoe?" Ferrell was back, pressing the issue. "Yes or no? We're split evenly three for and three against. You're the tie breaker."

"Yes, well, I think, under the circumstances…" Roscoe racked his brain, searching for some clue that would tell him what they were voting on. "Perhaps we should appoint a committee to study the issue and report back in say…" He knew it was a lame response but that was the best he could do under the circumstances.

"To decide to whether to adjourn for supper?" Ferrell stood and walked around the table mumbling, "See, that's why we need new leadership in the Community. He can't stay focused on the issues long enough to know what we're talking about." He got within inches of Roscoe's ear and said. "Yes or no? Yeah or neigh? In or out? Up or down? For or against? Go or stay?"

Roscoe looked around the table and saw the other members of the Committee leaning forward, anxious to hear his decision. Three were nodding yes, vote to adjourn, and two were shaking their heads no. He assumed Ferrell was the other no vote.

"Yes," Roscoe said. "Definitely yes." He stood to leave so quickly he and Ferrell almost bumped heads.

Roscoe found Edgar standing with a paw resting on the Big Rock and staring into the woods. He watched his shoulders lift and drop and heard him sigh. Roscoe figured he was still thinking about going the way of all squirrels before knowing the family line would continue.

"Ah, Edgar, sorry to bother you but I…' Roscoe wondered if he shouldn't have gone straight home and talked to him later.

Edgar turned slowly, his sad face reflecting his thoughts. He reached up with a paw and brushed away a tear. "Oh, it's you Roscoe, was there something…" His voice shook and was barely above a whisper.

"Yes sir. It's about our discussion, earlier at my, ah…" Roscoe fought to push back a smile.

"Our discussion about…" Edgar seemed to have forgotten.

"Children. Great grandchildren. The unbroken circle." Roscoe was having trouble, he'd never seen Edgar so disconnected from things.

"Children?" Edgar scratched his chin and looked like the thought had never occurred to him.

Roscoe started to say something to clear up the apparent confusion but Edgar spoke before he could. "Oh, that discussion. In your nest. Earlier. Yes, I see. Pay no attention Roscoe it was just the meaningless ramblings of a former Chairman on the fragile nature of life. Forget it ever happened." Edgar turned back to the woods.

"Well, that's just it sir. I did some serious thinking about it after you left and I must say I agree with you." Roscoe wondered if it might have been better for Penny Sue to have this conversation, she knew her grandfather a lot better then he did.

Edgar nodded his head slightly.

Roscoe continued, "So that's why I want you to be the first to know. We're expecting. A baby. Or babies. Not all at once of course. But certainly…" Roscoe knew he was rambling but he was so excited he couldn't stop.

Edgar continued to look at the woods, as if he hadn't heard him.

Roscoe started to say it again but stopped when Edgar raised his paw. "Have you completely lost your mind?" He spun around and walked towards him. "What were you thinking? You can't possibly raise a family on the pittance you make as Committee Chairman. You're still making payments on your nest if I'm not mistaken. Penny Sue will be too busy to work outside the nest so more of the burden will fall on your shoulders." Edgar stood in front of him and poked Roscoe's chest with his paw. "It's the wrong time Roscoe. All the economic indicators are down. Prices are up." He stopped with his face inches from Roscoe's. "Are you crazy?"

"But what about you and Edna almost waiting too long to have Edgar Jr.?" Roscoe was confused by his reaction, he thought he'd be pleased to learn he was going to be a great grandfather. "What about discovering Edna was…"

"You've been joined what? Six months. Why you barely know each other. The medical bills will pile up and who knows if the seed school will still be in existence by the time he or she is…"His voice trailed off as he marched down the path to the Clearing where Roscoe knew he'd tell the first person he met that that he was about to be a great grandfather.

"Well," Roscoe shrugged, "at least he's got something new to think about." He looked at the position of the sun and decided he had an hour before the start of the second half of the SquirrelFest meeting. He figured that was enough time to make it back to his nest and see how Penny Sue was feeling.

Turning Pro

Roscoe couldn't remember a time when the members of the Community were more content. Because of Sparky's latest encounter with Bird Man there was the feeling they could deal with anything humans threw at them. And, if that wasn't enough, they heard from friends outside the Community that one of their own had become an urban legend.

Whether Community members came to the Clearing to do business or just to kill time, their conversations invariably swung around to what they called, "the night of the dark streets." As could be expected, they weren't satisfied with repeating the story without adding a few details of their own. Before long, the entire city of Centerline was blacked out, the neighbors deck caught fire, and Bird Man was so upset he moved taking Sylvia, his cat, with him.

That's why it was such a shock when the rumor began to spread that Sparky was leaving Abner and moving to the Community of Ben.

Roscoe's meeting with the Neighborhood Cleanup Committee ended early which meant he had just enough time to run home and have lunch with Penny Sue before going to the bowling alley for the seed school fund-raiser. This years theme was, *"Lanes of Learning-Rolling To Higher Test Scores."*

He closed the meeting room door and was surprised to find a large crowd at the foot of the stairs demanding to know if the rumor was true.

"What rumor? I've been in meetings all morning." It bothered him that the Community members could take something they were pretty sure wasn't true and turn it into a cold, hard fact.

Besides, on any given day there were half a dozen rumors circulating through the Neighborhood, he'd been the receiving end of several himself.

"Well, duh, will you get with the program for heavens sake? Why is our Chairman always the last to know?" Ferrel had missed the morning meeting so he'd heard the rumor before Roscoe and had time to think about its impact on the Community.

Roscoe decided not to take the bait and respond in kind. "If someone will tell me what's going on I'll be happy to answer. But, if it's about Bird Man putting barbed wire around the top of his fence forget about it, it's not going to happen."

"I'm not saying your right about the barbed wire but this is far more serious than that." Ferrel pushed his way through the crowd and moved to the foot of the stairs before saying, "It's about your buddy Sparky."

Roscoe waited, hoping Ferrel would continue. Instead, he looked at the ground and shook his head in disappointment.

"And the rumor about Sparky is?" Roscoe put his paws on his hips and decided to wait him out.

"He's leaving." Ferrel sighed as if the burden of carrying the information was too much for him.

"On vacation? Or a field study?" Everyone knew Sparky did that from time to time. He'd be gone for a week or two and then return. If he wasn't on a field trip he could usually be found working in his lab when everyone else had turned in for the night. Roscoe didn't see anything wrong with that.

"Vacation?" Ferrel said with a laugh, "You wish. Don't you get it Roscoe? He's leaving. His lab. His friends. The Community that raised him. Everything. He's turning pro. I hear he's signed a big contract with the Community of Ben." Ferrel looked at Roscoe with a, *How do you like those acorns?* look on his face.

"No way. Not Sparky. He wouldn't do that." Beneath his show of confidence, Roscoe began to experience the first pangs of doubt. "Abner's his home. He was born here."

"Check this out *Mr. Chairman*, his laboratory is up for sale. At least, that's what Morgan told me, he put the sign up this morning."

TWO FEEDERS, NO WAITING

Roscoe was stunned. It had to be a mistake or a practical joke by one of the kids in the Community. The same thing had happened to him. He'd received an early morning caller who climbed in his nest and wanting to know how much he was asking for it. When he climbed down his tree on the way to work he found a **For Sale** sign leaning against the trunk.

The meeting room had received its share of for sale signs in the past month. It was spring, and this years seed school graduates were feeling frisky.

"I'll talk to him. But in the meantime, everyone should remain calm until I get back." Roscoe had to push his way through the crowd that had followed Ferrel to the Clearing.

"What will we do if Bird Man pulls something else?" Someone in the crowd asked as Roscoe passed by.

"We can't make it without Sparky," another shared his concern.

Roscoe finally broke free of the crowd and hurried to Sparky's lab.

He slowed when he got close enough to see the *For Sale* sign stuck in the ground next to the entrance and thought at least Ferrel had that part right. He walked to the place in front of the lab Sparky had shown him and said, "Roscoe to see Sparky." Usually, when he said it the door in the base of the tree swung open and Sparky was waiting for him with a visitors badge.

This time however, he heard a recorded voice say, "If you're here to look at the lab with the idea of buying it, say one. If you're here to purchase used lab equipment say two. If you're here for another reason say three."

Roscoe said, "Three," and had to wait a few seconds before the door swung open. He entered the lab but couldn't find Sparky. Finally he heard a noise in the back of the lab and walked cautiously in that direction. He was surprised to find Sparky taking books and catalogs off the shelves and putting them in boxes.

"Sparky, what's going on?" Roscoe was at a loss.

"Oh hey Roscoe. I planned on coming by your place later," Sparky closed the lid on the box he was packing and slid it across the floor to join others stacked in the center of the room. "Everything has happened so fast, I, ah..." he stopped for a moment while he looked for an empty box.

"Oh? What happened?" It was not Roscoe's way to come right out and say, "I heard you were leaving, please tell me it's just an ugly rumor."

"It's all about taking advantage of my fifteen seconds of fame." Sparky made quote marks when he said, fifteen seconds of fame. "You know, seize the day, grab the brass ring, go for the gold, that kind of thing."

"Why? You've got everything you want right here. Everyone knows and respects you. Why would you leave all this? You'll have other moments." Roscoe had trouble believing he was having this conversation.

"It all comes down to seeds Roscoe. I've invested every thing I've earned in my lab and have put nothing away for a rainy day." Sparky looked at the title of the book in his paw before tossing it into an open box. "So, someone comes along from the Community of Ben, makes a fantastic offer…" he shrugged. "What am I supposed to do?" He looked at Roscoe hoping he'd understand. "What would you do?" He paused before adding, "Did I mention a signing bonus? Working in a state of the art lab? And, most important of all, having a chance to work with Dr. Nels?"

He finished with a shrug, "For a person in my position it's a no brainer."

"I'm sure we could come up with something to keep you here. At least give us the opportunity to make a counter offer." Roscoe was grasping at straws. Abner was a working class Community, living from feeder to feeder. Other than the a few seeds set aside for emergencies, that was it, they had nothing in reserve.

"It's not really about seeds Roscoe." Sparky knew there was no way they could match Ben's offer. "The big thing is I have the chance to study with Dr. Nels." Tears welled in his eyes when he thought about leaving his friends.

They stood quietly, facing each other. Roscoe knew there was no point in arguing. Even if they could somehow match the signing bonus they had no one in the Community equal to Dr. Nels.

He stepped forward, gave Sparky a hug, and mumbled, "Take care buddy." He started to walk away but stopped and said, "The door is always open if you want to come back, you know that."

TWO FEEDERS, NO WAITING

Sparky couldn't speak. He could only nod yes, he understood. For him, the promise that he was welcome back if things didn't work out was the strongest argument Roscoe could have made to convince him to stay.

Roscoe took his time going back to the Clearing, he had a lot to think about. He knew Ferrel and his crew would be waiting to hear the results of his meeting with Sparky. He also knew Ferrel would never understand that Sparky felt he needed to go someplace else if he wanted to continue to grow as a scientist, he could only go so far working alone.

When he got close to the Clearing he heard voices discussing the Sparky situation. He stopped and gathered his thoughts, trying to find the best way to tell them the rumor was true, Sparky was leaving.

Ferrel's voice rose above the others. "I'm telling you, this wouldn't be an issue if I were Chairman." The others quieted when they heard the anger in his voice.

"You don't let a resource like Sparky walk right out from under your nose. Webster the Librarian, yes he could leave and we'd go on like nothing happened, librarians are a dime a dozen, **BUT** you don't let someone like Sparky wriggle off your hook, he's one in a million."

Roscoe was surprised how quickly things had changed. Ferrel had been one of Sparky's harshest critics.

Roscoe heard murmurs of agreement from the crowd. Someone spoke up. "That's exactly what I've been telling Clude here. I call it the brain drain, letting the best and brightest leave our Community as soon as the graduate from seed school."

"Think back to how Roscoe became Chairman in the first place." Ferrel's voice was filled with emotion. "He pushed, get this, **his own father-in-law** right out of the meeting room door."

Someone in the crowd spoke hesitantly, "Actually Ferrel, he wasn't his father-in-law at that time and if you remember Edgar was acting kind of…"

"Whatever!" Ferrel cut him off with a dismissive wave of his paw. "Don't get lost in the details of that ugly affair and miss the big picture. And, don't forget, it was Roscoe who convinced us to go to Bird Man's in the first place. What a disaster that's turned out to be."

"Seed Man moving had a lot to do with it." Darin couldn't let him keep telling half truths. "And, we went there at the recommendation of the search committee. It wasn't Roscoe's decision."

"As usual, you've missed the point, Darin. There are dozens, maybe hundreds of feeders in the Neighborhood and which one does he pick? The one with a cat who will smack you six ways from Tuesday if she catches you putting so much as a foot in her yard." Ferrel paced back and forth as he talked. He surprised them when he brought his paws together with a smack to illustrate the sound of the cat hitting the fence.

"If you mean Sylvia, well, she's a friend of the Community. In fact, if it wasn't for her, Sparky wouldn't have known about…" Roscoe recognized Marvin's voice.

"What is the first rule we learn in seed school? N*ever trust a,*" Ferrel ignored Marvin and put a paw to his ear waiting for the crowd to provide the answer.

"Cat," a few of them answered. No one dared tell him that was the third rule. The first rule was never trust a human and the second was, if the snow is over your head, stay in bed.

"I'm sorry, I didn't hear you." Ferrel leaned toward them with his paw still behind his ear.

"Cat," more of the crowd joined in.

"If that's the best you can do it's no wonder you elected a wimp like Roscoe to be your Chairman." He glared at them, upset they couldn't work up enough enthusiasm to answer a simple question.

"Cat!" They said so loud it sounded to Roscoe like everyone had joined in.

Ferrel shook his fist at them. "The elders who established the rule knew from bitter experience it was true. And what's the first thing Roscoe's does? He trusts a cat."

"What are you saying Ferrel? What's your point?" It was Jules who spoke this time.

"Just the kind of question I would expect from one of Roscoe's **buddies**." The way he said buddies made it sound like it was a bad word. He crinkled up his face like he'd taken a bite of a stale nut cake. He raised his voice and pounded one paw in the other. "Being Chairman is like running a business. You make decisions based on what's best for the Community, **NOT** what's best for you and your friends."

He lowered his voice. "Now, to get back to your question. What I'm saying Jules is this, Sparky's leaving is the latest in a long line of poor decision making and maybe we should take another vote to decide who we want as Chairman, Roscoe or me."

The crowd was stunned. As far back as they could remember no one had ever volunteered to be Chairman; they had been selected by the Committee for the Protection of Neighborhood Resources.

In the quiet that followed, Roscoe retraced his steps to Sparky's lab, turned around, and started walking back to the Clearing, whistling so they wouldn't be surprised when they saw him. When he joined them he acted like he hadn't heard what they'd been talking about earlier.

Ferrel slipped back in the crowd and gave no sign he'd been the one doing all the talking while Roscoe was gone. Everyone looked at the ground like they'd been caught doing something they weren't supposed to.

"Well?" Ferrel asked when Roscoe got close enough to hear him.

Roscoe sighed. It was hard to act like he hadn't heard what Ferrel said about replacing him as Chairman. There were so many things he wanted to say in his defense like there was nothing he could do about Seed Man leaving. That it had been a stroke of luck that Marvin had discovered Bird Man's yard and became friends with Sylvia. That perhaps the rule about cats did not apply to all cats. And that once in awhile you had to let a friend do what he thinks is best regardless of the consequences.

Instead he simply said, "The rumor is true, Sparky is leaving." He started to walk away but stopped and said, "Now, if it's all right with everyone, I'm going home for lunch."

As he passed through the crowd he felt someone give an encouraging pat on the shoulder and say, "We'll be okay Roscoe. You've bailed us out of some pretty tough jams in the past." Roscoe mumbled, "Thanks," and continued to his nest.

He stopped when Ferrel stepped in front of him, blocking his way. It was obvious he was struggling to keep his feelings under control. His face was bright red and he was taking quick, uneven breaths. "Don't get too comfortable with the title of Chairman. Losing Seed Man and now Sparky may be the one two punch that knocks you off that pedestal everyone has put you on."

Roscoe looked directly at Ferrel. "Thanks, I'll write that down as the thought for the day in my planner."

On his way to his nest Roscoe marveled at his self control. Six months ago he would have torn into Ferrel and exposed him for the trouble maker he is.

Maybe, he thought as he stepped off the main path and followed the one that leads to his nest, I'm growing up.

Sparky stood by the Big Rock and looked sadly down the path. From his position he could see all the way to the Clearing and he wondered what life will be like without his friends stopping by his lab to visit. He sighed and when he turned around he saw Chairman Ben and Dr. Nels waiting for him on the boundary between the two Communities.

Ben was the first to speak. "Welcome to our Community Sparky. Here, let me help you with those books." Most of Sparky's books had been moved to his new lab, and the ones he carried with him were those he felt he couldn't live without and didn't trust anyone else to handle.

"Well, well, I finally have a chance to meet the famous Sparkles," Dr. Nels stepped forward to touch paws.

"Ah, that's Sparky sir, not Sparkles." Sparky hated to get their first meeting off on the wrong foot but, he was afraid a name like Sparkles might catch on.

Dr. Nels looked at the small piece of paper in his paw. "So you say sir and so it is. Allow me to apologize for that unfortunate slip of the tongue." He held out has paw in a gesture of reconciliation. Sparky took it and immediately wished he hadn't as a sharp pain shot up his arm as Dr. Nels tightened his grip.

It dawned on Sparky this must be the way Dr. Nels greets every new employee that comes to work in his lab. Mispronouncing their names and squeezing their paw were his ways of letting them know who was boss.

Ben stepped between them and said, "If you'll walk with me Sparky,

I'll take you to your nest and introduce you to some important members of our Community." Ben picked up Sparky's box of books and led him away from the Big Rock to the deep part of the woods.

Sparky understood why Roscoe thought so highly of Ben. He was the Chairman and founder of his Community yet it was not beneath him to lend a hand with his books. No such offer came from Dr. Nels who, without saying a word, walked away taking a short cut to his lab.

When the *Welcome To Our Community* dinners were over and with his security clearance finally out of the way, Sparky was allowed to enter the working part of the lab. He was about to have his first official meeting with Dr. Nels and was anxious to make a good impression.

He knocked softly on the door to his office and received an, "It's open." He pushed the door open and walked into the spacious room. He couldn't help thinking his old lab in Abner would fit comfortably inside a space this size.

"Sparky how good of you to come by. Settling in are we? Meeting your coworkers? Found the walnut tea machine?" Dr. Nels didn't bother getting up but gestured for Sparky to sit in the chair across from him.

"Yes, sure, everything's fine. I was wondering when I could start…"

"Working on something? Well my boy, your wait is over." Dr. Nels opened the top drawer of his desk and removed a yellow folder. "I have five problems I'd like you to solve. I must tell you in advance they are problems of such complexity they have vexed the best minds in our Community. I thought you might take a swing at them. You can bring the answers back when you're finished." He tossed the folder to Sparky, smiled, lifted a letter from his desk, and started reading.

Sparky got the hint the meeting was over and slowly backed out of the room

"Close the door on your way out, I need to finish this by noon." Dr. Nels didn't bother to look up.

Sparky did as he was told and hurried down the hallway to his cubicle where he would have his first look at the problems in the folder. He zipped through the first two then rubbed his paws together and smiled when saw the third problem dealt with two of his favorite subjects; electricity and magnetism.

He spent that afternoon, night, and most of the next morning working out what he thought was a clever solution to problem three. By the end of the next day he'd finished the last two. He had no way of knowing everyone who'd worked on these problems had taken twice as long as he had to finish them. Or that many had never made it past problem three.

The following morning he was back at the door to Dr. Nel's office. He knocked and was invited in. Dr. Nels sat back in his chair and folded his paws across his ample stomach. "Having trouble with the problems are we?' He said in a smug voice and lifted his paws creating a barrier between him and Sparky. "I'm not allowed to give hints or help in any way. Remember? we talked about that."

Sparky hadn't slept in two days. There were dark rings under his eyes and what little fur remained on his head stuck out in all directions. He looked terrible. "Ah, no sir, nothing like that, it's, ah, well, what I mean is, I'm finished, with the problems and was wondering if there was something else..." He placed the folder on the surface of the desk and slid it across to Dr. Nels.

"Well, well, very good Sparky, very good indeed. Maybe what Ben has been saying about you is true after all. Once one gets past the unkempt appearance they may actually discover there's a mind in there somewhere." He smiled at Sparky and opened the folder. "Be seated while I go over these." He pulled out a page and hummed quietly as he checked Sparky's answer to the first problem. He wrote something at the top of the page, turned it face down on his desk, and went to the next one. When he finished reading the last problem, he looked into the bloodshot eyes of an exhausted Sparky and shook his head in disappointment.

"Done it," he said sliding the first paper across the table without taking his eyes off Sparky. "Done it," he repeated the same motion with the second one. "Done it. Done it. Done it." He said as he worked his way through problems three, four and five.

He shook his head letting Sparky know he wasn't pleased with his answers. "You're going to have to do a lot better than that if you expect to make it in my lab buster. You've repeated the same, dull answers I've received from everyone else." He shook his head sadly. "To tell you the truth Sparky, I was expecting something a little more, oh, original I guess is the word I'm looking for."

"Am I missing something or…" Sparky was puzzled. He wanted to say he'd done the best he could but if the answers were as bad as he said they were he'd go over them again.

"You most certainly are." Dr. Nels forced a smile. "You're missing the one element that has become the trademark of my work in the Community of Ben." He tapped the end of his pencil on the top of his desk as if trying to think of where to begin.

"Trademark sir? I'm not sure I follow…" Sparky quickly went over his answers to the problems in his mind and couldn't think of anything he'd left out.

"Dynamite, my boy. I don't see where you have used a single stick of dynamite in any of your answers." Dr. Nels smiled at Sparky. "Let me explain in a way that will illustrate in simple terms what I'm talking about."

He left his chair and walked to the chalkboard. He drew a plan of Bird Man's house and backyard. When he finished Sparky saw he'd included the houses on either side of Bird Man's.

"Your trick of attaching the live electrical wire to the fence was, I'll admit, somewhat creative. **BUT,** if you returned to the Big Rock a few days later, you would have noticed everything was back to normal, nothing had changed. The lights in Bird Man's house were working properly. His neighbor was on his deck reading his newspaper." He smiled at Sparky in a fatherly way.

"You're solution to the problem was only temporary." He wrote, **TEMPORARY!** in large letters across the board. "It's like nothing happened." He set the chalk down and blew the dust off his paws. "As far as Bird Man is concerned, it's business as usual. Nothing remains that would connect the Community of Abner with the power outage.

"Now, had **I** been consulted on the problem I would have added the one vital piece of equipment that would have taken weeks, maybe months to recover from. I would have sent a message to Bird Man that you don't mess around with my Community and walk away unscathed. Do you have any idea what that piece of equipment might be?" He smiled and raised his eyebrows when he finished, encouraging an answer.

"Dynamite?" Sparky ventured a guess.

"My you are quick on the uptake Sparky, I'll give you that much. Yes my boy. Exactly. Dynamite. With it," he swept his paw across his sketch wiping out the back of Bird Man's house and a good part of the neighbor's deck to demonstrate the destruction that would have followed if a stick of dynamite, properly placed, had been used. "You don't bounce back from a blow like that my boy." He said and tapped the board with his paw to emphasize his point.

"But aren't you afraid you might hurt..." Sparky stopped when he saw Dr. Nels shake his head.

"**Me? Afraid?** No Sparkles, I'm never afraid. I go with my instincts and focus only on the immediate problem. I never worry if there's, what's the word everyone is using today? Collateral damage? If an innocent bystander is injured in the explosion," he shrugged nonchalantly, "it's a risk I'm willing to take."

"Do you really think that's necessary? Blowing things up I mean. Humans could get hurt and..." Sparky knew he was tired but even in his condition causing so much damage didn't make sense to him.

Dr. Nels leaped across the room, slammed his paws on the top of his desk, and leaned into Sparky. "Let's get one thing straight Sparklet, right from the get go; I'm in charge here, not you. I had grave reservations about bringing you on board because you represent what I call the soft side of science. You're worried that your precious little experiments might hurt the air or damage the grass." He said the last part in a high pitched, whiny voice. Then he switched back to his normal voice and said with disgust, "Humans indeed."

He paused a moment to catch his breath. "Do you think they're concerned about those things when they blast away at us with their guns? Or how about their favorite, the poison peanut? Were they thinking of our safety when they built a gadget like Mr. Fling-Um?"

He walked to his desk and sat on a corner. "It's a tough world out there Sparklet. It's time you came down from your ivory tower and join the rest of us in the trenches where the real work of science takes place." He poked Sparky with his paw and left a chalk mark on the chest. "In my tenure as director of this lab, I have accomplished things you've only dreamed of."

He reached across the top of his desk and picked up the folder with Sparky's answers. He shoved it toward him and said with a sense of pride, "I was solving problems like these when I was in seed school."

He moved within inches of Sparky's face and spoke in a voice a little above whisper, "It's crunch time Sparkles. It's the fourth quarter, the bases are loaded, and the fat lady is ready to sing. It's time to take a seed or get off the feeder." He stood for a moment looking Sparky in the eye, then tossed the folder in his lap. "Redo problem five only this time, let me see a little **dy-no-might**."

He waved his paw telling Sparky he should leave. "Oh and Sparkles," he called as he settled in his leather chair, "don't catch your tail in the door on the way out."

Sparky went back to his cubicle, removed the test questions from the folder, and spread them on his desk. He put his chin on his paw and studied each page. "Where in problem five," he wondered, "is the best place to put a stick of dynamite?"

Ferrel had continued pressing the members of the Committee for a vote on who should be their Chairman. Finally they said okay just to keep him from bringing the subject up again.

The night before the election, he and Roscoe stood on the small platform outside the meeting room.

Since he was the challenger, Ferrel was given the choice to speak first or wait until Roscoe was finished before taking his turn. He chose to speak first and had been going on for twenty minutes, pointing out the failures of the Community under Roscoe's leadership. He covered everything from Roscoe almost missing his own joining with Penny Sue to when he got squirrel fever attending an emergency conference meeting.

"His biggest failure though, has to be letting Sparky, one of our own, a graduate of our fine school system, and an acknowledged genius by the scientific community, slip through his paws and go to work for the Community of Ben. Why if I were…" Ferrel stopped when he saw heads in the crowd turn away from him and look toward the path that leads from the Clearing to the Big Rock.

He heard a murmur start at the back and roll toward him like a wave. "Why if…" He raised his voice but was unable to pull his audience back. Their eyes were fixed on a lone figure walking toward them in the strange, lurching gait they all recognized immediately. "It's Sparky," someone at the back of the crowd whispered to person standing next to him and pointed.

"It can't be. Didn't you hear Ferrel say he'd moved to the Community of Ben?" The one next to him said as he stood on his toes for a better look.

"I'm telling you it's him, I'd recognize that walk anywhere." The one speaking backed up, clearing a path for Sparky to walk through on his way to join Ferrel and Roscoe.

After climbing the steps Sparky set the box of books he was carrying on the platform. He nodded to Ferrel as he crossed over to Roscoe and gave him a hug, a rare show of affection for him, especially in front of others. "Thanks for keeping the door open," he said quietly, then turned around and stood next to Roscoe.

"It's all a show folks." Ferrel recovered quickly and shook his paw at the crowd. "Don't be fooled. It's a sham. Sparky waltzes in here and gets a few sympathy votes for his old buddy Roscoe, but tomorrow he'll be back with his new friends at…"

Ferrel's tirade was interrupted by someone who said, "Let us hear it from him? We can figure out if he's telling the truth or not."

The rest of the crowd picked up the idea and chanted, "Sparky. Sparky." They refused to stop until he stepped away from Roscoe and waved.

He cleared his throat, pushed his glasses back in place, and looked at the crowd. "I made a mistake. I thought I was at the top of the heap after the blackout at Bird Man's. So I agreed to move to the Community of Ben for a big salary and a signing bonus that would keep me in seeds for the rest of my life."

He looked down at the platform then back at the crowd. "I told

Roscoe about it and he did what I'm sure was the hardest thing for him to do but what turned out to be the best thing he could have done, he let me go."

Ferrel started to ask what kind of leader would let someone like him just stroll away but those at the front of the crowd told him to pipe down and let Sparky finish.

Ferrel mumbled something no one could understand and stepped back.

"But Roscoe told me if I left, the door to the Community was open if I wanted to come back." He smiled and looked at Roscoe. "Well my friend, I'm back."

After he said it, a cheer went up from the crowd and members of the Community shouted how happy they were he'd changed his mind.

He raised his paw to quiet them. "To say I'm back doesn't really say it all. You see, I've discovered this is where I belong but I never would have figured it out if Roscoe had used our friendship to talk me into staying. I would have always wondered what it would be like to work someplace else." He swung his arm in a circle indicating any place other than Abner.

He didn't know what else to say so he shrugged, and walked back to his place next to Roscoe.

"Why wait until tomorrow to vote?" A woman at the front of the crowd asked. "I'm casting my vote to keep Roscoe in office right here and now."

"Me to," the person next to her agreed.

Eventually someone said, "Let's make it unanimous.".

Ferrel stomped off the stage and pushed his way through the crowd. "Better luck next time," someone hollered after him.

"If there is a next time," someone on the other side of the crowd shouted and her comment was followed by laughter.

Gradually everyone left the Clearing and headed to their nests pleased that things in the Community were returning to normal. Sparky was back and Roscoe was still their Chairman. They seemed to sense that days like this don't come along very often.

Sparky was telling Roscoe something funny that happened when he was with the Community of Ben when they heard a thud come from somewhere near Bird Man's yard.

"What was that?" Roscoe looked up and asked.

"My guess would be a small charge of dynamite." Sparky scratched his head and fought to keep from laughing.

"Dynamite?" Roscoe was puzzled. "I don't get it."

"Dr. Nels sent me back to my desk and said I should find a place to put a stick of dynamite in the answer to my biggest problem." Sparky stopped, he'd learned that telling a good story required a few long pauses. "So, it finally dawned on me that my biggest problem was him." He smiled.

"You didn't, I mean he's not..." Roscoe couldn't bring himself to ask if he'd blown up the lab.

"Oh no, nothing like that. It was more like a firecracker in a bag of talcum powder. You know, the old seed school trick."

Roscoe had no trouble remembering Sparky doing the same thing to Coach Bobby. The coach had made fun of the way he ran, lifting his feet like he was crossing a field of hot rocks.

"So where did you put it?" Roscoe was starting to see how funny the situation was.

"In his study. I rigged it up so it would explode when he opened his office door." Sparky closed his eyes and pictured Dr. Nels covered from head to tail with white powder.

"What goes around," Roscoe started.

"Comes around," Sparky finished. He put his arm around Roscoe's shoulder and said, "What do you say we get Webster and go to the feeder for a snack? I'm starved. I haven't eaten in days."

Roscoe smiled and said sincerely, "It's good to have you back. I missed you."

Sparky nodded. "I guess sometimes you have to leave someplace if you want to end up someplace else, even if where you end up is back where you started." He made a funny face and asked, "Does that make sense?"

"Almost," Roscoe answered, "why don't you take it to your lab and work on it?" They both laughed and Roscoe hollered over his shoulder as he crossed the Clearing, "Last one to the feeder has to clean up Dr. Nels' office."

"That may take awhile." Sparky said as he picked up his box of books and ran after him.

Incident at Big Rock

"Roscoe have you got a moment?" Edgar opened the door to the meeting room and leaned in.

"We're just about finished." Roscoe smiled at Nadine and Eldon who were seated across from him. They'd been meeting for over an hour and were almost ready to make a decision.

Roscoe started to tell him to wait outside until they were finished but before he could, Edgar entered the room and moved behind his desk.

"Selling your nest Eldon?" Edgar raised an eyebrow and started to ask if this was a good time since there were already a number of nests on the market.

"Excuse me Edgar but this is rather personal." Roscoe shifted in his chair so Edgar could only see a corner of the contract and not the asking price. "I'm sure Nadine and Eldon would prefer for you to wait…"

"Understood Roscoe." Edgar raised his arms in an act of surrender. "Message received loud and clear." He turned to face Nadine and Eldon. "Please, accept my apologies. I meant no harm." He bowed, and remained bent over as he walked across the room, and sat down on the wooden bench beneath the window. "I'll wait here while you wrap things up. Don't hurry on my account. I've got nothing but time."

Nadine gave Roscoe an uncomfortable look. They'd gone to great lengths to keep their appointment with Roscoe secret but now, with Edgar looking over her shoulder, it only confirmed her thought that it was impossible to keep anything from the Community.

Nadine got up and gestured for Eldon to join her. They stood awkwardly for a moment expecting Edgar to take the hint and leave but when he showed no sign of moving, she told Roscoe they'd talk with him later about the, "You know what."

Edgar hurried across the room and opened the door for them. When they stepped out on the platform at the top of the steps he quickly closed the door, and took the chair Eldon had been sitting in moments before.

He looked at Roscoe and forced a nervous smile.

"Is there something you want Edgar?" Roscoe knew if he'd done that to Nadine and Eldon when Edgar was Chairman he would have been thrown out of the room.

"You think I? Me? Want? No, no." He picked at a worn place on Roscoe's desk.

"Then why…"

"Since you brought it up, there is one thing," he scooted forward in his chair, "but, if you're too busy my simple request can wait." Edgar looked at Roscoe and smiled.

Roscoe pointed to the papers crammed in his in box. "Well, I do need to review these before I leave. So if there's…" He pulled a folder from the top of the stack.

Edgar moved closer to Roscoe's desk, glanced over his shoulder to make sure no one had entered the room, and said in hushed tones, "I have been asked by an unnamed source to publish an account of my years as Chairman." Edgar fought to keep the excitement out of his voice.

"That's wonderful news Edgar, I'm sure it will make fascinating reading." Roscoe smoothed the paper in front of him.

"Are you kidding Roscoe or do you mean it?" Edgar's voice changed, worry replaced optimism.

"Of course I mean it Edgar. You did some pretty interesting things when you were Chairman." Roscoe tried to move the paper so he could read it but Edgar put his paw down and pinned it to the desk.

"What I have in mind is a little more, how shall I say it?" Edgar continued to hold Roscoe's paw. "Complicated." He tilted his head hoping Roscoe would get what he meant.

"Complicated?" Roscoe was having trouble seeing how a review of his years as Chairman could be complicated, it was all a matter of public record.

"Maybe blended is a better word." Edgar let go of Roscoe's paw and stood up; he found pacing helped him think.

"Blended? Edgar, I'm not sure I…"

"Borrowed. From you. A little." He hurried across the room and knelt in front of Roscoe. "The things I did as Chairman are so boring even I wouldn't buy the book. Who wants to read about issuing a permit for SquirrelFest? Or getting enough signatures to put up a statue of Abner?"

He stayed on one knee and, when he looked at Roscoe, he was almost pleading. "So I thought, if its okay with you, I could change a few things and say the encounter with Dr. Nels took place on my watch, so to speak."

"I really didn't do that much Edgar, it was mostly…"

"See the thing is," he got up and stood next to the conference table, "the thing is, you could have. And I thought, with a little help, I could sort of pump it up. A little."

"Pump it up?"

"Embellish. Add to. Blow things out of proportion."

"I'm familiar with what pumping something up means Edgar. But, if the book is meant to be about you and your time in office, everyone knows the event you want to borrow took place six months after you were remov…I mean, after you left."

"Rod said it has to have market appeal." Edgar stopped, he hadn't intended to mention Rod, the marketing representative for *ReadMore Publishing* who'd brought up the idea about the book.

As if on cue the door to the room opened and a short, extremely thin person Roscoe had never seen before, entered. His face was unusually long and his beady eyes made him look suspicious. His ears appeared larger than they actually were because of his bald head. Roscoe could see the beginning of a soul patch beneath his lower lip.

"Sorry to interrupt but I was passing by and heard my name being bandied about." He walked confidently to Roscoe and said, "I'm Rod, Edgar's literary account representative." He held his paw at an odd angel and when Roscoe touched it, it felt like he'd grabbed a paw full of wet grass. His voice was surprisingly deep for someone his size and each word sounded like it had been thoroughly inspected before being released for public consumption.

"You are?" He dropped his chin and studied Roscoe as if trying to remember if they'd met before.

"Roscoe, current Chairm..."

"Chair," Edgar blurted out and turned a chair toward Rod. There were a few things he hadn't told Rod and the fact that he was no longer Chairman was one of them.

"Roscoe," Rod ignored Edgar's offer of a chair and rubbed the fuzz beneath his lip. "Where have I heard..." He looked at Edgar, pointed to Roscoe and mouthed the words, "The dimwit?"

"Oh no, I'm sure you have him mixed up with someone else." Edgar waved his paws trying to get Rod's attention and tell him to change the subject. "We've talked about so many things. Rascal? I may have mentioned someone named Rascal who was..."

"I'm in the remember names business Edgar and I'm sure you told me about someone named Roscoe who was one seed short of a full..."

"Feeder anyone? My treat. Ha ha." Edgar took a step toward the door. When he saw neither of them move, he fanned his face with his paw and said, "Is it warm in hear or is it just me?"

"I take it you've told him about *The Project?*" Rod asked as he leafed through the notebook he'd pulled from his leather backpack.

"Yes. Of course. We were discussing it when you, ah..." Edgar looked at Roscoe and made a gesture that he should say something.

Roscoe shrugged, he had no idea what Edgar expected him to say.

Rod interrupted the silent dialog taking place between them. "Then I'm sure you will not hesitate signing these so we can get the ball rolling." Rod handed Roscoe two sheets of paper. "A copy for you," he explained, "and one for my records in case somewhere down the line you get cold feet and claim the story as your own. I can assure you sir, in the publishing business this is S.O.P."

When he saw the confused look on Roscoe's face he said in a way that suggested everyone except Roscoe knew what S.O.P. meant. "Standard Operating Procedure," he said as he pulled a pen from his backpack, unscrewed the cap, and handed it to Roscoe.

Roscoe read the first line out loud. *"I relinquish henceforth and forever more any claim, attachment, or remembrance of the Incident at Big Rock.*" He lowered the paper and looked at Edgar. "What incident at Big Rock?"

"You know. What we were talking about earlier. Sparky. Dr. Nels. The explosion." Edgar was anxious to get this part over with. He knew he was on shaky ground and he wouldn't even be here if Rod hadn't talked him into it.

"But it didn't happen there. Nothing happened at Big Rock." Roscoe felt if they were going to borrow a story henceforth and forever more, they should at least get the facts straight. "Dr. Nels wasn't involved…"

"Roscoe. Roscoe." Rod stepped between Roscoe and Edgar. "Have you heard of poetic license? Who's going to know?" He paused as if searching for an explanation simple enough for him to understand. "Okay, let's say Edgar's book sits on a library shelf for fifteen or twenty years. Are you with me so far?" Without waiting for an answer he continued. "And let us further imagine that someone removes it from the shelf because after reading the title they think, 'Wow, that looks interesting.' They don't remember you. They don't remember Edgar, and the Big Rock has probably been moved a half a dozen times."

Rod smiled and leaned closer to Roscoe. "But they do know something about book titles and this one grabbed them." When he said "grabbed them" he reached out with his paws and clutched the air in front of Roscoe's face.

He paused long enough to let the idea sink in before finishing with, "At the Big Rock, near the Big Rock, who's going to know?"

Roscoe started to say something about since it involved Edgar's years as Chairman telling the truth might be important but Rod held up a paw, cutting him off.

"Okay, I can see you're not on board." He looked at the floor, thought for a moment, and slowly began nodding his head. "Let's say, for the sake of argument, we do it your way. The same person I mentioned earlier stands in front of the same shelf in the same library. She stops when she comes to a book called, *Something That May Or May Not Have Happened In The Basement Of A Laboratory In A Community That Was Once Called Ben But Is Now Called Something Else.* Now I ask you who wants to read about that?"

Rod shrugged and answered his own question. "Not me. Not you. Not someone standing in front of a library shelf twenty years in the future. That's who."

He put a paw on Roscoe's shoulder and spoke like a teacher explaining something to a slow wittted student. "When you've been in the book publishing business as long as I have you realize there is one, and only on, marketing rule. You only get one chance to make a first impression and believe me, *Something That May Or May Not Have Happened*, will impress no one. Edgar's mother, may she rest in peace, wouldn't be tempted to give the book a second look." He winked, nudged Roscoe with an elbow and said, "Sign the paper and we'll let you get back to whatever it is you do here."

"I'll look it over and get back with you." Now it was Roscoe's turn to smile. He knew they needed his signature and he hoped buying a little time would give Edgar a chance to come to his senses.

"Roscoe, please." Edgar was almost in tears, this could be his last chance to regain some credibility in the Community after losing his job as Chairman over the little problem of stealing Roscoe's nest and lying about attending an emergency conference meeting.

"Fine." Rod threw his arms in the air and took a step back. He was obviously struggling to keep from saying what he was really thinking and what he was really thinking was definitely stronger than calling him a dimwit. He backed away from Roscoe's desk and threw his paws in the air. "No harm, no foul. Take as much time as you need." He crossed the room and opened the door. "I'm sure you won't mind if we use the meeting room for a while, we have some serious work to do." Rod said as he handed Roscoe the stack of papers he'd taken from his in-box.

Before the door closed behind him, Roscoe heard Rod say, "Sparky? What kind of name is that? You have to connect with the reader Edgar and I think Brad has a softer, more reader friendly sound to it. I'm sure there are a number of guys out there named Brad who know a thing or two about science."

Roscoe stood on the small platform outside the meeting room before descending the steps to the Clearing. Why am I so concerned about signing the paper? he wondered, no one will recognize the story when Rod is finished with it anyway.

TWO FEEDERS, NO WAITING

A week later Roscoe opened *The Abner Echo* and was surprised to see the following review written by investigative reporter Toby in his column, *Toby Or Not Toby*.

> *"It came to this investigative reporters attention recently that a certain former Chairman of the Committee For the Protection of Neighborhood Resources is about to release a book he claims to have written about an event that the most casual reader of this publication knows* **did not take place during** *his years in office. This, many of my readers will remember, is the same Chairman who consistently fell for any scheme that walked into the Clearing.* **Hello!** *Does the name Dr. Ernst ring a bell? Need I say more? This same* former *Chairman, who left office* under a cloud of uncertainty *concerning a missing nest and a prominent member of our Community now asks us to believe he single handily brought down the notorious Dr. Nels? Now there's one doctor you don't want to go to if you come done with a case of squirrel fever. Oh, and about his book Incident At Big Rock…only read it if you want a good laugh. My advice, take two medicinal seeds and call me in the morning. Better yet, don't call me, call Brad if you can find his number."*

No sooner had Roscoe put the paper down than the meeting room door flew open and Edgar stood on the threshold with a copy of *The Echo* in his paw. He was in tears and unable to speak; his lips moved but no sound came out.

After several tries, he was finally able to say, "I remember when Toby was in seed school." Edgar's voice was flat. He spoke like he was in a trance. "He interviewed me once. For the school paper. He seemed like a nice kid. How could he do this to me?" He held the paper up for a moment then lurched toward the wooden bench. He sat down, placed his elbows on knees, and buried his face in his in his paws. "I'm ruined Roscoe. Destroyed. Everything I accomplished in office will be held up for ridicule."

"Edgar, it's Toby. Who remembers what he wrote a day later. Today's Echo will be insulating someone's nest tomorrow."

"Apparently more than you think. There's a petition going around to have my name removed from *The List of Chairman* on the base of the statue of Abner."

"I wouldn't worry about it Edgar, give it time, it will blow over. You know how the members of the Community are, tomorrow morning they'll forget they read it."

"Edna signed it." Edgar buried his face deeper in his paws then, to Roscoe's surprise, he quickly stood, looked out of the window, made an odd gesture with his paw, and turned around, and sat down.

"Edna signed the petition? About removing your name?" Roscoe couldn't believe it.

Edgar tapped his foot and looked anxiously toward the door. "She's mad that I listened to Rod instead of her."

There was a light tap on the door and Edgar quickly asked, "Who is it?"

The door opened, and someone Roscoe had never seen before stepped in.

"Ah, Edgar," the stranger said in a youthful voice, "there's an emergency. Out there," he pointed over his shoulder toward the Clearing, "that only you can…". He glanced at something in his paw and seemed to be having trouble reading it. "Is that handle or candle?" He waited a moment for Edgar's answer.

"Oh right." Edgar jumped to his feet. "A problem you say? That only I can handle?" He moved quickly to the door. "Excuse me Roscoe but this sounds pretty serious. I better get on it."

"It's Rod, your literary account representative. He says he's made a mess of things and he's going to," the stranger paused as Edgar ran past him and flew down the front steps. "End it all," he hollered to Edgar who was already half way across the Clearing.

Edgar stopped when he came to the tall oak near the statue of Abner. He could see Rod, balanced on a limb high in the tree, clinging with both paws to a branch above his head.

"It is no use Edgar," he hollered to the crowd that had quickly gathered in the Clearing, "nothing you say will stop me. I've ruined your good name by convincing you to borrow an event in someone else's life when you had so many…" He temporarily lost his balance and dropped the piece of paper he was holding. "Ah, anyway, it's all my fault, and I can't live any longer knowing what I've done to your good name."

Edgar studied the ground for a moment like he was expecting an answer to appear in the dust at his feet.

"I'm going to jump Edgar," Rod had managed to reach his script that had caught on the limb he was standing on and found his place. "Nothing you say will stop me. It's too late."

Roscoe was curious so he followed Edgar to the Clearing and stood next to him, "Did he say he was going to jump?"

"Yes Roscoe, that's exactly what he said. But, fortunately I've received training in this kind of situation." Edgar stood beneath the tree and looked up. "Rod, it's okay. I'll talk you down. Over time, I can repair my broken reputation but you can never repair a body broken after a fall from that distance." He wished he'd paid more attention when he attended a *Crises Intervention Seminar* at Annual Conference. "We can go to the feeder and…"

"Excuse me Edgar." Roscoe interrupted the obviously staged event. "Think about it for a moment. We're squirrels. We live in trees. Jumping from one limb to the next is what we do." Roscoe turned and headed back to the meeting room. "It's all over folks," he waved his arms and said to the few spectators that remained. "There's nothing going on here, the show is over."

Several looked at Edgar and shook their head in disappointment as they walked away. It was obvious the whole thing had been set up to help Edgar bolster his sagging image. As far as they were concerned it had the opposite effect. Their former Chairman, who they'd kept in office because they didn't want to hurt Edna's feelings by replacing him, had fallen from the pedestal they'd placed him on and he couldn't seem to climb back on.

Edgar stood alone in the Clearing. He'd never felt so stupid in his whole life. After he'd climbed down the tree, Rod said something but for the life of him he couldn't remember what it was.

He wondered why he couldn't have been proud of the things he'd accomplished while in office instead of allowing Rod to talk him into making things up.

He started down the path with no idea in mind where he was going, all he knew was he needed some time alone, away from the suspicious looks from members of the Community. He took the path that led toward seed school. He'd found the sound of children's playing in the field in back of the school relaxing. Besides, he knew the story of his phony attempt to regain the respect of the Community by stopping Rod from taking his life had failed miserably and would be the topic of conversation at the feeder for weeks. It wouldn't do any good to explain it was Rod's idea; he knew it was time to stop hiding behind someone else and take responsibility for his own actions.

He sat down where he could see the school yard, lost in thought.

It slowly dawned on him something was wrong, the normally boisterous playground was strangely silent. He got up and looked at the position of the sun to make sure it was the right time for recess. The field behind the school was normally filled with youngsters anxious to get outside between classes and burn off some energy.

He wandered over to the edge of the field and checked to see if they were playing where he couldn't see them and discovered no one was outside. He looked but couldn't see the member of the safety team who was required to be on hand during recess in case someone got hurt.

He pushed the door to the school open and stepped inside. The main hallway, normally bustling with activity, was empty and the classroom doors were closed.

As long as he was here he thought he'd drop by and see his old friend Professor Digby, the *Our Origins and Beginnings* teacher.

He heard a voice coming from the gymnasium and changed his course to see what was going on. That explains the empty hall and playground he told himself, they're having an assembly.

He peeked through the window in the door to the gym and wondered what kind of play they were performing, the students were huddled at one end of the room and someone with his back toward him had an arm around the neck of Nelda, the gym teacher.

Edgar eased the door open enough to hear what was being said. Maybe it's a self defense class, he thought or a safety demonstration.

"…my kid. That's all I want and I'm out of here. Okay?" He heard an obviously distraught person say.

He heard Nelda squeak, "Your son does not leave this school without a permission slip signed by the principal." He watched whoever it was, tighten his grip around her neck. One of the students was crying and shaking his head in disbelief.

He quietly closed the door and thought about what he'd seen. He decided from the terrified look on the children's faces this was not a classroom demonstration and hurried through the empty halls and out the front door of the school.

Roscoe had rescheduled his meeting with Nadine and Eldon, it had taken some work to find a time convenient for both of them. They'd just picked up the discussion where they were before they were interrupted the last time when the meeting room door opened and Edgar ran in.

"Ah, Roscoe. You've got to get…" Edgar threw his paws in the air in frustration, he couldn't think of who or what committee Roscoe should get. "Someone." He walked further into the room unaware Roscoe had visitors. "Seed school. Emergency. Quick."

He turned and headed toward the door thinking Roscoe would pick up the sense urgency and follow him.

"Edgar I'm sorry. I can't do anything until we're finished here. You're going to have to leave. Now." Roscoe wasn't sure what he could do to keep Edgar from continually interrupting his work as Chairman. He'd hoped the disaster in the Clearing earlier had brought an end to his sudden need for attention but, apparently he'd been wrong.

"Roscoe. This is the real thing. It is not made up. The school. Nelda. A parent, is acting crazy." Edgar ran out on the platform at the top of the steps but when he saw Roscoe hadn't moved he ran back inside.

"It will have to wait Edgar, we're busy." Roscoe gestured for Nadine and Eldon to stay seated and gave Edgar a look that said, enough is enough.

Edgar ran out of the room hoping to find someone in the Clearing to help. The few Community members milling around turned away in disgust at his obvious attempt to fool them again.

He knew time was running out for Nelda, the last time he saw her she didn't look like she could hold on much longer.

He gave a final look around for help before running as fast as he could back to the school.

When he got to the gym, things hadn't changed much; the angry parent was still holding Nelda and it looked like the students hadn't moved since the last time he'd seen them.

He took a deep breath, pushed open the door, and stepped inside. "Do we have a problem?" He heard a voice that sounded like his and it took him a moment to realize it was.

"We?" the parent spun around dragging Nelda with him. "I'm the one with the problem. I don't think there's any we here unless you have a mouse in your pocket."

"Buster?" Edgar ignored the comment and took a step closer. "Is that you? Vernon's boy?"

"Yea, what's it to you Edgar? **Former** Committee Chairman."

Edgar brushed aside the obvious insult and asked, "What's going on Buster?"

"What's it look like? I'm having a horrible day. I lost my job, came by here thinking I'd pick up Buster Jr. so we could spend a little time together and she says," he jerked Nelda around so she was facing Edgar, "it's against the rules." He said the last part in a whiny voice trying to imitate the sound of Nelda's voice.

Edgar laughed.

"You think this is funny?" Buster's voice rose a notch higher.

"No. No. It's definitely not funny. I'm sorry. It's just that you seem to think you're they only one having a bad day, that's all." Edgar thought for a moment and said to Nelda with a tone of authority, "It's okay, he can go."

"You think all you have to do is say is he can go and it happens?" Buster scoffed.

Edgar had no idea what to say next, then a thought popped in his head. "Are you familiar with section 3C in *The Big Book Of Important Things* about the rights and privileges of former Chairman?"

"Rights and privileges?" Buster looked at him like he was crazy. "What are you talking about? There is no section like that, you're just making it up." In spite of the rough sound of his voice Edgar thought he heard a glimmer of hope as Buster saw a way out of this mess.

"*The Big Book* states, and I quote, 'A former Chairman will serve on the seed school board until such time he is deemed unfit to do so.' I have not been so deemed and as a member of the board I say in all seriousness, you may take your child. No ifs, ands, or buts about it."

Buster didn't know what to do. He looked at Nelda and then back to Edgar. "You're saying we can leave?"

Edgar nodded yes, he was too frightened to speak.

Buster released Nelda and she collapsed at his feet, rubbing her neck where he'd held her. He stood over her for a moment then all traces of defiance slipped away as he squatted down and buried his face in his paws.

Edgar motioned for the children to leave the gym and Nelda recovered enough to follow them. Buster Jr. didn't go with the others but crossed the gym floor and took his father's paw in his.

"I don't know what came over me," Buster moaned, "it was just too much to handle."

Edgar, feeling more confidant than he had in weeks, closed the distance between them, put an arm around his shoulder, and knelt beside him. "You want to hear about too much? Let me tell you about too much." He helped Buster to his feet and led him to the bleachers at the far end of the gym. He motioned for Buster Jr. to join them.

When they were seated, Edgar began. "It all started when a literary account representative named Rod stopped me when I was on the way to the feeder."

Word of what was going on in the gym quickly spread through the school and eventually everyone in the Community heard what Edgar had done.

Roscoe stood by the gym door with Principal Charles and looked at the trio sitting together in the bleachers.

"…and, to make matters worse, Rod had this idea…" Edgar was just warming up. His voice, that started out as a whisper was now strong and changed easily as he imitated the voices of Rod and Roscoe.

Buster Jr. fell asleep leaning against his father's knee. Buster Sr. yawned and fought to stay awake as Edgar launched into another part of the story.

When he saw he was about to lose his audience Edgar realized he was talking too much. He mumbled, "Sorry," and decided if he were in Buster's place the last thing he'd want to do was face an angry crowd as he was leaving. He pointed to a door that led outside and away from the front of the school and said, "Why don't you go out that way?"

After a brief, clumsy hug from Buster Sr., Edgar watched them leave.

As soon as they were gone Roscoe hurried across the gymnasium floor and sat down next to Edgar.

"I'm sorry I didn't listen when you came and asked for help. It's just that you've been acting kind of..." He stopped when Edgar raised his paw.

"No problem Roscoe. I understand." He looked toward the door that moments before Buster and his son had walked through. "Take it easy on him will you? I know how he feels."

"Of course. We'll give him a warning but that's all. I'm sure Nelda doesn't want to cause a problem."

They sat quietly for a moment.

"What are you thinking?" Roscoe was the first to break the silence.

Edgar spoke through a yawn. "I guess it was a case of being in the right place at the right time."

"And doing the right thing," Roscoe added and put an arm around his shoulder.

The next morning Roscoe walked to his desk and saw a copy of *The Abner Echo* open to the editorial page. He sat down and saw someone had circled Toby's editorial with a black marker.

Toby or Not Toby.

> *Wow! Did you hear the one about the former Chairman who made a bold move and averted disaster for a room full of school children? If you haven't you're either stuck in your nest or out of the Neighborhood because it's the only topic of conversation this investigative reporter heard as he talked to the residents of Abner this week. The old saying that cream rises to the top is certainly true in this case.* **Edgar and The Incident In The Seed School Gym**...*now there's a story just waiting to be written.*

The Seed-O-Rama Show

The door to the Committee meeting room flew open and a stranger wearing a black sweater and matching beret marched in.

"Roscoe D. Squirrel, today is your lucky day." He announced as he crossed the room. He was followed closely by someone with a camera and someone else carrying a microphone on a pole.

"Lumus, catch the look of surprise on his face," the one in the sweater ordered. "Then pan around the room and try to capture the flavor of this room, it's outrageous."

Roscoe stood. "I don't…"

"Of course you don't, that's the point. If we'd made an appointment you'd be stiff as a board and we want the, *relaxed, surprised Committee chairman* look," the one wearing the sweater explained.

"No, I mean I wasn't…I'm not." Roscoe was having trouble figuring out what was going on. The one in the sweater looked vaguely familiar, but the other two were complete strangers.

"Relax Roscoe, chill a little, okay?" The one in the sweater smiled and started to introduce himself when Edgar walked in the room. He had a folded copy of *The Abner Echo* under his arm and was chewing a piece of nut cake.

"Oh great. Lumus, get a close up of that guy. When was the last time you saw a face like that?" Lumus swung the camera from Roscoe to Edgar.

Edgar looked surprised at first but quickly warmed to the possibility of having his picture taken. "Yes, well, all right then." Edgar tried to think of something clever to say but couldn't, so he repeated, "Yes, well then."

"Marvelous, just marvelous." The one in the sweater smiled and clapped his paws. "Vintage stuff. Classic material." He moved the microphone closer to Edgar.

"Yes, well, I, ah, that is we..." Edgar looked to Roscoe for help but saw he was as confused as he was.

"I'm at a disadvantage here," Roscoe shrugged. "You seem to know me but I don't think we've met." He stuck his paw in the direction of the stranger.

"Exactly. Understood. Message sent and received." The one in the sweater moved toward Roscoe and touched his paw. "I'm Randall, but I'm on the road so much promoting *The Seed-O-Rama Show* everyone calls me Roady." He stepped back and smiled hoping Lumus was catching all this on tape. "When we started doing these promotional pieces for the show they were live but one of our guests didn't take surprises well and threw us out of his office. Literally. Picked me up and threw me out." He chuckled. "That's when we went to tape."

"*The Seed-O-Rama Show?* I'm afraid I'm not..." Roscoe started to say he wasn't familiar with the show but before he could, Edgar interrupted.

"Sure you are Roscoe." Edgar smiled at his grandson-in-law. "Why Penny Sue was practically raised on it." Edgar moved closer to the technician with the microphone and began to sing the Seed-O-Rama theme song.

"Don't leave the room,
put down your book
that's a mystery or a drama."

Edgar motioned for Roscoe to join him but he shook him off, he wasn't familiar with the song. Having been turned down by Roscoe, he threw his arm around Roady and continued.

"For the next half hour,
we'll test your wits
as we play..."

Edgar encouraged the camera and sound man to join in as he shouted, **"Seed-O-Rama."**

When they finished, Edgar and the technicians slapped paws and laughed.

"Roady I'm Edgar, former Chairman of the Committee for the Protection of Neighborhood Resources, welcome to our Community." Edgar was all smiles as he touched paws with Roady. "I am at your beck and call sir. Although I must tell you, and you're going to find this hard to believe, I have very little acting experience." He stopped for a moment and put his paws behind his back. "I was, however, in the seed school play my third year." He looked at the floor, back at Roady, and shifted into a funny accent. "Will my lady be having her nut cake in the kitchen or the drawing room?" He smiled expecting him to remember the play. When he saw the look of confusion on his faces he said, "Act 1, scene 3? *Midnight At The Feeder?*"

"Yes, quite right," Roady was the first to recover from Edgar's performance, "but I'm afraid it's him were after." He pointed to Roscoe. "You may not be aware of it sir but you're quite well known in the area," he smiled and nodded. "That's why the producer selected your Community as the location for our next show."

"I'm not very good at games." Roscoe waved a paw. "Sorry, but I'm not interested."

"It's not just you Roscoe," Roady explained. "There'll be two others from your Community to help answer the questions." He smiled. "And, the winner gets a month's supply of seeds for his Community. You aren't going to walk away from a prize like that are you?"

Roscoe was weakening, he knew the difference a month's worth of seeds would make. It would improve morale, ease their dependence on Bird Man, and restock their nearly empty emergency supply. "I'll talk it over with…"

Roady shook his head and leaned toward him. "Sorry Roscoe but no can do. It's decision time." He rested his elbows on top of the desk, his face inches from Roscoe's. "The future of your Community hangs in the balance. What's it going to be? Yes? Or No?"

It was a tough moment for Roscoe. He hated doing things in front of others but, on the other paw, if he was part of a team it might not be so bad.

"I was wondering..." He started to ask about the nature of the questions but stopped when Roady lifted a paw stopping him. "Yes?" he waited a moment and then brought his other paw up and held it next to the first one, "Or no?"

Roscoe saw Edgar standing behind Roady, moving his head up and down, mouthing the word, "Yes."

Roscoe shrugged and said, "Sure, why not. I mean, yes, of course. I'll do it. Or, we'll do it since there will be..."

"Wonderful. Couldn't be better. Top notch." Roady spoke over his shoulder as he helped his partners gather up their equipment. "You have," he walked to the small window and looked out, "until sundown tomorrow night to pick two of your Community's best and brightest."

Lumus and the one with the microphone hurried out of the room.

"Do you know who our opponents are?" Roscoe realized he was going to need some help learning what they do on *The Seed-O-Rama Show*.

Roady flipped through the pages of his notebook. "You will be competing against," he ran a finger down the page before saying, "a team from the Community of Ben." He looked at Roscoe and smiled. "I understand Dr. Nels is a pretty smart cookie." He winked and closed his notebook. "Tomorrow night at the Big Rock. We encourage our contestants to get there a little early in case there are any last minute program changes." He was almost out the door when he waved over his shoulder and said, "Choi."

Roscoe and Edgar stood quietly for a moment, then Roscoe said, "Tell me all you know about the Seed-O-Rama Show."

"I'm surprised you missed it when you were at Squirrels Of Fun. It's the number one show there and is usually sold out." Edgar was ready to continue but Roscoe cut him off.

"What I mean is, what do the contestants do?"

"Well, for one thing it can be pretty funny. I mean, I remember a program where they had to see which team could stack safflower seeds the highest..." Edgar laughed just thinking about it.

"So, it's what? A series of challenges to see who gets done first?"

Roscoe was beginning to have second thoughts about his decision to be part of the show.

"Sometimes. Other times there are questions about Community history, stuff like that." Edgar placed a paw under his chin as he thought. "Okay, a typical question would be something like, what is the name of the squirrel who stowed away on the Mayflower?"

Roscoe was sure they'd covered that his second year in seed school but that was a long time ago.

"Dormer. The name of the first squirrel to come to America is Dormer. But don't worry, they asked that question on the program last spring, so they probably won't use it again. Everyone knows the answer by now."

It was obvious to Roscoe that Edgar had spent a lot of time watching the show.

"It's a quiz show?" Roscoe was still having trouble getting a feel for what to prepare for.

"More like a quiz game show. Once they had a two legged race to a feeder and back. They tied the legs of the contestants together and they had to run like that." Edgar paused wondering if this was a good time to suggest, since he knew so much about the show, he would make a perfect team member.

"Thanks Edgar. As you can tell I've never seen the show." Roscoe walked out of the room leaving Edgar wondering if he'd missed the opportunity to play the, *member of the family* card.

That night Roscoe had trouble sleeping. Names of who to choose kept flying in and out of his thoughts. When he wasn't dreaming about that he was making a fool of himself in one of the contest events. He was standing at the end of a conveyor belt and was supposed to pick up ten seeds and put them in a bag. If he put in too many or too few, he had to start over. The belt picked up speed and he wasn't able to keep up. Pretty soon seeds were piled around him and he couldn't find the sacks he was supposed to put them in. When he woke up he discovered he'd pulled the blanket off the bed.

He sat up and felt his heart pounding in his chest. He looked around the dark bedroom and was relieved to see the seeds and conveyor were gone. He let his head fall back on his pillow but wasn't sure he wanted to risk closing his eyes and returning to the conveyor or some equally frustrating challenge.

He woke up when he felt someone poke his shoulder. He opened his eyes but could barely make out the figure of Edgar standing at the foot of the bed. "Edgar? What are you…" He looked over and saw Penny Sue was still sleeping.

"I brought your breakfast," Edgar whispered. "I know how busy you are and thought I'd save you a trip to the feeder." He stepped back and pointed to the small table beside the bed. "I brought a cup of water in case your thirsty."

"Edgar I don't…" Roscoe was still half asleep and had no idea what time it was other than way too early.

"It's nothing Roscoe, really, I was coming back from the feeder and thought, why not drop some seeds off for my favorite Chairman who happens to be joined to my granddaughter and therefor a part of **the family**."

"This doesn't have anything to do with *The Seed-O-Rama Show* does it?" Roscoe was out of bed and moving Edgar toward the edge of his nest.

"The Seed-O…you think? Good heavens no. Why I'd forgotten all about it until you brought it up. No, no, this was just an act of kindness from a happy member of the Community who appreciates all you do for us." He gave Roscoe a hug before climbing over the side of the nest.

"Who…that?" a sleepy Penny Sue sat up and asked.

"Your grandfather." Roscoe yawned. He would like to lay back down but knew he wouldn't be able to go back to sleep after his strange conversation with Edgar.

"What…want?" She rubbed her eyes and leaned back on her elbows.

"To be on stage." Roscoe picked up a seed, bit into it, and was surprised to find it tasted pretty good.

"Oh," she said and let her arms straighten so her head fell back on her pillow.

Soon Roscoe heard the slow breathing that accompanies deep sleep. He shook his head and wished he could fall asleep that quickly.

Roscoe was on his way to the meeting room when Ferrel joined him. "3.2 miles," he said confidently.

"Three point... I don't get it. Is that the end of a joke or something?"

"The average number of miles a typical Community member travels in a day." Ferrel was proud to display this newly acquired piece of information.

"Tell me this doesn't have anything to do with Seed-O-Rama show?" Roscoe couldn't believe it was starting already. He'd passed by Marvin earlier juggling three acorns and singing the seed school fight song.

"Of course it does. It's a great show with all kinds of interesting questions. Like what's the maximum number of members on a Find The Nut team."

"There's a maximum number?" Roscoe tried to remember if Coach Bobby had said anything about that.

"Seven!." Ferrel shook his head at Roscoe's lack of knowledge about a popular game like Find The Nut. "You have to know that kind of stuff Roscoe. This isn't about you, it's about the Community. It's about Abner. I mean, the questions will be coming at you right and left. You won't have time to think, you have to react, and just repeating the question is not going to get the job done." He threw an arm around Roscoe's shoulders and the tone of his voice became friendlier. "You need someone like me on the team Roscoe. A true, dyed in the wool, trivia buff."

"I'll keep that in mind Ferrel thank you." Roscoe hoped he wouldn't follow him into the meeting room.

"If you put the decision off too long you may find the cupboard is bare. A friend in need is..." he waited for Roscoe to finish the saying. When he saw nothing that suggested he had any idea what he was talking about he finished with, "A friend indeed." Ferrel squeezed Roscoe's shoulder and walked away.

Roscoe shook his head and started to ask, "What cupboard? Which friend?" but it was too late, he was gone.

When he opened the door to the meeting room he saw Jules standing in a corner, tossing seeds into a basket on top of his desk. He noticed his planner and a folder with the papers he needed for his next meeting had been moved to the conference table.

"Jules, what's going on?" Roscoe asked and waited for him to complete a throw before crossing the room and picking up his planner.

"They had to do this on show twelve, only someone from the other team was blindfolded and sitting on a stool trying to knock the seeds away." He tossed another seed in the basket.

"I'll let you know Jules, I really don't have time to think about it right now." Roscoe put his paw on Jules elbow and hurried him toward the door.

Jules grew serious. "The clock is ticking Roscoe. You can't put making a decision off forever."

Roscoe mumbled, "Yes, I know, you're right," and closed the door before Jules could say anything else.

He returned to his desk, put his head on his paws and wished the whole *Seed-O-Rama* thing would go away. He knew who he thought would be best to put on the team but was sure the minute he announced his selections everyone would blame him for playing favorites. And, if they didn't do well, he'd be second guessed for the next month.

He knew he couldn't count on Edgar to stay focused during the show and he ruled Ferrel out because he wanted the team to represent the best the Community had to offer. He was sure Ferrel would argue with Roady over every wrong answer. If Jules and Marvin were truly his friends they would understand why he picked Sparky and Webster. And, if they didn't...well he didn't want to think about that.

He announced his choice to the Committee that afternoon. A normally talkative Edgar grew quiet and didn't say a word for the rest of the meeting. Ferrel, on the other paw couldn't keep his thoughts to himself. "That's just plain stupid Roscoe. Have any of you even seen the show? Do you have any idea how it works? You'll end up giving the whole Community a black eye." He banged his paw on the table to emphasize his point. "What were you thinking when you picked Webster for heaven sakes? Why, he couldn't find his way back from the feeder if the directions were written on the back of his paw. He gets tongue tied when he gives his annual library report to the Committee. What's going to happen when he discovers he's on stage with hundreds of screaming *Seed-O-Rama* groupies? He'll freeze up quicker than a bird bath in December.

"And Sparky? He looks like the before picture in one of those advertisements for a health club. You know, the twenty seven ounce weakling and everyone kicks sand in his face."

He stomped around the room before saying, "Just forget it," and slammed the door behind him as he left the room.

Gradually the other disappointed Committee members followed him.

Edgar was the last to leave. He looked at Roscoe and said, "I guess family ties aren't as strong as the used to be." He pushed his chair back in place and walked quietly out of the room.

Roscoe sighed and hoped the worst was over.

Members of the two Communities gathered around the Big Rock, anxious for the show to start. They watched quietly as the Seed-O-Rama crew set up the portable stage and making sure the microphones were working properly. Those who'd arrived early hoping to get seats close to the stage killed time by trying to guess which one was Roady, the host of the program.

When the team from the Community of Ben arrived a program assistant took them to their chairs on the stage. Chairman Ben had sent Sparky a card saying he was sorry things had worked out but he understood. Dr. Nels however was still upset about the trick Sparky pulled on him during his brief stay in his laboratory.

Everyone was surprised when they saw that Ben, founder and permanent Chairman was on the team and they almost fell over when they discovered Elmer, a security guard at the lab was their third selection. But they figured with Dr. Nels on the team, they could give him an acorn for one partner and a paw puppet for the other and they'd still win.

Finally Roscoe, Webster, and Sparky were taken to their seats and the crowd quieted down sensing the program was about to start.

Roady, wearing a tuxedo and with the fur on his head slicked back with safflower oil, stepped to the middle of the stage, lifted his arms and said, "Hey, hey, hey friends far and near." He held a paw to his ear and leaned toward the audience.

"*The Seed-O-Rama Show is here*," the crowd hollered back. Most of them had seen the show while on vacation and knew what they were supposed to say, they didn't need a stagehand holding a sign to tell them.

They joined Roady in singing the show's theme song, the one Edgar sang when he came to the meeting room.

When they finished, Roady waved his paws, a signal for them to quiet down. "Tonight we have as our contestants the Community of Ben on this side," he swung his arm in their direction. The crowd on their side of the audience went crazy, jumping up and down and screaming, "Ben! Ben! Ben!"

"Okay. Take it easy folks. Save some of that energy for the rest of the show." Roady acted like he was trying to get them to quiet down but he knew from focus groups this was the favorite part of the show.

"And, on this side, let's give it up for Team Abner."

The members of their Community shouted, waved their arms, and held up signs that said, "Abner rules." Several in the audience had painted their faces in bright colors while others yelled and slapped foam sticks together.

"I'm sure you are familiar with the rules. But let me point out the importance of working as a team. You must agree on an answer and, a word to the wise," Roady waited a moment before finishing. This was a standard Seed-O-Rama trick to keep the audience involved.

He shook his head and looked confused. "You're not going to believe this but I've forgotten the third rule. Maybe you can help me out," After he said it he held the microphone toward the crowd.

"Read the whole question before answering it," they hollered back.

He popped his forehead with his paw. "Of course, that's it. You've got it." He tucked the microphone under his arm and applauded them. "You're wonderful, really. Best audience ever. I don't know what I would do without you. No kidding."

A stage hand made a rolling motion with his paw telling Roady to

TWO FEEDERS, NO WAITING

speed it up. He nodded he got it then looked at the audience and asked, "Are we ready to play?"

"Yes," they shouted back.

Dr. Nels sat forward in his chair, waved a paw nonchalantly, saying with his gesture that he was ready.

Webster tried to ask how points were scored since he'd never seen the show but Roady couldn't hear because of the crowd noise.

Roady made a sweeping gesture with his paw and the noise dropped to a whisper, "Question number one is a toss up for either team and the first one with the correct answer gets one point. But, a wrong answer gives the other team a point. Got it?"

"Yes," the crowd responded.

Webster stood to ask what happens if both teams give the wrong answer but he was too late because Roady had already pulled a card from the bright red Seed-O-Rama Question Box. When he saw the game had started, he sat down.

"Name the two parts of a nut." He didn't get a chance to finish because a buzzer from Team Abner went off.

"Hey, you guys are quick. It looks like it's…" he checked with one of the judges to find out who'd pushed the buzzer, nodded and said, "It looks like Webster has the answer."

Webster appeared to be surprised at what he'd done. "I wasn't, I mean, I must have…" he looked confused and said, "I don't know where my buzzer is." He got an odd look on his face when one of the stagehands pointed out he was sitting on it.

Webster blushed and was so embarrassed he forgot the question.

Roscoe heard Ferrel tell Edgar, "Can you believe that? He didn't even know he was sitting on the buzzer."

"Since Abner couldn't answer the question goes to Team Ben. Can you handle this one? To those in the audience who are keeping track of the score knew this could be a two point swing since Webster failed to answer the question." Roady pointed his microphone towards Team Ben.

Dr. Nels crossed one leg over the other, picked a piece of lint off his fur, and leaned back confidently. He spoke as if he was addressing a class of first year students. "That's an easy one Roady since it's something everyone learns during their first year of seed school." He waited a moment before adding, "If they're paying attention that is." He shot a glance at Webster and wondered if his opponents couldn't answer a softball question like this one, what they would do when they got to the hard ones.

"There's the part you throw away and the part you eat." He smiled confidently at the Ben fans in the audience.

"That is correct. Team Ben has…" Roady stopped when he realized Dr. Nels hadn't finished.

"But, I think if your research crew had delved into the subject a little deeper, they would have discovered a third layer has been added to the list." He used his paw as a visual aide. "Beneath the part you throw away and around the part you eat, a new layer has been discovered. It's officially called the decorative layer because some nest keepers have chosen to *decorate* with it. Hence the name, decorative layer. The nests I have seen adorned in this manner are surprisingly attractive."

Dr. Nels smiled broadly and accepted the congratulations of his teammates.

"Thank you doctor for that update." Roady turned toward the audience and said, "He's a pretty special guy isn't he?" The Ben side of the crowd screamed, "Yes," and congratulated one another for having someone as clever as Dr. Nels in their Community.

"With Dr. Nels answering the questions it's like taking nut cake from a baby." One Ben fan said to the one sitting next to him.

"That puts Team Ben up by two points." Roady waited while an assistant carried a card with a big two on it across the stage and put it in front of Dr. Nels. When the assistant left the stage Roady put his paw in the question box. "Are you ready for the question number two?" Roady asked and the fans from Ben responded with an enthusiastic, "Yes."

Those on the Abner side gave a lukewarm response, not convinced their team would ever be ready to answer a question.

"For one point, who knows Coach Bobby's real name. As I'm sure you know I'm referring to the legendary seed school coach and creator of the Find The Nut game?" Roady dropped his paw signaling the clock had started.

TWO FEEDERS, NO WAITING

The members of Team Ben tried to huddle but Dr. Nels pushed them away. "You've served up another easy one Roady and we're going to knock this one out of the park." He smiled, scooted to the edge of his chair, and said confidently, "That would be, Robert."

His fans sat back and relaxed, when they realized their team had been first to answer and could do no worse than tie on this one.

Webster leaned toward Roady and started to say he agreed with the answer but Roscoe pulled him back.

"Hold on a minute Webster. I did some paperwork for Coach Bobby recently." Roscoe stared at the floor like he was expecting the papers he'd signed to miraculously appear and reveal the coaches signature.

"Robert is close but I think…" Roscoe clapped his paws together letting the other members of his team know he had it. "Roady, out of respect for Coach Bobby could I whisper the name to you? I'm not sure he'd want it spread around."

"**I think not!**." Dr. Nels stood up so quickly he sent his chair tumbling over the back of the stage. An assistant ran after it. "You didn't hear me try to weasel out of it when I answered the seed question did you?" He looked toward his fans and gestured with his arms they should get involved in his protest.

"**No way,**" they yelled and chanted, **"Answer! Answer!"**

"Roady please, this is a little more serious than naming the parts of a nut. Think about the impact something like this could have on his life?" Roscoe moved closer to Roady and spoke quietly.

"I understand you're concern Roscoe but Dr. Nels has a point. I'm afraid you'll have to answer loud enough for the judges to hear." Roady looked to the judges who nodded they agreed with him.

Roscoe shook his head no. He was not about to reveal the middle name of a well known and much loved seed school gym coach was Roberta. He'd been the last of seven children, all boys and his mother, thinking it might change her luck, had named him Roberta before he was born and was so upset she'd never bothered to change it.

Roady could see what Roscoe was trying to do and appreciated his concern. But this was show business where you smile when you are down.

"Sorry Roscoe but you'll have to answer the question or give up the point."

Roscoe shot a glance at Dr. Nels and saw he was sitting back in his chair, with his feet stretched out in front of him, amused at Roscoe's dilemma and not willing to lift a finger to help.

A gong sounded, signaling their time was up.

Roady gestured for the assistant to remove the two from in front of the Team Ben and replace it with a one. "Sorry guys, your answer is wrong. Coach Bobby's name is not Robert."

Team Ben was not celebrating. They felt Roscoe had pulled a fast one by refusing to answer the question. Dr. Nels flipped through the program rules to see if there was something in the fine print that said a contestant had to answer a question. When he didn't find what he was looking for, he rolled up the rule book and threw it on the floor.

Roscoe wished he'd gone ahead and given Coach Bobby's name, if he had, they score would be even.

"The team from Ben has a one point advantage. So we'll move on to question three." An assistant placed a jar of seeds on a table between the two teams. "You must determine how many seeds are in the jar. Who ever gets closest to the correct number wins."

Dr. Nels snorted. His reaction suggested this was child's play for him. He whispered to Ben as a youth he'd practiced this kind of thing with various sized jars.

"Remember, you cannot touch the jar, lift it, or weigh it." Roady looked at both teams. "Understood?"

The teams nodded yes, they understood.

Dr. Nels pushed his buzzer before Roady finished.

"I recognize the size of the jar Roady. So, the only thing left to do is determine its volume. Fortunately for Team Ben, I developed a chart years ago which I happened to have with me this evening." He reached in his brief case and removed a piece of paper. "As you can see, it reflects the number of seeds required to fill various sized containers." He ran his paw down the side of the chart and stopped when he came to the size of the jar on the table. He took his time returning the chart to his briefcase before turning back to Roady and saying, "The jar in question contains exactly two hundred thirteen seeds."

TWO FEEDERS, NO WAITING

He nodded confidently to the members of his team, returned the paper to his briefcase, folded his arms across his chest, and gave Sparky a look that said, "Let's see you top that lab boy."

Roscoe signaled to his teammates they should go along with Dr. Nels so, if he was wrong, they would only lose one point. He hoped there would be a bonus round coming up that would give them a chance to at least break even.

"Hold on a minute Roscoe." Sparky left his chair and walked over to the table. He crouched down and studied the lid of the container. He straightened, went back to his seat, and removed an envelope from his backpack.

He went back to the container and sprinkled a fine powder on the lid.

"Apparently our opponents weren't listening when you read the instructions!" Dr. Nels bellowed and was on his feet, protesting what Sparky had done.

Edgar shook his head and stared at the ground thinking if Roscoe had only chosen him he could have prevented this kind of thing from happening. At least he could follow a few simple instructions.

"Did I touch the jar?" Sparky calmly asked. "Have I lifted or moved it?" He held his paws up showing he was innocent. "And, I think it's pretty obvious I haven't weighed it."

"Roady, explain the rules to the contestant please, he must not have understood them the first time. Only this time speak a little slower, Sparkles isn't as quick on the uptake as some of the rest of us." Dr. Nels drew a laugh from the Ben side of the crowd when he called him Sparkles.

The Abner side sat quietly, embarrassed at the poor decisions being made by their representatives.

Roady looked to the panel of judges for an opinion. They were frantically turning pages in the rule book, looking for something that would cover sprinkling powder on the lid. Finally they looked at Roady and said as far as they were concerned no rule had been broken and they could find nothing wrong with what Sparky had done.

"Perhaps the letter of the rules was not violated," Dr. Nels stammered, "but surely it is an abuse of the spirit of this delightful program."

Roady gave Dr. Nels a look that suggested if he said another word, he'd take away the one point they had.

Dr. Nels slumped in his chair, folded his arms across his chest, and pouted. "I don't see the point in what he's doing anyway, unless it's some weak attempt to stall for time hoping his teammates can think of something." He poked Elmer in the ribs with his elbow and they both laughed.

"What's going on Sparky?" Roscoe whispered, he didn't see the point either.

"I noticed a slight dent in the lid." Sparky whispered. "And verified it when I sprinkled powder on it. I knew I was kind of pushing it rule-wise."

"And," Roscoe knew Sparky had to walk him through the thought process so he'd understand what he'd done.

"And, there's a cylinder of some type attached to the inside of the lid taking up room in the jar. Now, it's anybody's guess as to how close to the bottom it is." He scratched his head. "I'm thinking it's pretty close."

"What are you saying?" Webster didn't see where he was going with this.

"He guessed too many seeds. The cylinder takes up room so his answer is too high." Sparky looked at the ground, thought for a moment, and then back at Roscoe. "Say two hundred, we only have to be closer to the actual number than they are, we don't have to be exact." He stepped back, satisfied with his answer. "I could run some numbers if you'd feel more comfortable."

"Team Abner, I need an answer. Time is almost up." Roady lifted his eyebrows to encourage them.

Roscoe gulped and took a deep breath. He knew if they lost this one the contest was over, the best they could do was tie. "Two hundred?" he answered.

Dr. Nels exploded with laughter and slapped his knee with a paw. He leaned toward Ben but said in a voice loud enough for everyone to hear. "And you thought old Sparkles was so smart." He turned and smacked the back of Elmer's chair in celebration.

The crowd from Ben stood and cheered. They were beginning to see the possibility of a shutout.

TWO FEEDERS, NO WAITING

Ben wasn't so sure Sparky was wrong.

Roady waited patiently while the audience celebrated, he knew how to take advantage of crucial moments in the program. He waved the card with the answer trying to get them to quiet down.

"The exact number of seeds in the jar is," he announced and those on the Abner side held their breath, "one hundred ninety seven." Roady started to say the contest was even but gave up because the Community of Abner fans were making so much noise no one could have heard him.

"There is no way," Dr. Nels kicked his briefcase across the stage.

"The score is even." Roady watched his assistant carry a one sign and place it in front of the team from Abner. "Now, for the tie breaker, the fourth and final question." Roady looked at the crowd and asked, "Is the audience ready?"

"Yes," they roared back.

"Contestants?"

The members of both teams nodded yes except for Dr. Nels, who continued to glare at judges.

"Okay then, the fourth and final question." As he spoke he handed both teams a piece of paper that had the question written on it, then opened the one he'd kept for himself. "Three squirrels have to go through a foreign Neighborhood. They come to a fenced in yard and see a sign that says only two can cross the yard at the same time **but** they can only make one trip. How do they get to the other side of the yard?"

Dr Nels smacked his paw down on his buzzer. "Roady your panel of judges is going to have to dig a little deeper for more challenging questions. I certainly hope this isn't the best they can do." He stood by his chair and put a paw on his chest and moved the other behind his back. "I recognized this problem after I read the first line. It may interest you to know I wrote an article on this very conjecture that was circulated among scientists of merit for their review." He shot a glance at Sparky making sure he got the point that he was not included in that elite group. "It is known as *The Malcom Variation* and was named for the famous mathematician Malcom of the Community of Fred." He waited while several of the judges wrote the name in their notebooks.

When they were finished, Dr. Nels took the paper with the question from Elmer's paws, tore it in half, and let the pieces fall to the floor.

"The solution is really quite simple. The two squirrels allowed to cross represent eight feet, four per squirrel if my memory is correct." He smiled and the Ben side of the audience roared with laughter. "They simply carry the third squirrel so only eight feet are on the ground at any time."

The crowd went crazy. Most of them didn't care much for Dr. Nels, he was a little too arrogant for their taste, but when it came to a contest like this they were glad he was on their side.

Edgar's shoulders sagged. He'd never heard of whatever variation Dr. Nels mentioned but the answer made sense. It looked to him like it was over for Team Abner.

Roscoe looked at Sparky hoping he could think of some other way for the three squirrels to get across the yard. Sparky bit his lip and shook his head no, his mind was blank. He hated to think that Dr. Nels was able to beat them on a question he could normally handle easily.

While Dr. Nels was giving his answer, Webster had been reading the question hoping he could find something the others had missed. Maybe their was a fourth squirrel or another yard."

He sat up, blinked, and did the unthinkable. Without consulting his teammates, he folded the piece of paper in half, walked across the stage, and handed it to Roady.

Ferrel was furious. "He quit. He caved in like a moldy nest." He wadded the commemorative Seed-O-Rama program in a ball and threw it on the ground. "He should have tried something," he complained to the person seated next to him, "even if it was wrong. But does he try? No, he just throws in the towel."

Dr. Nel's touched paws with his teammates, then pumped his arm. and shouted an enthusiastic, "Yes!"

Roady waited for the noise to die down before announcing, "I declare the twenty-third *Seed-O-Rama Show* officially over." He swept his arm around taking in both sides of the audience. "And, it gives me great pleasure to announce the winner of tonight's contest."

The crowd from Ben cheered as they moved to a position in front of Roady so the moment he announced the winner, they could rush on the stage and lift Dr. Nels to their shoulders. They knew he didn't like a public show of affection but this was different, he'd just defeated the team from Abner all by himself.

Ben, Elmer, and Dr. Nels formed a circle with their arms around each others shoulders. Dr. Nels stepped back, pointed at Sparky, and slowly rotated his wrist until his thumb was pointing down. He hollered across the stage, "Don't mess with the best sonny boy." Fortunately there was too much noise for Sparky to hear.

"Hold on. Quiet down." It took Roady a while to get the crowd under control. When it was finally quiet he looked at both teams. He took a step toward Team Ben and the crowd from their Community crouched down, ready to leap in the air the moment the victor was announced. "I'm sorry gentlemen, but," he spun around and pointed to Webster. "Tonight's winner, by one point, is Team Abner."

The crowd was stunned. They couldn't believe what they heard. A moment ago the Community of Ben was sure they'd won and were thinking about where in their Neighborhood they could store a months supply of seeds.

The Community of Abner crowd had walked away in disgust that one of their own members, their librarian for goodness sake, had given up when the chips were down. They were so surprised they'd won they didn't know what to do. They kept asking one another, "Did he say what I thought he said?"

When it finally sank in they went wild. They rushed back to the stage and roared when they saw Roady hand the Seed-O-Rama trophy to Roscoe.

After the celebration, Roscoe, Sparky and Webster stood alone on the stage, drained of energy, and too tired to move.

"I don't get it Webster. You read the paper and handed it to Roady." Roscoe paused, he didn't want to say anything that would hurt Webster's feelings but he couldn't figure out what happened. "You didn't answer the question. How did we win?"

"I read the problem all the way through. To tell you the truth, it wasn't until I read it the second time that I saw it, printed on the bottom of the page. It said to ignore everything written above and hand the paper back to Roady. Dr. Nels was so sure he knew the answer he didn't see any reason to read any farther." Webster smiled and pushed his glasses back in place. "The writers of the show probably figured no one would read the entire question, they never do."

It was quiet for a moment, then Roscoe said proudly, "You did."

Webster blushed. "It's the third rule Roscoe, read the instructions before answering the question."

They raised their arms in the victory and walked toward the celebration just getting started in the Clearing.

Where There Are No Seeds the Squirrels Perish

From the Wisdom of Abner
Volume 3, Page 7

Roscoe couldn't believe it. The month supply of seeds they'd won on *The Seed-O-Rama Show* was gone in a little over two weeks. In spite of his warnings that they should slow down, the Community went through them like there was no tomorrow. One night they got into a food fight and threw seeds all over the Clearing.

"What's the big deal," Ferrel asked after Roscoe stopped the fight and forced everyone to clean things up, "Bird Man will come through for us."

Roscoe tried to explain that if they would take it easy they wouldn't have to depend on Bird Man who could shut the feeder down any time he wanted.

"Listen to yourself Roscoe," Ferrel argued. "Where's the excitement? Where's the thrill of living on the edge?"

Don't fight it, you can't win, Roscoe told himself. If you try to show a sense of responsibility they say you're too serious. If you throw caution to the wind and join the eating frenzy they say you're wasteful.

He sighed and tried to concentrate on the contract he'd been working on all morning but gave up. He kept thinking about how quickly they'd gone through a months supply of seeds when Marvin opened the door.

"Got a minute Roscoe?" He crossed the room and pulled a chair away from the conference table before Roscoe had a chance to answer.

"Sure. Why not?" Roscoe tossed his pencil on his desk and gave up hope of getting anything done.

"I just came from Bird Man's and the feeder tubes are empty." Marvin pushed the pencil around the desk with his paw.

"That's to be expected, didn't Sylvia say he's on vacation?"

"Well, yes and no," Marvin answered as he swiveled back and forth in his chair.

Roscoe hung his head and wondered why no one answered a question with a yes or no anymore? It seemed lately every time he asked someone a serious question the one he was talking to did everything they could to keep from giving him a direct answer.

He looked at his friend and said, "Look Marvin, he's either on vacation or he's not. Which is it?"

Marvin was surprised by the tone of Roscoe's response. "Yes he was on vacation doing something Sylvia called skiving, but he's not now. He came back early because he ran into something."

"Hold it Marvin. Did Sylvia say anything about what he does when he's skiving? Did she mention what he hit that caused him to come home early?" Roscoe wondered if this discussion was going anywhere but at the moment he didn't hold out much hope that it was.

"Well, I think it's done on snow. At least that's what I got from Sylvia. You can check with her. She said he left with these stick things on top of his car and when he came back one of them was broken."

"I think it's called skiing Marvin, not skiving,

Marvin thought for a moment before asking, "What was the other thing?"

"You said he hit something. I asked what he hit?"

"Oh yeah, I remember, two things actually, a pole and a tree."

"And?" Roscoe rolled his paw encouraging him to go on.

"She said he broke his body." Marvin looked at Roscoe and smiled.

"Can humans do that? Break their body? Don't they usually break something like an arm or leg?"

"Sylvia said when they carried him from his car he had a full body cast, all she could see was his head and one foot."

"So she's saying he can't put seeds in the feeder because he's injured?" Roscoe couldn't believe it had taken this long to get an answer. They'd finally completed a full circle back to the original question.

"Right," Marvin nodded his head. "His neighbor comes over and feeds her but he doesn't want to mess with the bird feeder. Besides, Bird Man can't see it from his room in the house."

"How long does she think it's going to be before he's well enough to fill the feeder on his own?" Without Bird Man putting seeds in the feeder, the Community was facing a bleak future; after finding his yard, they'd given up looking for other sources of food.

"She said, maybe a month, possibly more." Marvin hadn't made the connection between Bird Man not being able to fill the feeder and the Community going hungry.

"Come with me, I need to talk to her immediately." Roscoe announced as he moved toward the door pulling a reluctant Marvin along with him.

They stood by the fence and watched Sylvia pace nervously back and forth. She was so engrossed in her own thoughts she hadn't seen them arrive. She jumped when Marvin called her name and seemed surprised to discover they'd been standing there for a while.

"Sylvia? Are you okay?" A concerned Marvin asked when she came over to meet them.

"It's owner, he doesn't do anything; no television. no visitors. He doesn't pet me when I jump on the bed." She waited a second to collect herself, she appeared to be on the verge of tears. "I'm…worried that's all." She looked at Marvin, forced a smile, and said, "Thanks for asking."

"What happened to the feeder?" Roscoe noticed it wasn't in the usual place in the yard.

"The neighbor took it down. He said it wasn't doing any good since he wasn't going to keep it filled. Besides, my owner can't see it anyway." She motioned to the side of the house and the window to Bird Man's bedroom.

"Where'd he put it? I don't see it anywhere." Roscoe had been looking around the yard while Sylvia was talking.

"Under there." She pointed to the neighbors deck.

"Why'd he put it under there?" Marvin thought it was odd knowing how much Bird Man loved watching birds fly around his yard.

"Well," she sighed, "to be honest, he's not happy with you guys. He said he's pretty sure you were the reason the lights went out the night of the big explosion although he's not sure how you did it. I heard him tell Owner from now on you guys were on your own. He said as far as he was concerned, there's no such thing as a free lunch."

Roscoe moved along the fence and studied the yard. He noticed the fence went past Bird Man's bedroom and half way to the street before turning and connecting to the house. He pointed to a window. "Is that his room, where the shades are drawn?"

Sylvia didn't need to look. When he mentioned the shades being drawn she knew which room he was talking about and nodded yes. "Why?"

"Oh nothing, I just had a, ah..." Roscoe turned to Marvin. "I'm going back to the meeting room, you can stay and talk with Sylvia if you want."

Marvin looked at Sylvia who quickly nodded yes, she could use some company. He smiled and said, "Thanks Rosc, See you later."

Roscoe was headed down the path to the Clearing when he glanced back and saw Marvin and Sylvia, their heads close together, with only the fence separating them.

He had an idea but he knew it would be a tough sell. What he was going to recommend went against the first rule taught in seed school; he was going to help a human in trouble.

"Are you ought of your seed picking mind!" Ferrel shouted and stood so quickly he knocked his chair over.

Roscoe had just finished explaining to the Committee his plan to cheer Bird Man up by moving the feeder from beneath the neighbors deck and installing it in front of his bedroom window. He'd gone to great pains to point out that while Bird Man had given them trouble in the past it was time to get over it and let bygones be bygones. Yes, they'd had their difficulties but he had kept the feeder tubes full of seeds.

Ferrel was the most vocal of the Committee members, the others were too astonished by his suggestion to say anything.

"You just don't get it do you? The seeds are there for the **birds**, not us. Everyone knows that for goodness sake." Ferrel banged his pencil on the conference table to help make his point and struggled to keep his voice under control. "What's the first thing the teach us in seed school? **NEVER TRUST A HUMAN!**" He said the word human so loud some of the Committee members covered their ears.

"Much as I hate to say it, I have to agree with Ferrel on this one Roscoe, I just don't see why we should do it." Darin, usually an enthusiastic supporter of Roscoes ideas, picked at something on the top of the table, unwilling to make eye contact with him.

"Can't we just talk about it?" Roscoe had seen them like this before; locked in on some outdated saying and unable to consider there might be an exception.

"Okay," Ferrel threw his paws in the air. "Just for grins, let's suppose, and as long as I'm on the Committee it's never going to happen, but for the sake of argument, let's suppose we go along with **your** half baked idea." Ferrel paced back and forth in the small space between the conference table and the door.

Word had spread through the Community that something big was going on so every inch of space in the meeting room was filled. Someone stood in the doorway and repeated everything that was said to those who'd arrived late and were forced to stand outside.

"First, there's the matter of getting the feeder pole and tubes from under the neighbor's deck without getting caught. Then there's the chore of getting over the fence and traipsing across the yard," he put his paws together like he was carrying the feeder pole across his shoulder and acted like he was sneaking across the yard. "**If** we made it that far without being detected, then we have to plant the pole in the ground which, in case you've forgotten, **is like concrete** since it hasn't rained in two weeks." Ferrel stepped back to catch his breath before continuing.

"**If**, and I emphasize if, we're able to do that, there is still the small matter of getting the seeds in the feeder tubes." He moved closer to the table and looked Roscoe in the eye. "I'd say the chances of that happening are somewhere between slim and none." He looked at those lining the meeting room walls and grinned as he finished with, "And Slim just left town."

The person in the doorway hollered, "Slim left town." The crowd outside was confused. They'd missed the first part about Roscoe's chance of success.

Some thought he said Tim left town and were trying to figure out which of the three Tims in the Community he was talking about.

Ferrel's comment was followed by a nervous laugh from several in the room.

If there's one thing the members of the Community are uncomfortable with it's tension, and this was definitely a tension filled moment.

It was so quiet Roscoe could hear the person at the door trying to explain what Ferrel meant about Slim leaving town. "It's a figure of speech meaning there's not a chance Roscoe's idea will work." The person in the doorway waited as someone outside asked a question. "Tim?" he answered, "who said anything about Tim?"

"You've heard how Ferrel feels about this, are there any other opinions?" Roscoe didn't know what else to do, he hoped his question would buy some time, and give him a chance to think of something.

The members of the Committee remained silent; no one wanted to take Ferrel on.

"Let me just say it's off the wall ideas like this that suggest we should seriously consider removing Roscoe as Chairman and install…" He didn't get a chance to say, "me," because someone in the back of the room said, "I think it's a great idea."

Ferrel spun around, expecting to see one of Roscoe's buddies come to his aide and prevent their friend any further embarrassment. Instead, he was surprised to see his son Ferrel Jr., push his way to the center of the room.

"No one asked for your opinion Junior so zip it," Ferrel motioned for him to go back where he'd been standing. "This is a Committee matter and we don't need any help from you." He shook his head, embarrassed that his own son didn't know the first thing about Committee procedure.

Ferrel Jr. dropped his head, looked at the floor, and muttered, "Sorry, I thought…"

"You thought? I don't think so. If you'd **thought** you'd have kept your mouth shut." Ferrel glared at his son. He started to tell him to go home, or back to school, or someplace other than the meeting room. He stopped when he heard Darin say, "That's perfectly okay Ferrel Jr., it's a Community problem and this is an open meeting. You said something about Roscoe having a good idea?"

Ferrel started to protest but when he saw the other members of the Committee nod they agreed with Darin, he found his seat at the conference table and sat down heavily. He gave his son an angry look and folded his arms across his chest, daring him to speak.

"What, I was, ah…" Ferrel Jr. was caught off guard. He wasn't used to anyone listening to what he had to say, let alone ask for his opinion on something as important as this. He wasn't sure how to handle it.

"Well, see, I thought, I mean, was thinking," he looked around the room trying to avoid his father's angry glare. He tugged nervously at the fur on his shoulders as he spoke. "It's just that at seed school there's a third year project, I think its every year, at least it has since I've been going there. I think it's like a tradition or something?" He looked at the Committee members for confirmation. They nodded yes, the school had a number of traditions and the third year project was one of them.

"Anyway, like I was saying, or started to say until, ah, the third years have to complete a project before they, we actually, can graduate so I thought, you know, with Bird Man hurt and the feeder down…like that would, ah…" He shrugged and looked at the floor. That's as far as he could go and he hoped someone on the Committee would be able to connect the dots and figure out what he was trying to say.

"Let me get this straight," Ferrel stood, towering over his short, scrawny son. "A bunch of snot nosed kids, not even out of seed school who don't know the difference between an acorn and an Irish Wolfhound when it comes to practical experience, think they can waltz over to Bird Man's in broad daylight, **remove** the feeder from beneath the neighbors deck, and **plant** it by his window. Is that what you're trying to say?" He stood inches away from his son. The tone of his voice suggested that was the dumbest thing he'd ever heard in his life.

"Well see, I suppose, what I mean was, is…" Ferrrel Jr. looked around trying desperately to think of something to say. "They, our sponsors I mean, said we can have help. They allow that, help I mean, so I…"

Ferrel face grew red. Partly because he wasn't used to his son talking back to him but mostly because he knew exactly where this conversation was going. "So, what do you plan to do, ask your super hero Sparky to come up with some weird way to get the job done? Maybe he could mix up some magic potion in his lab?"

Ferrel Jr. stared at the corner of the conference table and shook his head no. "Not really. I ah, was actually…" he didn't get to finish.

"Or Roscoe? Or maybe weak kneed little Webster who sits around the library all day and sorts books?" Ferrel Sr. leaned forward causing his son push against the crowd.

"No. See, I was thinking we could ask," Ferrel Jr. hesitated for a moment trying to drum up enough courage to say what he had in mind. "You," he finally blurted out. "I was going to ask you to help us. That's all. I thought you could, you know," he shrugged, "show us how."

The room grew quiet. Everyone was waiting to see how Ferrel would react to his son's comment about him helping the third year class.

Ferrel was stunned. The last person he expected his son to ask to help was him.

"Well now, I'm, ah, awfully busy." He slowly backed toward the door. "You know with the Committee and of course there's the, ah…other thing" He looked around expecting someone on the Committee to speak up and agree it would take up a lot of time but no one did. He raised his paw like he was going to say something else and then, unexpectedly pushed through the crowd and ran out of the door.

The silence after his departure was broken when Darin said, "I move that Ferrel Jr. and his third year class relocate the feeder from under the neighbors deck and, that Ferrel Sr. be declared an official Community helper on the project."

His motion was enthusiastically seconded and was followed by a chorus of, "Aye's." Several in the crowd joined in even though they knew their vote didn't count.

Penny Sue shook Roscoe's shoulder, waking him from a deep sleep. He opened one eye and saw that it was still dark outside. "Wha…?" was all he could say, it felt like his tongue was stuck to the roof of his mouth.

TWO FEEDERS, NO WAITING

"There's someone at the base of our tree, I can hear him walking around." There was a sense of panic in her voice.

"They probably lost their way in the dark and came to the wrong tree. They'll figure it out." Roscoe rolled over and closed his eyes.

"I don't think so, they've been down there too long for that. You better take a look." She shoved him again. "I heard him call your name."

"Penny Sue I have a busy day tomorrow and I was late getting home tonight. Couldn't I..." He stopped. Even though it was dark he knew she was giving him a look that said, "If you don't do something I won't be able to go back to sleep."

He sighed, "Okay," and rolled out of bed.

"Who's there?" He asked when he was almost to the ground. "Who's down here?" His question was met with silence.

Whoever it was stopped walking and stood motionless at the base of Roscoe's tree.

"It's me, Ferrel. Ferrel Sr." He spoke so softly Roscoe had trouble believing it was him. He'd never heard him speak in anything other than a loud, angry voice.

"Ferrel, it's after midnight, is there something..." Roscoe waited.

"I'm sorry to bother you but it's about the meeting. Today or yesterday I guess. Last night." He was surprised when Roscoe had said it was after midnight. "You know. Ferrel Jr., the third year project." Ferrel seemed to be having trouble finding the right words to explain why he'd come to Roscoe's this time of night.

"You probably heard, after you left we voted to support the third year project if that's why you're here." Roscoe found he was getting upset, their conversation could just as easily have taken place at his office in the morning, after they'd both had a good night's sleep.

"Right, I heard." There was another pause and Roscoe heard him clear his throat.

Finally Roscoe said, "Well, if that's it then I'll just go back up and try to get back to sleep before..." When he didn't get a response from Ferrel, he assumed their conversation was over so he started climbing his tree.

"I don't know how." The hopelessness in his voice caused Roscoe to stop. "I've never done anything like this, you know, helped on a project. Helped on anything actually."

As far back as Roscoe could remember, Ferrel had never admitted to not being able to do something. Usually he'd argue about the details of a plan until whoever he was talking to threw their paws in the air and said, "Oh, never mind I'll do it my self." Roscoe hadn't guessed it was because he didn't know how to tell someone what to do without insulting them.

"So you want..." Roscoe was still not sure where this was going but he hoped he didn't ask him to take his place sponsoring the class project. Or, after what he said at the meeting, get him to talk Sparky into doing it. Or Webster.

"Help." It was almost a squeak but Roscoe heard it.

"How can I help you Ferrel?" Roscoe was back on the ground standing in front of him.

"Everything. I've thought about it all evening and I haven't come up with a way to get the feeder up. I have no idea how to work with kids Ferrel Jr's age." He shook his head sadly and dropped his voice to almost a whisper. "We barely say two words to each other any more."

Roscoe couldn't see him very well, but he was sure he was looking at the ground, embarrassed at having to admit he didn't know where to begin.

"Let's meet at Sparky's lab in the morning, He's never at a loss when it comes to ideas." Roscoe went with the first thing that entered his mind.

"Yea well, that's just it isn't it? What will the others say. I mean, I shot off my mouth during the meeting and now I'll look, well, you know, kind of stupid, if I..."

Roscoe smiled. "Ferrel, no one will know unless you tell them."

Roscoe waited until he could no longer hear footsteps. He knew Ferrel had a big decision to make and he was glad this time he wouldn't be the one losing sleep over it.

As he climbed in bed Penny Sue asked sleepily, "Who was it?"

"Just someone trying to find his place, but he's gone now."

Just before she drifted back to sleep he heard her say, "I hope he finds it."

The next morning Roscoe was almost to Sparky's lab when he heard Ferrel call his name. He was hiding behind a tree and looking back toward the Clearing, making sure no one followed him.

Roscoe understood. He knew for Ferrel, asking for help was a big step. "Stay where you are, I'll get Sparky to open the door and we can go in together. If he's working on an experiment this may take a while. His helper Buford may be with him, I don't want you to be surprised if he is." Roscoe spoke over his shoulder as he walked to the circle in front of Sparky's tree.

"Whatever," Ferrel flicked his fingers telling him to get on with it. He glanced up the path, making sure no had seen him come to the lab.

Roscoe said his name when the automated voice said, "Identify." He waited patiently while the security system scanned the list of names cleared to enter the lab.

He heard the familiar, "Enter friend," and watched the door to the lab slide open. As Roscoe walked toward the lab he gestured for Ferrel to join him. As soon as he stepped from behind the tree the area around Sparky's lab exploded with applause. He looked around as members of the Community walked toward them shouting words of encouragement.

Ferrel glared at Roscoe. "Who did you tell?"

"No one honestly, I didn't even tell Penny S…" He thought back to breakfast when she asked what was on his schedule for the day. He'd told her he was going to stop by Sparky's then go to the meeting room. He remembered her asking why he was going to Sparky's and he'd hesitated for just a second, trying to think of something to say without giving away the real reason of his visit. Eventually he said something about a technical matter but he remembered seeing her raised eyebrow and curious look.

"No one." Roscoe answered and blushed. "Honest I didn't tell anyone."

Ferrel shot an angry look his way and hurried into the lab.

Sparky looked awful. There were black circles under his bloodshot eyes. What little fur remained on his head was in clumps where he'd nervously tugged on it while he was deep in thought. On the table in front of him was the result of his nights work, a model of Bird Man's house and backyard. It included part of the neighbor's house and deck. He and Buford had spent all night working on it.

Roscoe could see Buford curled up on a bench in a corner of the room sleeping.

"This is fantastic Sparky." Roscoe couldn't believe the detail he'd gone to. He'd even made a replica of Sylvia and positioned her by the cat door at the back of the garage.

"What is it?" Ferrel asked, his mind still locked on the surprise visit by the Community at the entrance to the lab.

"It's Bird Man's yard," Sparky answered in a scratchy voice.

"What's that? Over there?" Ferrel pointed to a coiled piece of string by the side of the house.

"Well, I guess that's as good a place to start as any." Sparky yawned and took a sip of cold, walnut tea.

Roscoe could tell Sparky had planned to give a more formal, step by step presentation of his plan to the Committee but after staying up all night working on the model, he decided to hit the high points and leave the rest for any questions Ferrel might have.

"First, we have to soften the ground in front of Bird Man's window for at least two days before *Operation Raise the Feeder* gets under way." Sparky spoke through a yawn, "If you'll come over here I'll show you how to turn the faucet on and off."

They walked a few steps to a place on the wall where a water faucet that looked exactly like the one on the back of Bird Man's house was mounted. Roscoe remembered seeing it at the dump and was surprised when Sparky picked it up and put it in his backpack.

The plan was simple; soften up the ground so the feeder pole would go in more easily, have Sylvia keep the neighbor busy long enough to move the feeder and pole from beneath his deck, and fill the feeder tube with seeds from the garage.

Ferrel was stunned. He'd been trying to figure out how to get the feeder from under the deck and had completely forgotten about Sylvia.

"Brilliant," he said as he walked around the model. "Absolutely brilliant." Now that he had a plan, Ferrel was feeling more like himself again. "All that's left is to figure out how I can get out of here without being seen and we're good to go." He was half joking when he said it.

"There's a back door," Sparky gestured toward the back of the lab.

Roscoe opened the front door to the lab, made a big deal about saying goodbye and thanking Sparky for his help on, "That extremely difficult technical problem." He was hoping this would cause anyone hanging around to come to the front of the lab to find out who was leaving.

He might as well have saved his breath. He shook his head when he heard cheers and clapping coming from the other side of the tree, the side where the back door to the lab was located.

Never try to keep a secret from the Community, he told himself. He glanced at the crowd gathered around Ferrel as he angrily pushed past them on his way to the meeting room. He saw Penny Sue clapping her paws and jumping up and down with the others. Or from Penny Sue, he added to his observation about keeping secrets.

Roscoe agreed to let Ferrel use the meeting room for his introduction to the third year class. In turn, he'd had asked for Roscoe to introduce him to the students and hang around to make sure things didn't get out off on the right foot.

When they were finally assembled, Ferrel got his first look at the members of the *Raise the Feeder* team and fought the urge to get up and leave. One of the males had a small earring in his ear. The other one had shaved his head and let the fur around his face grow way past what was considered acceptable by the Community. The two females on the team did not inspire confidence; one chewed nervously on a tree root while the other kept getting up and looking out of the window to see if her boy friend had come by to pick her up.

Compared to the others, Ferrel Jr. was looking a lot better in his father's eyes.

Roscoe smiled and stepped forward. He'd had second thoughts about Ferrel sponsoring the project, working with him was like walking through a mine field, one false step and he would explode.

"Good afternoon. I'm Chairman Roscoe and I want to welcome you to the kickoff meeting of your third year project. Ferrel Sr. has graciously offered to help," he gestured in Ferrel's direction, "and has developed an excellent plan that will not only teach you how to work together as a team but will also help a friend of our Community through a difficult time."

A paw shot up from one of the team members. "I thought, like we weren't suppose to have nothing to do with humans. Professor Digby told us that the first day of class. Right guys?"

The other members of the team nodded they agreed.

"Well, this is a little different situation," Roscoe smiled remembering he used to have the same black and white view of things. "The one we call Bird Man has provided our Community with seeds for the last several months and is hurt so this is our opportunity to..."

A team member interrupted. "Didn't he like, try to blow you up or something. I read about it in *The Abner Echo*."

Ferrel Sr. got up from his chair and began pacing at the back of the room.

"No, no, that's not quite right. See, Sparky came up with a way to rewire the feeder so it..."

"How come the feeder was wired in the first place," the one looking out the window asked as she walked back to the table disappointed her boyfriend hadn't come by to get her. "I don't remember seeing any wires on Seed Man's feeder."

Roscoe raised his paws. "Let's get back to your first question. Before Bird Man got to know us he had a different view..." Roscoe stopped because the one with the shaved head was frantically waving his paw. Roscoe nodded in his direction. "Doesn't he have like a huge cat that chases us out of his yard and smacks the fence to scare us?"

"You mean Sylvia?" Roscoe chuckled trying to convey seeing her as an enemy was a misunderstanding. "As it turns out, she's on our side and has played a key role on several..."

"How do you know it's not just an act? You know, play along until we get in there and then she tears us limb from limb?" The one with the facial fur looked concerned. "You know, the second rule, never trust a cat."

Roscoe forced himself to remain calm; he knew getting upset wouldn't accomplish anything. He decided not to mention that never trust a cat

TWO FEEDERS, NO WAITING

was the third rule. "Look, Sylvia has helped us in the past and we have no reason to doubt…"

"Right, like you thought you'd seen the last of Pete O'Malley until…"

"That's enough out of you pip squeak." Ferrel stepped in front of Roscoe. "You've gotten way off track. No offense Roscoe but you've let this thing go on far too long." Ferrel made a gesture with his head toward the door. "You want to close that on your way out?"

He turned to the four terrified third years. Ferrel Jr. was the only one smiling, he was used to this kind of talk.

"Look, we only have so much time to get this done and if you think I'm going to let you goof around and then give you a passing grade you'd better think again." He took a step toward the team. "The way I see it, there's a time for talk and a time for action." He glared at them and finished with, "So the question for you is, what time is it?"

The last thing Roscoe heard as he closed the door was Ferrel Sr. lecturing the students. "Don't you know who that is? He's the Chairman of the Committee and from now on when you see him I want to hear you call him Mr. Roscoe. Got it?"

Five heads nodded yes, they understood.

Ferrel had decided to present the plan devised by Sparky and have the students choose which part the wanted to work on. But, when he finished walking them through the model and explaining the details of the plan, he saw very little interest on their part.

"Why can't we do what they did last year?" one of them asked. "They just sat around and talked about what they were going to do after they graduated,"

"Yea, and the year before that they painted a class room at pre-seed school." One of the females said. "There's no danger involved doing that unless you get paint on your fur."

Ferrel looked outside and saw shadows creeping across the Clearing. He realized they'd spent all afternoon talking about the project and hadn't accomplished a thing. He smacked the conference table with his paw. "Okay, listen up. You," he pointed to one of the females, "and you," he nodded to Ferrel Jr., "come with me, were going to wet down the area under Bird Man's window." He looked around, "The rest of you have a decision to make. Either be here in the morning ready to go to work or be the first class in the history of the school to fail to complete their third year project. You're either in or out. And let me be the first to break the news to you. Your mommy and daddy aren't going to be able to bail you out of this one." He glared at each of them before adding, "Got it?"

To everyone's surprise, the team under Ferrel's direction gradually began to work together. So much so, that when the project was complete and the bird feeder was filled and in position outside Bird Man's window, they hung around together after school and looked for other things to do.

Knowing that Bird Man enjoyed watching birds attracted to the feeder, they worked out a deal with Sylvia. She'd walk around the yard when he was awake and go inside and close the cat door when he fell asleep or was watching a television program. That was the signal members of the Community could use the feeder.

The students wore arm bands and acted like guides and signaled to Community members when it was safe to get seeds.

On graduation night, Ferrel was given the *Helper of the Year* award and several attempts were made by the *Raise the Feeder* team to lift him onto the shoulders but he managed to avoid them.

During the ceremony he was asked to come to the front of the gym and say a few words about his experience as a class project helper. A normally talkative and opinionated Ferrel was reduced to sobs as he tried to describe what working with the students had meant to him. When he finally pulled himself together he said, "There's someone in this room, without whose help and encouragement this project would never have gotten off the ground."

He looked at Roscoe and was ready to point him out as the true hero of the evening but stopped when he saw him shake his head no.

He shifted to Sparky who did the same as Roscoe.

"It's, ah, I…" Ferrel was stuck. Not being able to recognize Roscoe and Sparky caught him off guard. He blinked and smiled when the thought hit him. "My son, Ferrel Jr."

Ferrel Jr. stood thinking he'd just wave to the crowd and sit down but found himself running to the front of the auditorium, leaping on the stage, and hugging his father. He was followed closely by the rest of the third year class.

As Penny Sue and Roscoe were walking to their nest after the graduation ceremony she asked, "Do you remember the night the stranger was walking around our tree and said he was lost? Do you think he found his way home?"

Roscoe smiled and said, "I'm sure of it."

Playing Chess with the Man

"All I'm saying is if the Community's birthday falls during the middle of the week, you celebrate in the middle of the week. It loses its meaning if you move it to a weekend." Darin sat down after giving his opinion.

Ferrel threw his paws in the air. "The whole point of celebrating the birthday is to bring visitors to Abner and they won't come unless it's on a weekend."

Darin leaned forward and struggled to keep his voice under control. "That's where you're wrong Ferrel. It's not about the visitors it's about the Community. It's our birthday, not the birthday of a bunch of strangers. If it falls on a weekend fine, they're welcome to come but only under those conditions."

Ferrel shook his head hoping to send a message to others on the Committee that Darin was out of touch with the economic reality of the time. He sat back and picked at something on the arm of his chair. "Ask Owen down at *The Squirrel's Nest* and see how he feels about visitors. He'll tell you it's all about visitors you lunk head."

The *Squirrel's Nest* is a popular spot for having a slice of nut cake and enjoying a cup of walnut tea before turning in for the night. Owen had recently purchased three nests and was hoping to attract the bed and breakfast crowd.

Roscoe was having trouble staying awake. He'd planned for the meeting to last an hour at the most and so far they'd been going twice that long and he saw no end in sight.

It was a warm morning so the Committee had voted to keep the meeting room door open. It had taken the first hour for them to agree on that.

Roscoe could see members of the Community standing around the Clearing, sharing stories about their children, or talking about what they were going to do over the weekend. Could life be that simple he wondered and, in a way, envied them. How long had it been since he and Penny Sue had time to do that? To do anything really.

He watched Jules run down the path to the Clearing and thought it was odd, because he never runs, even in games.

He lost him for a minute and guessed he'd taken the path to the bowling alley. He was surprised when he suddenly appeared in the doorway of the meeting room.

"Psst. Roscoe. You've got to take a look at this." He was out of breath from the trip from Bird Man's yard and was bent over with his paws on his knees, trying to catch his breath.

Roscoe held a paw to his lips and gestured he was in the middle of a Committee meeting and couldn't go with him even if he wanted to.

"But this is so cool. Really, you've got to take a look."

"Jules, I can't leave, we're trying to decide…" Roscoe stopped when he realized the members of the Committee were no longer arguing with each other but looking at him.

"I'm sorry guys, Jules was just…" Roscoe was embarrassed at being caught not paying attention. He was usually on top of things during a meeting but today he felt restless and was having trouble following the arguments. He could care less when they celebrated the Community birthday but as Chairman, he had to keep his thoughts to himself.

"We heard," one of them said.

"Why don't we take a break for lunch. A little time away will clear our minds and help us find a solution to the birthday business." Darin stood and started toward the door.

Ferrel smiled. "I think you've finally got it Darin, the birthday celebration is all about business."

Darin told him to give it a rest and left the room. Soon the others on the Committee followed.

TWO FEEDERS, NO WAITING

Jules and Roscoe stood at the back of Bird Man's yard. "Okay, what's so important that you had to interrupt a Committee meeting to show me?" Roscoe had scanned the yard twice and, as far as he was concerned, nothing had changed since the last time he was here.

"Right. Look again, more, shall we say, at the base of the feeder pole." Jules seemed to enjoy being the only one who knew what was going on.

Roscoe sighed and wondered why he didn't just tell him what to look for insisted on making him guess.

"Okay," Roscoe reluctantly turned and looked at the feeder. "I see the feeder pole and the…what's the feeder tube doing on the ground?" He saw it and the small group of squirrels eating the seeds that had spilled when the tube hit the ground.

"I did it Roscoe. No kidding. I was about to drop down for some seeds and I heard this voice say, *'Pick the feeder tube off the hook and drop it.'* So, I did." He poked Roscoe with his elbow, barely able to contain his pride. "Cool isn't it? Think about it, no climbing poles, no waiting around for someone to finish before it's your turn." He gestured toward the group huddled around the fallen feeder tube. "And, best of all, you can dine out with your friends."

"I don't know Jules. Did you think about it from Bird Man's point of view? He won't be able to see if a bird flies over for a seed. Every time a feeder tube ends up on the ground he has to stop what he's doing and put it back up. Then he has to rake up the seeds and put them in the tube."

Jules looked at the ground, disappointed. "Thanks for the encouragement, buddy. I show a little initiative and look what I get for it."

"And, with seeds in short supply, this is not a good time to get on the bad side of Bird Man." He stopped talking when he saw Bird Man walk out of his garage and stomp angrily toward the feeder. At the sound of the door to the garage opening, those around the fallen feeder tube ran up the closest tree or found a hiding place beneath an evergreen.

You could tell by the way he walked that he was upset. He studied the hook on the feeder pole trying to find an explanation for how the tube could have fallen. As far as he could tell the wire at the top of the tube was okay and the day was too mild for the wind to have blown it off.

He placed the tube back on the hook, looped something around it, looked around the yard to see if one of his neighbors was playing a practical joke on him, then went back inside.

When he was sure it was safe, Jules ran over to the fence.

"Jules, come back here," Roscoe whispered but he had the feeling he wouldn't stop even if he'd heard him.

Jules went up the pole and tugged at the hook that held the feeder tube in place but it wouldn't budge. He squatted down and inspected whatever Bird Man had used to secure the hook to the feeder tube. He jumped to the ground and came back to the fence where Roscoe was waiting.

"Well, so much for that. He's tied something around the hook and it won't move." Jules sighed. He was hoping this would be his big contribution to the Community. So far, he'd done nothing special to help during the seed shortage and he saw this as his chance.

"Aw, just forget it," he mumbled as he walked away.

"It was a good try Jules, thanks for the effort." Things had worked out well for Roscoe. The feeder tube problem had been taken care of and he didn't have to be the bad guy squelching Jules creativity, Bird Man had done it for him.

If they had just left it at that, written it off as a nice try, the problem would have blown over and Roscoe could have returned to part two of the weekday versus weekend debate. But, as luck would have it, he glanced over his shoulder and saw Bird Man watching them from his kitchen window. When he was sure he had Roscoe's attention, he raised his hand, pointed a finger at him and lowered his thumb, like he'd pulled the trigger on a pistol. He took a step away from the window and blew on his finger, clearing the imaginary smoke from the barrel, and returned the gun to its holster.

Roscoe felt something stir inside his chest. Moments before he was ready to go back to the Clearing, have lunch with Jules, and forget about the whole dropping the feeder tube issue. But now, having been insulted by Bird Man, he had only one thought in mind and that was to get Sparky.

"He did what now?" Sparky had only been half listening when Jules told him what had gone on at the feeder. He'd been filling in numbers on what he called a *Periodic Seed Chart*. He'd been recording how many days passed between the times Bird Man filled the feeder. He'd been keeping track for almost three months, starting shortly after they discovered the feeder in his yard and could predict to the day when he'd fill it again.

Jules repeated the story and Roscoe finished it off by describing Bird Man acting like he'd shot him.

The threatening gesture seemed to do it for Sparky. He put his notebook down and said, "Let's take a look."

After a thorough inspection of the hook on the feeder tube Sparky joined them at the back of the yard.

"Jules you could have taken care of it yourself. He just looped a couple of rubber bands over the wire, you can chew through them." Sparky said it like he couldn't understand why they'd called him when they could have figured it out on their own.

Jules took off for the feeder and with a few well placed nibbles, snapped the rubber bands. He lifted the feeder tube triumphantly in the air, turned so he was facing the back of Bird Man's house, and let go. When it hit the ground the top flew off, scattering seeds around the yard.

"Piece of nut cake," a smiling Jules said as he climbed the fence and joined Roscoe.

"That was very impressive Jules, excellent work." Sparky turned and started back to his lab. He stopped when he saw Bird Man step through the garage door and watched intently as he put the feeder tube back in place and tied something around the hook.

He gave a menacing glance around the yard to frighten off any squirrels waiting for him to go back inside before venturing out and eating the seeds off the ground. It wasn't long before he could be seen taking his position at the kitchen window.

Sparky walked past Jules and Roscoe, climbed up the Big Rock, and sat down. From his position he had an unobstructed view of the yard and his head was even with the top of he feeder.

"Its just string Jules," Sparky called down, "you can untie the knot with your fingers."

Jules looked at Roscoe and wondered if it was really a good idea to go back to the feeder again. He was thinking of suggesting they call it quits and find something else to do.

Roscoe started to say maybe they should leave it alone, the feeder was full and that was the point of the whole thing anyway. There was nothing to be gained by going any farther. In fact, if this continued, there was a chance it would have the opposite effect; Bird Man deciding to take the feeder down and if he did the whole Community would suffer.

Jules cringed when he heard Sparky say, "Anytime Jules."

Roscoe shrugged and gestured it was okay, he should do what Sparky said.

It didn't take him long to loosen the string. When he did, he lifted the feeder tube off the hook and let go. There was no celebration or taunting this time. And, he felt no joy in watching the tube hit the ground and turn upside down. In fact, he felt just the opposite. It was like telling a joke and realizing you told the same joke a few minutes before.

He hopped off the feeder pole and walked straight to the fence. He knew Bird Man was watching from the window and he didn't want to spend any more time in his yard than he had to. He didn't stop to pick up seeds, his only goal was to get over the fence and out of the yard as fast as he could. It had been exhilarating the first time he'd done it but now the whole thing seemed kind of childish.

He came back and stood next to Roscoe. They could see just enough of Sparky to know he was sitting at attention, not taking his eyes off the garage door.

Before long, Bird Man came out and walked straight to the feeder. He was on a mission and had no time to look in the trees for misbehaving squirrels. He picked the tube off the ground and put it back in place. Then he used a tool of some kind to zip something around the hook. When he finished, he stood silently, and stared at the rock where Sparky was sitting.

"What's going on?" Jules hollered to Sparky.

"I'm not sure. Go back to the lab and get my utility knife. If he's used what I think he's used, you're not going to be able to untie it, you'll have to cut it off."

"Can't we just leave it alone?" Roscoe was concerned where this was going. Bird Man was not required to provide them with seeds, he did it of his own free will. Sparky needed to keep that in mind before things spun out of control.

"Don't you see what's going on Roscoe?" There was a hard edge to Sparky's voice. It was obvious this was more than fun and games to him, it had gone beyond that. "He's mocking us to our face. Because he's a human and we're just dumb little woodland creatures, he thinks he's smarter than we are."

His earlier request for Jules to get his utility knife changed to a command. "The bench in the lab Jules, middle drawer. And you better step on it, there's not a lot of daylight left." They couldn't see him but could only hear his voice. While giving instructions to Jules he continued to look at the kitchen window. Roscoe was worried, this was a side of his friend he hadn't seen.

It was dark when Jules returned. He was surprised to find Bird Man had turned on his porch light and had talked his neighbor into doing the same with his. As a result, the yard was flooded with light. A quick check by Jules showed Bird Man was still at the window but, with the backyard lit up, he was having trouble seeing what was going on. His face was pressed against the glass as he searched the corners of the yard for signs of activity.

Sylvia was frightened by her owners appearance. He had a wild look in his eye, hadn't shaved, and his legs shook from standing at the kitchen sink for so long. Each time he walked through the garage she stood, ready to receive a pat on her head or a back rub, but he walked by like he hadn't seen her.

Sparky didn't look much better. He hadn't eaten all day and had missed his afternoon nap. Instead of the erect posture he'd assumed when he first climbed the Big Rock, he was leaning noticeably to one side. His attention was no longer focused on the feeder but had shifted to the kitchen window and the face of Bird Man. If someone from the Community walked by, Sparky would appear to be spending a pleasant evening looking at the stars. But Roscoe knew that was not the case, he was studying his opponent and anticipating his next move.

"It's getting late Sparky," Roscoe called up to him. "We need to get back to our nests. You've made your point. You've matched him move for move. What do you say we call it even and go home?"

"Cut the binding Jules," Sparky ignored Roscoe's request and gave directions to Jules in a cold, detached voice.

"Sparky, I'm bushed. I've been over the fence half a dozen times. Couldn't we wait until tomorrow?" Jules put his paw over his mouth to cover a yawn.

"Leave the knife, I'll do it." Sparky said from on top of he rock.

Jules looked at Roscoe for permission to not go to the feeder, he was exhausted. The trips over the fence and running back and forth to the lab had worn him out. Adding to his fatigue was the tension in the air and knowing if he went in the yard Bird Man would be watching every move he made.

"Sparky, couldn't it wait…" Roscoe didn't have a chance to finish because Sparky cut him off. "I said leave the knife and go home Jules. You too Roscoe. I'll do it myself."

Roscoe didn't know what to do. He was fighting sleep and he knew Sparky was too. But, he was the one who'd asked him to come to Bird Man's yard so he felt obligated to stay. What started out as a practical joke had spun out of control. He was sure Sparky had gone over the edge and he didn't know how to pull him back to safety.

He heard movement on top of the rock and within seconds Sparky was standing next to them. He took the knife from Jules and walked purposely away from them. They watched him climb awkwardly over the fence, a task made more difficult because he was carrying a knife.

When Sparky dropped to the ground on the other side of the fence he landed awkwardly. They heard him yelp and figured he'd sprained an ankle when he hit the ground. They watched him limp to the feeder, climb the pole, and cut through the binding around the wire hook.

Fighting to keep his balance, he turned to see if Bird Man was watching. When he saw he was, he slowly lifted the tube off the hook and dropped it.

Roscoe switched his gaze from Sparky to the kitchen window. He saw Bird Man lower his head, frustrated the nylon strip he'd installed hadn't stumped his opponent. He stood for a moment, with his head resting on his arms, as Sparky cleared the fence and limped back to his friends.

"Okay, that's taken care of. Let's go home and get some sleep." Roscoe and Jules took a step toward the Clearing but stopped when they heard Sparky say, "It's not over Roscoe, not by a long ways. You can go if you want, this may take awhile."

"I'll wait with you Sparky, you shouldn't be out here alone. We can take turns watching Bird Man." Tired as he was, Roscoe knew he couldn't leave his friend alone, on top of a rock, in the middle of the night.

"Thanks Roscoe but it's no longer about you, or Jules, or dropping feeder tubes." There was a sound of resolve in Sparky's voice. Somehow he knew he'd been drawn into the age old battle between man and the creatures who live in the woods. "It's about him and me."

He'd refused Roscoe's offer of help as he struggled to climb to the top of the Big Rock. When he was finally in position, he turned toward Bird Man's house and sat down, ready to continue his silent vigil.

"If you want to help Jules, see if you can find my brother Louis. I'm going to need him." When he said it, his voice was flat and empty of any emotion.

"Louis? Do you mean Light Paws Louie?" Jules stared at Sparky and saw a slight nod of his head.

"Why does he need Light Paws?" Jules asked Roscoe quietly.

Roscoe shrugged. "You know Sparky, he's thinking three or four moves ahead." Roscoe put a paw on his shoulder. "Go ahead, I'll wait here."

He heard Jules walk down the path, the sound of each step magnified in the still night air.

He took a deep breath, climbed the rock, and sat down next to Sparky, who barely noticed he'd joined him. He was waiting for Bird Man to make his next move.

The next morning Jules and Light Paws came up the path. Light Paws had other plans for the morning but dropped them when Jules told him, "Something's going on at the Big Rock, your brother needs you."

As they approached the rock they saw Roscoe spread out on his stomach, sound asleep. Sparky however, was still wide awake with his eyes locked on the back of Bird Man's house.

"Sparky, Louis is here." Jules said softly. "Do you want me to send him up or...?"

At first there was no answer, then they heard Sparky's dry, raspy voice say, "No, he'll wake up Roscoe, I'll come down."

"Hey, Sparky, you okay man?" A concerned Louis asked his brother when he finally made it to the ground.

"Yeah, fine, couldn't be better." Sparky leaned against the Big Rock in an effort to keep weight off his swollen ankle. His answer was followed by a long, drawn out yawn.

Their attention shifted to the back of the house when they heard the door to the garage open. They were shocked by Bird Man's appearance as he stepped into the yard. Sometime during the night, he'd thrown a robe over the clothes he'd worn the day before. His hair was uncombed and pressed down from resting his head on his hands. There were dark circles under his eyes from lack of sleep. His normal determined walk had changed to a lifeless shuffle as he slowly made his way to the feeder and picked the feeder tube off the ground.

They watched with interest as he slid the wire hook on top of the feeder tube over the arm of the pole. They heard a snap as he secured the hook in place. He tugged on whatever he'd put there and turned, searching the area for his adversary. He found him and looked straight at Sparky. He smiled a wicked, defiant smile and seemed to be saying, "That should put an end to this nonsense." He shuffled back across the yard to the garage. When he got there, he placed a hand against the door frame, hoping to rest long enough to gain the strength to go on. After standing motionless for several minutes, he let go and stepped inside.

He turned to close the door but decided not to, it required too much energy.

Roscoe saw Sylvia stick her head out and look around before walking dejectedly back to her bed in the garage.

"That was predictable," they heard Sparky say in a whisper. "Louis, could I see you up here for a moment."

TWO FEEDERS, NO WAITING

Something had changed in Sparky's voice, like he'd just received a new boost of energy.

Louis listened as his brother explained the situation. He nodded he got it, slid off the rock, and started for the fence. He spoke to a sleepy Jules as he walked by. "I'll be right back, I've got some work to do."

"What's going on Louis? What work?" Jules hadn't heard the conversation between Sparky and his brother but even if he had, it wouldn't have made sense. Growing up together, they'd developed a secret code to keep others from figuring out what they were saying. "Sparky's one step ahead of Bird Man on this one. He guessed he'd put a combination lock on the feeder and sure enough he did." Louis blew on his paws and rubbed them against his chest, pleased his brother had called him. "It just so happens," he grinned at Jules, "I'm pretty good with locks."

"But you don't know the combination. How could you possibly..." Jules stopped and smacked his forehead with his paw when he remembered how he got the name Light Paws. In his first year at seed school he delighted in opening lockers and either moving things from one to the other or just moving the locks around. It was also why he was taken from the school in Abner and sent to *The School for the Gifted* two Communities away.

"It's all in the paws Jules," he called over his shoulder. "Look after Sparky, okay?"

Jules was amazed at how calm he was. He looked like someone who did this every day. Then it dawned on him he probably did.

Sparky poked Roscoe and told him to wake up, he didn't want to miss this.

Louis took his time going over the fence. That's the way the great ones do it, Jules thought, they're never in a hurry. He remembered reading somewhere that for the professional at moments like this, everything moves in slow motion.

As Louis made his way to the feeder, Roscoe saw Bird Man lift his head and stare in disbelief. He looked worse than he had when they saw him earlier. His greasy hair was plastered to his forehead. A dark shadow had grown on his cheeks and it seemed to take him longer to switch from looking from one thing to the other. His gaze moved slowly from Louis to Sparky and then back to Louis. He fought to keep his eyes open and seemed confused when a different squirrel entered the yard.

A grin slowly spread across Sparky's face and he put a paw across his mouth to stifle a yawn. "This is going to be good," he said through a laugh, "really good."

When Louis was on top of the feeder he lifted his arms and shook his paws like a pianist warming up before a concert. Then he crouched down, put his ear close to the lock, and began twisting the dial.

A look of panic spread across Bird Man's face and he stumbled backwards as he pushed himself away from the sink. Something was wrong. The squirrel on top of the feeder looked far too confident and seemed to be doing all the right things. At first he thought it was just a show, that he would fumble around with the lock, get frustrated, and that would be it. But the easy, deliberate way he was going about his work bothered him.

He left his place by the sink and returned a moment later with a radio. He opened the kitchen window far enough for the music to escape into the yard. "If he can't hear the tumblers, he can't open the lock," he giggled uncontrollably and cranked the volume as high as it would go.

It was difficult for Roscoe and Jules, standing by the Big Rock to hear what the other one said, they couldn't imagine what it was like for Louis on top of the feeder pole much closer to the house than they were.

Fortunately, Louis heard the last click from inside the lock before Bird Man turned on the radio. He stood and put his paws to his ears like the music was destroying his concentration. He turned to face Sparky and shook his head, telling his brother it was impossible to open the lock when he couldn't hear himself think.

Jules gasped, unwilling to believe that Louis had failed. He wondered if this was the last of the legend of Light Paws Louie. He looked up at Sparky, expecting him to be crushed by the latest turn of events. He'd gone toe to toe with a human, so there was no disgrace in losing now. In fact, he should be proud he'd lasted as long as he had.

To his surprise he saw a smile play at the corners of Sparky's mouth. Not a lot, just a slight upward turn at the corners. He knew his brother well enough to know he'd never let a little distraction like loud music throw him off.

Bird Man brought his hands together and pressed them against his face. He was exhausted but at last, he'd won. "I can always catch up on sleep," he mumble to the empty kitchen. "I can always wash and change my clothes. But it isn't everyday I can meet a worthy opponent who pushed me to the limit of my endurance and beat him."

He started to turn away from the window but stopped when he saw Louis wobble on top of the feeder. He put his hands on the edge of the sink to steady himself, leaned forward, and watched with interest as Louis fought to keep his balance, leaning one way, then overcorrecting, in a hopeless attempt to keep from falling.

To Bird Man, it looked like he'd lost his battle with gravity and was about to fall. In one last act of desperation, Louis reached out and grabbed the bottom of the lock.

Something was wrong, Bird Man could sense it. Squirrels do not loose their balance and if they fall they don't grab things, they land lightly on the ground and scamper away. He turned the radio off in time to hear the lock click open. He watched in disbelief as the squirrel, in an athletic move, pulled the lock off the hook, swung into a standing position on top of the feeder, and raised his arms in victory. Then, in an obvious act of defiance, he lifted the feeder tube off the hook, snapped on the lock, spun the dial, held the tube at arms length for a moment. and let go.

He gave a deep bow toward the kitchen window before sliding down the pole and climbing the fence.

He slapped the paws of Roscoe and Jules as he passed by and confidently climbed the Big Rock. He hugged Sparky and said, "Got to go bro." Then he was off the rock and headed down the path like this was the first event in a busy day.

Roscoe was concerned about Sparky. He knew he was used to staying up all night when he was working on a project but not under these conditions. He hadn't eaten since before the standoff began and for most of the afternoon, the sun had beaten mercilessly on the top of the Big Rock heating it to a temperature that must have been unbearable. Roscoe could see Sparky's lips were chapped and his face was sunburned. His ankle, swollen twice its normal size, caused him to sit awkwardly, with one leg sticking out at an odd angle.

One thing hadn't changed however; his unblinking eyes remained locked on the kitchen window of Bird Man's house.

He perked up a little when Light Paws was opening the lock but since then, his condition had gone downhill.

There had been no activity at the feeder for over an hour.

"Maybe it's over," Roscoe whispered hopefully to Jules. "Maybe he's out of..." He stopped when he saw Bird Man throw the door of the garage open and stagger out. He stood for a moment trying to block the sunlight with his hand. He hesitated and seemed to have forgotten why he'd come outside. Then his head jerked slightly as he remembered and he stumbled toward the feeder with an odd, lurching gait. He would come to a complete stop, lean sideways, catch his balance, and move forward again.

When he finally got to the feeder he picked the tube off the ground and hung it in place. The combination lock was removed and replaced by a padlock that could only be opened with a key. He lifted a string with the key on it and waved it for Sparky to see before slipping it over his head and putting it around his neck.

He held on to the feeder pole to keep his balance as he lifted his bleary eyes and tried to focus on Sparky. When he finally located him, he made several attempts to smile but gave up and returned to the grimace that had been there since he left the garage.

On the way back to his house he stumbled and fell to his knees. He was too tired to stand without help, so he crawled to the garage. When he reached the door, he grabbed the frame and pulled himself to his feet. He swayed from side to side, waiting for his vision to clear before stepping inside. He made no effort to close the door.

It took awhile, but he eventually appeared at the kitchen window. He put his hands on the sink for support and pressed his face against a cool window pane, exhausted from his trip to the feeder.

"That's it. That does it." Roscoe got to his feet. Jules had already excused himself and gone to his nest, he couldn't stay awake any longer. "Sparky, I'm sorry to pull rank on you but as Chairman of the Committee,

I insist you put an end to this," he searched for the right word but he was having trouble thinking clearly, "contest or whatever is going on here."

He watched helplessly as his friend made the painful climb off the Big Rock and leaned against him for support.

"Okay. You're right." Sparky could barely speak. Two days on top of the rock with no food or water had taken him to the edge of exhaustion.

"You go," he whispered in a raspy voice, "I'll be along in a minute." He tried to stand but moaned as a muscle in his leg cramped.

"You're sure? You're not going to send for Buford or someone else to come out and help you?" Roscoe was puzzled by what had taken place. He knew Sparky had a stubborn streak and refused to give up when he was working on a complicated problem until he solved it. In public, however, he barely spoke a word and went out of his way to avoid any form of conflict.

Everone in the Community knew of his ability to concentrate fully and neglect things like sleep and eating regularly but this was a different, each problem he solved brought a new challenge.

Sparky nodded yes, he was sure and no, he was not planning on sending for Buford.

Roscoe looked at him, trying to decide if he'd really given up or just saying it to get him to leave. He decided to give him the benefit of the doubt. Sparky appeared to have accepted his loss and was ready to move on. Besides, it was obvious he was in no shape to do anything even if he wanted to.

"Well, okay, I'll see you later then. Should I send someone to help you get to the lab?" Roscoe saw his friend leaning forward with his paws on his knees, worn out from the climb down the rock.

"I'm fine." His throat was so sore he could only whisper. He paused and said, "Thanks for hanging with me Rosc, you're a true friend." His voice shook when he said the last part; it was obvious he was not only beat up physically but emotionally as well.

"I just want to think about this experience for a few minutes," he continued, "you know, try to make sense out of it. What's the word Sid uses all the time?" He closed his eyes and tried to think of the word. He opened them when it finally came to him. "Closure."

Roscoe stopped half way down the path and looked back. He saw the classic looking Sparky, leaning against the Big Rock, standing as straight as he could, struggling with the thought of losing what had been a monumental battle with a human.

He fought the urge to go back and help him to his lab. Then a wave of exhaustion rolled over him and he continued to his nest.

Sparky's eyes flicked to the path, saw Roscoe make the turn to the Clearing, and knew he wasn't coming back.

It took an enormous effort to keep from smiling as he brought his paws from behind his back and studied the lock pick Louis had given him when they'd hugged after he'd removed the combination lock.

It took him a while to make it over the fence, one leg had fallen asleep, and his ankle ached where he'd twisted it when he fell on his first trip to the feeder.

Bird Man jerked his head up. He'd fallen asleep, standing at the kitchen sink. He glanced at the clock and saw two hours had passed since he'd come back inside. He couldn't believe it, it seemed he'd only closed his eyes for a second. It took him a moment to figure out why he was standing at the kitchen sink. Then he remembered and he was almost afraid to look out of the window. When he did his mouth fell open in disbelief. His legs shook with fatigue and he had to grab a cabinet door to keep from falling.

Nothing had changed. The feeder tube was still hanging from the hook on the feeder pole.

He scanned the yard and then broadened the search to take in the large rock on the other side of the fence where his adversary had been.

Both were empty.

He smiled and leaned his head back. "Yes," he said out loud. He started to pump his fist but stopped when the simple act of lifting his arm caused pain to shoot through his shoulder. His arm was still numb from supporting his head while he slept.

He shook himself awake, reached down, and picked Sylvia up. He held her close to his chest and did a clumsy dance around the kitchen as he repeated several times, "Who beat the squirrels? I beat the squirrels." He wept and pressed his face against hers.

"Oh, Sylvia, if you could only understand what has taken place over the last two days…" His voice trailed off as he thought about it himself. He turned so they were both facing the feeder. "See the feeder pole out there?" He took her paw in his shaky hand and pointed at the feeder with it. "Well, Miss Sylvia, those bad squirr…"

He stopped in mid-sentence.

Something was wrong.

The feeder tube was still on the pole but something… He tucked her under his arm as he hobbled through the kitchen and out the garage door.

His lips moved and he mumbled something Sylvia couldn't understand.

He staggered to the feeder and stared at the hook that held the feeder tube in place.

He couldn't believe it. After the squirrel had opened the combination lock he'd run out of ideas and if he hadn't remembered the padlock he kept in the cabinet drawer next to the flashlight he would have had to admit defeat.

After putting the lock on the feeder and the key on the string around his neck, he grabbed the pole to steady himself. It took him a moment to remember why he was there then remembered when he felt the key on the string bump against his chest.

Now, as he studied the feeder he saw the padlock had been opened and was hanging loosely from the hook on the feeder pole and, even though he wasn't thinking clearly, he knew he'd been beaten.

He checked the rock again and saw it was empty. He let his gaze shift to the path to the woods and saw the squirrel who'd been sitting there moments before, limp slowly away.

Two Feeders, No Waiting

Ferrel stood by the fence at the back of Bird Man's yard and wondered why he hadn't thought of it before. That thought was followed by a second; why hadn't anyone thought of it?

He saw Community members waiting patiently in the tall grass for their turn at the feeder. Someone would drop from the feeder tube, hurry across the yard, and signal to the next in line it was his turn. As soon as he left for the feeder, everyone shuffled forward and filled the vacant place in front of them.

Amazing, he thought. And to make it even more unbelievable, not one of them thought it could be any different. All the great thinkers in the Community had failed to see the answer that was staring them in the face.

"It's too obvious," he muttered excitedly, "hidden in plain sight."

The idea that came to him was simplicity itself. He would build an alternate feeder and sell memberships. The price of the membership would cover the purchase of seeds, maintenance of the feeder, and hopefully provide a tidy profit for him.

Members of the club could reserve times at the feeder and eliminate the hours wasted every week standing in line. "Hold on," he said a little louder than he intended causing some of those in the seed line to look his way. "How about different levels of membership tied to the best time to go to the feeder?"

He pictured a gold level that covered the busiest hours in the morning and evening. A silver level for the second busiest, and bronze for the least desirable times.

He hadn't been this excited about an idea in a long time and knew this must be the way a successful business person feels when they come up with an idea they know can't miss.

He turned away from the fence and walked slowly down the path to the Clearing. There were a number of details to work out before he could get things started. Like where to put the feeders, how much to charge for a membership, and perhaps most important, what to name his business. Ferrel's Feeder? he wondered. Or Ferrel and Son? Both were good names for Communities around Abner but what if the idea caught on? What if I sell a franchise to some ambitious member of another Community who'd never heard of me? The benefit of name recognition would be lost.

He stopped walking when it came to him. It was like someone handed him an envelope with the answer to the name question written inside. He smiled a broadly as he pictured a sign that read, **"Two Feeders, No waiting."**

He felt a shiver of excitement and told himself, "This could be big. Really big."

Later in the afternoon he sat in his nest, thinking about what he was now calling his "two feeders" idea. He would need a location far enough from Bird Man's yard that members of his club wouldn't have to decide if they should go to Bird Man's feeder are his. He would need two feeder tubes. And, he would need seeds.

That was it.

He'd started business's before but realized the reason they failed was because they'd been too complicated. His seed processing plant for instance, required expensive equipment and a number of highly trained employees to run it. He was sure once the stale, moldy seeds he'd purchased were polished and attractively packaged no one would know the difference.

He discovered too late that the mood of the typical seed purchaser is fickle and advertising them as organic didn't explain why they tasted so bad.

He'd failed in the salvage business he'd inherited from his father because of neglect. His heart wasn't in collecting junk others in the

Community threw away. Then, when he was asked to serve on the Committee for the Protection of Neighborhood Resources, he'd become obsessed with replacing Roscoe as Chairman.

That left him, he would explain to others, between jobs which everyone knew was a round about way of saying he was currently unemployed.

He thought about the first problem and was sure the tree he owned at the edge of the woods by the shopping center would be a good choice.

It met the requirement of being far enough from Bird Man's but during the day there was human activity in the parking lot. He was sure the members of *Two Feeders, No Waiting*, would eventually get used to it but, to be on the safe side, he'd hang the feeder tubes on the side of the tree away from the mall.

That brought him to the question of feeder tubes. He could make them or…he decided to think about that later because the question of the size and type of tube depended on the answer to the third and bigger problem, where to get the seeds.

"There's the rub," he mumbled and scratched his head as he realized he'd hit on the one thing that stood between him and success, the seeds.

He left the chair he'd been sitting in and walked to the edge of his nest. He looked around and wondered where he could find enough seeds to keep the feeder tubes full. He knew they had to taste as good as those Bird Man provides or no one would sign up.

Thinking is not something that comes easily for Ferrel. He prefers to get one idea and go with it. Being on the Committee drove him nuts as its members took hours to examine every side of the simplest question that looked pretty straight forward to him.

Then, when they finally made a decision, Roscoe would ask if everyone was happy with it and that would send them back to square one.

He'd wondered more then once what would happen if they were forced to take on a really big problem.

Several times he felt like standing up during one of their endless discussions and shouting, "Will you make up your minds? Yes or no. Up or down. One way or the other. Forward or backward. It's as simple as that!"

But he'd waited because he had the bigger goal of becoming Chairman in mind and he couldn't afford to lose the vote of a single member when the moment arrived to make his move. Once he became Chairman, he'd streamline the decision making process by telling them how to vote.

He stopped pacing and stood perfectly still when the thought came to him. He blinked and stared at the floor of his nest. "It can't be that easy," he mumbled and shook his head in amazement. He laughed out loud and said, "Of course, Pete O'Malley." He'd been trying to get his seed distribution company into Abner for over a year but Roscoe had found ways to keep it from happening.

He rubbed his paws together as he considered the possibilities. He would be Pete's customer not the Community's. He would work directly with Pete and not some flunky picked by the Committee to represent them. And, when it became obvious to everyone that Pete was providing a valuable service, they'd realize Roscoe had been they one who'd kept it from happening sooner.

Two Feeders, No Waiting, was about to become a reality and with its success, he would be a step closer to becoming Chairman.

The only thing that stood in his way was finding Pete and Stubs and convincing them he was their guy in Abner.

It took almost a week to locate him. He probably could have done it sooner but he couldn't just walk up and ask someone if they knew where Pete O'Malley was, it would scare them to death. In fact, he realized he didn't need to say his whole name to cause them to panic. All he had to do was say, "Pete,"or, "Stubs," and whoever he was talking to clamed up and suddenly remembered he had an appointment somewhere else. If he said, "O'Malley," they'd get a wild look in their eye and begin shaking with fear.

He'd taken his time; a casual inquiry if there had been any news of trouble in another Community. Or he'd slip a question into a conversation about the last time Stubs had been seen and there it was. He discovered Pete's whereabouts and wonder of wonders, he wasn't that far away.

TWO FEEDERS, NO WAITING

"**P. O'Malley, Esq.**" was printed in large letters on a wooden board nailed to the trunk of a tree. Next to his name was an arrow pointing up.

"Mr. O'Malley?" Ferrel called timidly and got no answer. He said it a little louder and got the same result.

He was about to leave when he heard someone behind him say, "Is dat youse Ferret?" He knew by the sound of the rough, high pitched voice it was Pete. "Put youse paws in the air and stands still while my associanate Stubs checks to see if youse is carrying any of dem weapons of masked obstruction."

Ferrel felt the rough paws of Stubs start at his wrist and work their way to his ankels.

"He's clean boss." Stubs grunted and stepped back.

"Did youse check his paws Stubby. As youse is provisionally awares, sometimes our guests keeps things hidden in their paws."

"Nothing in his paws boss." Stubs hadn't actually checked his paws but from the way Ferrel was trembling, he knew he wasn't capable of hiding anything.

"Has youse investigationed his pockets? Under his arms? Between his toes?" It sounded like Pete was reading from a list of possible hiding places.

"Yeah boss. Nothing." Stubs didn't like being asked the same questions over and over again. "Like I told youse, he's clean as one of them whistles youse hears about."

"Youse may turns around Ferret." Pete said with a sigh and by the sound of his voice he seemed relieved to find his life wasn't in danger.

As Ferrel turned he almost let out a gasp when he saw Pete. He was shocked at how thin he was. There were dark circles under his eyes and he coughed a dry, hacking cough, that seemed to shake every bone in his body. He leaned on his cane as he slowly recovered from the coughing attack.

"So, whys did youse choose to pays a visits to my abodes?" Pete asked and Ferrel could hear a wheeze each time he took a breath.

"Well, sir, ah Mr. O'Malley. Pete. Sir…" He was having trouble recovering from the shock of seeing the drastic change in his appearance. The last time he saw him he was healthy looking and more Pete-like. But now…

"I don't gots much time here Ferret, youse aint de only entry on my agendification for todays. Am I right about dat Stubby or not?"

"Right boss, youse has like, a bunch of stuff to do." Something in Stub's voice suggested he had no idea what Pete had on his schedule. Ferrel had the feeling if he hadn't shown up the page for today in Pete's planner would have been blank. Encouraged by that thought he became bolder.

"I'm starting a feeder business sir and I have everything except the seeds. So, naturally, I thought of you and..." Ferrel lifted his paws hoping to convey the rest was obvious.

"So youse is going into de seeds business? Is dat what I hears him sayin Stubby?" Pete was shaking and Ferrel wasn't sure if it was because of a chill or if something he'd said caused him to become angry. He desperately hoped it was a chill.

"No boss, I think youse has misunder..."

"Why would youse do dat to me's? Youse comes here, takes a look at my current conditional, and decides youse is..." Pete started coughing and had to lean against the trunk of a tree to keep from falling down.

"No I...." Ferrel said at the same time Stubs said, "No he..."

"Youse starts out wit nothin and gradually builds something..." Pete looked away as if trying to remember where he was going with the thought.

"Boss?" Stubs said at the same time Ferrel said, "Mr. O'Malley?" Stubs motioned to Ferrel he'd handle this. "Dat aint what he's saying Petey. He's here to buy seeds. He's not going to, you know, like compete with youse or nothing along them lines."

"How many does youse need?" Pete asked and because his mood had changed so quickly, Ferrel wasn't sure if he was still talking about protecting his business from a hostile takeover or asking how many seeds he needed to start his business.

"Sir?" he asked.

"Seeds." Pete said slowly as if he was afraid he'd lose Ferrel if he talked any faster. "How. Many. Seeds. Does. Youse. Needs?" His face grew red and he smacked his cane against the tree as he repeated, "How." *Smack.* "Many." *Smack.* "Seeds?" *Smack.*

TWO FEEDERS, NO WAITING

"Well, a lot I guess. Many. A number. Numerous. Quite a few actually." While he answered, Ferrel kept his eyes on the cane to make sure the next smack wasn't aimed at him.

Ferrel had just set up his sign in the Clearing when Myron, his first customer, walked over and asked, "So, how's it work?"

Ferrel smiled confidently. This was going to be easier then he thought and made a quick mental calculation. He'd been out here less than a minute and already had his first customer. At this rate, he'd have the entire Community signed up before lunch.

"Suppose, instead of waiting in line in Bird Man's yard for some slow poke to finish up at the feeder, you choose when you want to eat? No waiting. No finally getting to the feeder only to discover the person ahead of you has taken the last seed." He paused and let Myron picture what he was talking about. "What if you could eat as much as you want, for as long as you want, when you want?" Ferrel had worked out the answer to this question and several others until he could say them without looking at his notes.

He finished by pointing to his sign and encouraged Myron to read with him., "**Two** Feeders," they said together, "**No** Waiting." When they finished Ferrel handed him an application.

Myron studied it for a moment before asking, "Okay, say I want breakfast at eight o'clock in the morning. Do I just show up and start eating?"

Ferrel nodded yes that was the idea. "You tell me what time you want to have breakfast, I enter it the official registration book, and you're all set. It's as simple as that."

Myron thought about his answer for a moment before asking, "What if I oversleep one morning and don't get here until eight fifteen?"

Ferrel hadn't thought of that one but figured that was the benefit of being out early, he couldn't be expected to have an answer for every question could he?

"If you sign up for the gold level you will have priority over someone with a silver or bronze membership." Ferrel saw Myron was having trouble grasping the idea of his plan so he put an encouraging arm around his shoulder, pointed to the bottom line of the sign and read, "At *Two Feeders*, you're always first in line."

"Okay, but suppose someone else with a gold level membership, had the same problem I did? Over slept, that kind of thing."

Ferrel sighed and wondered what the chances of that happening were. "You're forgetting there are two feeders."

"Oh, right." Myron had forgotten about the second feeder tube. "Okay, let's say someone else, a third someone, shows up at exactly the same time we do, the other late sleeper and me. I mean, we're running late but it's at the time he, the third person, signed up for."

"Myron you're over thinking this. Trust me, it will work out, okay?" To emphasize his point, Ferrel dropped his paw to the part of the sign that said, "No waiting."

Two of Ferrel's friends walked into the Clearing and caught the last part of his explanation to Myron. They strolled over, picked a brochure from the table, and pretended to read it.

"Hey, this is a great idea," one of them said to his friend but loud enough for Myron to hear. "I wonder why someone hasn't thought of it before now?"

Ferrel smiled and fought the urge to tell them no one had thought of it because no one in the Community had the vision and creativity to make it happen. Instead he looked at the ground and mumbled, "Thanks."

"When it comes to ideas, this has to be the best I've seen in a long time." The second one added while the first one checked to see if Myron was listening. "Am I mistaken or did it say for a few extra seeds I can join the golden circle?"

Ferrel motioned with his paw that was enough, they could stop any time.

"That will be sweet, wearing a gold bracelet to let everyone know I'm a member of the inner circle." The one doing the talking missed Ferrel's signal.

Myron turned to leave.

"Is there something wrong?" Ferrel finally got the other two to stop talking and hurried after Myron.

"No, not really, unless, I mean, I was wondering why should I pay for seeds when I can get them for free at…" he pointed toward Bird Man's yard.

Ferrel was ready for that one. "Some things go together Myron." Ferrel smacked his paws to emphasize his point.

"You mean like no waiting? Or?" Myron was confused, that only sounded like one thing to him.

"No, like not having to stand in line and not being watched by Bird Man or his nosy neighbor." Ferrel was pleased with Myron's reaction when he mentioned Bird Man's neighbor. "He will be over there," he gestured toward Bird Man's house, "and you will be," he pointed in the opposite direction, "over there."

He had him. He could tell. He'd saved the part about Bird Man and his neighbor until the exact moment it was needed and he saw the minute he mentioned them it was like a light bulb turned on in Myron's eyes.

"Where do I…" Myron didn't get to say, "sign up," because he was watching Lester, the head of the safety team, walk slowly across the Clearing and stop at Ferrel's display.

"Hey, no crowding in line," Myron said defensively, "you can sign up after I do."

"I'd like to speak with Ferrel for a moment." Lester said pleasantly; Myron had no idea he was upset. "Could we have the Clearing?" Lester asked politely.

"Sure. No problem. But," Myron looked at Ferrel and said in a whisper, "don't forget, I was here first." He winked and walked away.

"Can I see your permit Ferrel?" Lester asked when he was sure Myron was far enough away not to hear.

The two Community members Ferrel had asked to help on the promise of not having to pay for a bronze membership walked over and joined them.

They picked up a brochure for *Two Feeders, No Waiting* and pretended to study it. The first one said, "Hey, this is a great idea. I wonder why someone hasn't…"

"Not now guys." Ferrel interrupted him.

"But you said if someone…" The second one looked confused.

They'd done exactly what he'd told them to do which was, if they saw a customer come to his table, walk over, and say what a great idea it was.

"Not! Now!" Ferrel hissed through clenched teeth.

They looked confused as they hurried away.

After they'd gone, Ferrel put an arm around Lester's shoulder and said sweetly, "Look Lester, this is hardly a big enough operation to require a permit. But, to let you know my heart is in the right place, if you'll overlook the permit business, I'll give you a lifetime membership in the bronze circle, no questions asked." While he spoke he slipped a bronze colored bracelet over Lester's wrist.

"You know the rules Ferrel and, if I'm not mistaken, you were the one who said we were losing money by not requiring a permit for selling things in the Clearing." He gave Ferrel a stern look. "And now, you're not only selling without a permit but attempting to bribe an authorized Committee official with this." He held up the arm with the bronze bracelet and shook his head in disappointment.

"Bribe? You? With…that?" He tried to snatch the bracelet from Lester's wrist but wasn't fast enough. "You've completely missed the point. I was simply showing you what they look like and checking to see if I had your size in stock. You know I would be the last person in the world to…" He had to holler the last part because Lester had climbed the steps, gone into the meeting room, and closed the door behind him.

The next morning Myron cut across the Clearing on his way to the Bird Man's. He was surprised to find a cute little stranger hunched down and looking around like he was lost.

He changed direction, and walked over to the stranger. "What's your name little fellow?"

The stranger batted his big eyes and looked at Myron. "Bwuisew," he squeaked in a high pitched voice.

Myron suppressed a laugh and wondered what some parents were thinking when they named their kids.

"Are you lost? Or…" Myron tried to think of how a cute little guy named Bruiser ended up in the Clearing.

"Fewwet?" he squeaked.

"Fewwet?" Myron scratched his head and tried to figure out who he was talking about. "Sorry, but I…oh, I get it, you mean Ferrel."

The stranger nodded yes, and wondered why it had taken Myron so long to figure it out.

"I haven't seen him this morning so I'm not sure…" Myron stopped when he heard the stranger say something.

"I'm sorry, I didn't catch that." He leaned closer and cupped a paw to his ear.

"You gots Libwawy?" Bruiser asked.

Myron tilted his head and wondered why the stranger had switched from looking for Ferrel to asking about the library.

"Did you want to know if we have a library? Or…"

"Whewe is?" Bruiser said.

"The library? Over there." Myron pointed in the direction of the hollow tree that served as the Community library. "But I'm not sure it's…"

"Tanks," Bruiser said so quietly Myron almost missed it.

"Sure. No problem." Myron watched him hop toward the library. He fought the urge to help as he watched him stop halfway across the Clearing to catch his breath.

When he saw him open the library door Myron figured Webster could take it from here and turned to the path that leads to Bird Man's yard.

He stopped when he heard the sound of books being pushed off shelves and reading tables being turned over.

It was quiet for a moment then the library door opened and Bruiser hopped out. Before the door closed Myron caught a glimpse of the destruction inside. Book shelves were lying on their sides, the reading table in the juvenile section was upside down, and the floor was covered with books.

Bruiser hopped timidly back to Myron.

He settled into a small, furry ball, and sat quietly for a moment before asking, "Whewe Fewwet?"

Myron didn't know what to say. He was having trouble believing what he'd seen. Had he really witnessed someone half his size and so frail couldn't make it across the Clearing without stopping just destroy the Community library?

"'Scuse please, but whewe Fewwet. You see him?" Bruiser looked up innocently and blinked.

Myron didn't know what to say. He was having trouble dealing with the contradiction of the cute little creature and the glimpse of the library before the door closed. "He, ah…" Myron stammered, "I mean, I don't…"

Bruiser held up a paw signaling that Myron should wait before answering.

He hopped unsteadily across the Clearing and stopped in front of the statue of Abner.

He sat perfectly still for a moment and closed his eyes.

Myron thought he'd decided to rest after making the ten foot trip from where he'd been to where he currently was. He turned to leave but stopped when heard, *"Heeeyaaahh!"* followed by a *thunk*.

When he looked back, Bruiser was hopping unsteadily toward him and the statue of Abner was leaning at an odd angle.

"That way." Myron managed to say and was surprised he could speak at all. "Ferrel. There. Path. Take." He found himself pointing involuntarily toward the path that led to Ferrel's nest.

"Tanks," he heard Bruiser say and watched him take a deep breath before undertaking the long journey to Ferrel's.

Myron's knees were shaking and he felt light headed. He would have sat on the bench to pull himself together but the statue of Abner was leaning in that direction.

He watched Webster come down the path from seed school. He waved and said hello to Bruiser who was going in the opposite direction. He had several books tucked under his arm and Myron guessed this was story day at pre-seed school and thought how fortunate it was Webster had been gone while Bruiser was doing his destructive work in the library.

He watched Webster open the door to the library, step inside, and heard him exclaim, "Holy mackerel, what happened in here?" before closing the door.

TWO FEEDERS, NO WAITING

Roscoe liked the way his morning was starting out. He'd checked on the refreshment stand being built at the Big Rock and to his surprise, it didn't look as bad as he'd imagined. The owner had worked hard to make it blend into the surroundings. Having the *Seed-O-Rama* show here had opened new possibilities of holding other events in the area.

On his way back to the Clearing he'd swung by Bird Man's and was pleased to find both feeder tubes full of seeds and no gimmicks to contend with.

He was whistling when he entered the meeting room and did a series of dance steps as he made his way to his desk. He spun his chair around several times before sitting down. He'd just placed his feet on his desk and opened his planner to see what was next on his schedule when he heard someone ask, "Are you alone?"

He looked in the direction of the voice and squinted. He saw a figure in the shadows by the door. Whoever it was had placed something over the window and blocked out most of the light.

"Ferrel?" Roscoe asked and his question was quickly followed by Ferrel whispering, "Shhh. Bruiser might hear you."

"Bruiser?" Roscoe couldn't think of anyone in the Community named Bruiser.

"Will you keep your voice down?" Ferrel took a step toward Roscoe's desk before asking, "Did you see what he did to the statue?"

Roscoe shook his head no, he hadn't paid attention when he crossed the Clearing.

"Or the..." he stepped back in the shadows when the door to the meeting room opened.

"Roscoe, what's going on?" Webster entered the room and was obviously upset.

He was followed by his two assistants.

"We had to close the library." The first assistant said.

"Indefinitely." The second one added and wrung his paws nervously before continuing with, "Books on the floor."

"Tables turned over." The first one said.

It's a mess." From both of them.

"You have to get to the bottom of this." Webster slammed a paw on

Roscoe's desk in a surprising show of emotion. "Sure, we can straighten things up but what if whoever did this comes back?" He shook his head in frustration. "This goes way beyond a seed school prank."

Before Roscoe could say anything several members of the Committee rushed in the room.

"What happened to the statue of Abner?" the first one asked.

"It's leaning sideways and practically falling over." The second one tilted his body at an odd angle to demonstrate how far the statue was leaning.

"The bench should be declared off limits. I mean someone could be sitting there and..." The first one stopped and the second one finished for him. "Pow, Abner knocks them six ways from Sunday."

"Crushed."

"Pulverized."

"Incapacitated."

"Guys," Roscoe wasn't sure how long they could keep going so he cut them off with a wave of his paw.

While they were trying to explain what the statue of Abner looked like, others from the Community came in with questions about why the library was closed and who put the orange cone by the statue.

Soon the meeting room was so full there was barely room to turn around.

The last person squeezed in and asked, "Who's the cute little guy in the Clearing?"

If there would have been enough room, everyone would have rushed to the window and looked out but they were packed in like seeds in a feeder tube and had to depend on whoever was closest to the window to describe what was going on outside.

"I don't see any...hold on. Cute little guy? Long eye lashes? Looks like a fur ball?" the one by the window asked. "He reminds me of that doll that was so popular a few years ago. Baby SqueezeMe."

"That's him. He was out there earlier and said something about looking for a fewwet and asked where the libwawy was. I couldn't understand half of what he said." Myron worked his way through the crowd and stood next to Roscoe's desk.

Roscoe could hear the voices around him say, "Fewwet?" and try to guess who or what the stranger was talking about.

"It's me." Ferrel said weakly and worked his way closer to the front of the room. "He's looking for me."

Several in the crowd still hadn't made the connection between Fewwet and Ferrel.

"His name is Bruiser. He's the one who made the mess in the library and knocked the statue over." Myron was enjoying his few minutes of fame. "I was there. I saw it all."

The one standing by the window shook his head in disbelief and asked, "Are you sure we're talking about the same guy?"

Webster tried to push through the crowd and get outside, he'd teach this Bruiser character you don't mess around with his library.

"I wouldn't if I were you," Myron stepped away from the desk and grabbed Webster's arm. "I've seen him in action and, no offense buddy, but you don't stand a chance."

"I took a course in self-defense while attending library school, that taught us how to handle unruly patrons. I'm not completely helpless." Webster bristled at the suggestion that Myron thought he couldn't defend himself.

Myron nodded and said, "I'm sure," but didn't let go of his arm.

Suddenly Myron was the center of attention. Everyone wanted to know how this Bruiser character got into the library and if it was possible for someone his size to knock a three foot tall statue sideways.

Roscoe told everyone to quiet down and asked Ferrel, "Why is he here? This Bruiser character or whatever his name is."

Ferrel sighed and wished there was some way he could talk to Roscoe in private. He knew his idea of providing an alternate feeder for the Community was a good one but realized to late that going to Pete wasn't.

"Well, see, I had this idea about another feeder." Ferrel looked around and was surprised at how quiet the room had suddenly become. "And, to make a long story short, I needed someone to supply seeds." Everyone leaned forward, not wanting to miss a word he said. "So, I, ah, paid Pete O'Malley a, ah, visit."

The room exploded with talk as they considered the possibility of Pete and Stubs returning to the Community, they'd clung to the hope they'd never see them again.

"How does getting your seeds from Pete connect to Bruiser?" Roscoe couldn't see how the two things went together.

Ferrel shrugged, he had no idea.

"He was asking for you," Myron spoke up.

Ferrel started to correct him and say no, he was looking for someone named Fewwet but realized it was no use, they knew who he meant.

"Why don't you go out and see what he wants?" Roscoe suggested.

"Me?" Ferrel tried to take a step back but couldn't move because everyone was crowded around him. "Out there? With him?"

"See what he wants. Find out why he's here." Roscoe thought the reasons for him to meet with Bruiser were obvious.

Ferrel started to say the room was so crowded he didn't think he could get to the door but before he could, a path opened as everyone took a step back. They left enough room around the door for him to open it.

Ferrel tried to put on a brave face but failed miserably.

"Okay then, I'll just, ah, go out and, ah," he was helped along by encouraging paws until he was out the door and standing on the platform at the top of the stairs.

He started to go back inside and see if there was some other way of handling this when he heard the meeting room door close.

After a shaky trip across the platform, he made it safely down the stairs and was on the ground, standing in front of Bruiser. He wasn't sure if he should speak first and if he did, what he was supposed to say.

"Is you the Fewwet?" Bruiser asked in a way that sounded more like a sigh.

"I'm sorry I didn't…"

"I say, is you the Fewwet?" Bruiser spoke a little louder.

Ferrel had a decision to make. He could say, "Me? Ferrel? No. No. I'm Darrel. Ferrel moved to a different Community." But he knew that would only buy a day or two; Bruiser would eventually find out he was lying and he shuddered to think what would happen when he did.

So, he shrugged and said, "Yes, that's me, I'm Ferrel." He closed his eyes and tried not to think of what would happen next.

"Whewe want dem?" Bruiser asked.

"Dem?" Ferrel tugged nervously at the fur on his shoulder. "Where do I…you're….here to…deliver…" Ferrel felt light headed and tried but failed to hold back a giggle.

"Me say somethin funny?" Bruiser asked and Ferrel thought he heard a touch of anger in his voice.

"Funny? You say…no, no." Ferrel waved his paws hoping to wipe away any suggestion he thought something Bruiser said was funny. He was so relieved he wasn't lying in a heap beneath the leaning statue of Abner, he was having trouble thinking clearly.

"Seeds? Whewe delivew?" It took Ferrel a moment to figure out what he said and when he finally did, he decided to show him rather than give directions. He didn't want Bruiser to make a wrong turn, blame it on him, come back and turn him into a punching bag. "Follow me. I'll show you."

Bruiser made a gesture with his paw and four of his buddies, each carrying a large bag of seeds, stepped from behind the trees surrounding the Clearing.

As they walked along, Ferrel tried to point out the post office and the Senior Center but Bruiser told him to, "Shuts up, wes wunning wate."

Ferrel had been dreading this moment. Most of the seeds delivered by Bruiser were in the feeder tubes and the rest were stored safely nearby. He'd been prevented from signing up members of the Community to his *Two Feeders Club* because he'd failed to apply for a permit. He had no idea how many codes he'd violated at the location he'd selected for his business. He knew there were rules about how far apart and how high off the ground they should be but he hadn't bothered to check. He was sure someone from the safety team should have inspected the location and issued a permit to operate before he opened.

To make matters worse, the feeder tubes were filled with seeds he hadn't paid for.

What he didn't have were customers to pay for the seeds which, in turn, would allow him to pay Pete.

Bruiser had been by a couple of times. As usual he didn't say much but Ferrel was sure he was taking everything in and reporting back to Pete.

It was opening day for *Two Feeders, No Waiting* and so far he hadn't seen one curious Community member. He walked nervously around the trunk of the tree wondering at what point he'd made a wrong turn and started down the slippery slope to failure.

"I sees youse is opening for business, but like," Pete made a show of looking around before finishing his thought, "I aint seeing no business," His voice was the last thing Ferrel wanted to hear. Bruiser had said nothing about Pete being here for the grand opening. Then again, maybe he had and he hadn't understood him.

Ferrel knew word of Pete's appearance had circulated through the Community by now and no one would dare come to the opening.

"Did youse fail to publicate de days of youse inaugurals?" Pete asked as he walked slowly around the tree that held the feeder tubes.

"Yes, well, see, there are rules…" Ferrel stopped when he heard a snort from Pete.

"Rules, as my beloved father tolds me on numerous occasionals, is made to be broken. Has youse heard dat one?"

Ferrel wanted to say yes and so had every crook who was currently behind bars but he changed his mind and said, "Sorry, I must have missed it."

"Well, youse may wants to put dat in youse memories bank." Pete looked at the feeder tubes and then back at Ferrel. "Speaking as we has been about banks brings us to de questioning of payments for dem aforementioned seeds which, I am lead to believe, was delivered to youse by my good friend and associanate, the Bruiser."

Ferrel tried to remember if they'd discussed the terms of paying for the seeds but, with Pete standing next to him, he wasn't thinking clearly. He was sure if Pete asked, he wouldn't be able to remember his birthday.

"Stubby, what does de Ferret owe us?" After he said it, Pete turned and faced the parking lot.

"De Bruiser delivered four bags of seeds boss." Stubs was looking at a scrap of paper attached to a clip board.

"I am awares of de quantification of dem seeds Stubby, my

questionnaire was directed to the subject of what de Ferret owes us for the temporaneous use of dem seeds." Pete turned and looked at Stubs as he waited for the total number of seeds delivered to Ferrel.

"It's ah, well, let's see. Four bags with fifty seeds in each." Ferrel heard Stub's pencil scratch against the clip board as he mumbled, "Dat would be four bags with fifty…"

"Two hundred Stubs. The answer is two hundred seeds." Ferrel couldn't take it any longer. Stubs had grown quiet and other than his lips moving, was standing perfectly still.

"And, did youse informalize de Ferret here of dem late fees to which he has provisionally made agreementation?" Pete put his paws behind his back and started rocking slowly from side to side.

"No boss, I didn't add in no late fee because, as of today, he aint late." Stubs had a confused look on his face; he wasn't sure why Pete asked him about late fees.

"But Stuby, doesn't youse agrees with me de possibilitazation that the Ferret might be runnings a little late. Am I misinformationed about dat?" Pete stopped rocking and Ferrel noticed a change in his voice. The light, playful sound he'd heard earlier had been replaced by a more threatening one.

Stubs shrugged and said, "Sure, I guess but…" he stopped talking when he heard Pete say, "Stubby. I means, de Ferret has been opened for businesses for what, an hour, and I don't see no customers. Which leads me to concludes dat if the current trendification continues he aint going to sell no seeds today. Do you follow my trains of thoughtfulness here?"

Stubs had no idea what Pete was talking about but to keep from being yelled at he nodded yes and said, "Yeah boss. I follow youse," in case Pete had missed his nod.

After standing quietly for what felt to Ferrel like an eternity, Pete spoke again. "And you don't need to constructivate no visuable aides or nothing along dem lines to projectile that if his current sales patternization continues…" His voice trailed off and let Ferrel and Stubs come to their own conclusions.

Pete picked up where he left off. "So anyways Stubby, in the most recent past, what has we done to dem unfortunated folks who has failed to pay for dem seeds in what could be described as a timeless fashionable?"

Stubs wanted to say he couldn't remember what they'd done but shrugged his shoulders, and stalled for time. "Something pretty good I bet."

"What we has done in de past, in case youse is unable to recall from youse memorials, is to breaks a knee cap."

Ferrel let out a gasp.

"Oh dat, sure," Stubs said it like it was something that happened so often he thought Pete was talking about some other form of punishment like hanging him upside down from a tree limb and treating him like a piñata.

"And, continuing in dat same traditional Stuby, what if de same individualization fails to makes a payment after dat first rememberance?"

Stubs smiled because at last Pete asked a question he could answer. "De other one. Knee cap I means. Both." He stood quietly for a moment trying to catch up with a thought that had flicked briefly through his mind. He thought harder and finally had it. "Hey boss, how about we change de name of dis place to, *Two Kneecaps, No walking?*"

Pete thought about it for a moment and chuckled, "Dat's a good one Stubby." Then he grew serious. "To impress upon de Ferret dat we is not just joking around about de things of which we has been provisionaly speaking, perhaps you may demonstrate an exampling."

It took Stubs a moment to figure out what Pete asked him to do. When he did he said, "Sure, no problemo," and started moving toward Ferrel but stopped when he heard Roscoe say, "See, I told you he was open."

Stubs hid the club he was going to use on Ferrel's knees behind his back and stepped away from him when he saw the members of the Community of Abner walking down the path to *Two Feeders, No Waiting.*

Soon the area around the tree was crowded with eager customers, each wearing a gold bracelet.

As they stepped forward to take their turn at the feeder, they handed Ferrel a seed, some gave him two. Eventually there were so many seeds he had to get a bag to put them in. He stopped counting when he reached two hundred and handed the bag to Stubs. He was going to give the bag

TWO FEEDERS, NO WAITING

of seeds to Pete but discovered, in the confusion of everyone coming to his tree, he'd managed to slip away.

Stubs turned to leave but discovered Roscoe was standing next to him. "A Community looks after its *own* Stubs." He said it so only Stubs could hear.

Stubs looked at the ground and nodded he understood. For a fleeting moment he envied Ferrel. He knew better than anyone the number of times Ferrel had been willing to sell out every member of the Community for personal gain. He also knew of his ambition to become Chairman but here Roscoe was, helping him out of a jam and rescuing him from financial ruin and serious bodily injury.

Stubs said, "What youse has done, paying for dem seeds and all…" He was too choked up to continue so he stepped around Roscoe and hurried away, hoping to catch up with Pete before he'd gone too far.

Ferrel worked his way over to Roscoe and when he was sure no one could hear him said, "Thanks Roscoe, you got here just in time. He was going to…"

Roscoe waved him off like it was no big deal. He and the Community were willing to help their own even if it meant taking a risk with someone like Pete.

"Did you take the seeds from the Community reserve supply?" Ferrel grew serious. "If you did, I'll be happy to replace them." He stopped when he saw Roscoe shake his head no, they hadn't taken them from the reserve supply.

He looked at Ferrel and smiled. "It seems Bird Man has a feeder." He patted Ferrel on the shoulder before pointing toward a feeder tube and saying, "Excuse me but it looks like it's my turn."

SquirrelFest

Part 1: When the Acorn Is Ripe

"I'm telling you I can guarantee he'll be here. But, we have to act now if we want him. We can't piddle around and wait until the last minute like we usually do." Ferrel hit the table with his paw to drive his point home. The meeting of the SquirrelFest organizing committee was going into the fourth hour of the third day.

Half the Committee wanted to keep everything local, their experience with bringing in outsiders had not been good.

Ferrel had become the spokesman for the other side. Their point was, when you bring in outsiders you make a profit and the bigger the name the bigger the profit.

The one Ferrel wanted to bring to SquirrelFest was Shorty, also known as *The First Squirrel* because he lives on the lawn of the White House and has been fed by three different presidents. Few in the Community had any idea what a president was or why he lived in a white house but they'd all heard about Shorty.

"How can you be so sure?" Darin studied one of the brochures Ferrel had passed out. "A famous personality like Shorty is probably booked years in advance. Besides, I hear he's cut back to only a few appearances a year. Why would he want to come to Abner?"

"Okay, listen closely because I'm only going to say this once. I know somebody who knows somebody who heard another Community I'm not at liberty to name canceled so there's an open spot in his schedule."

Ferrel leaned casually against the wall, proud that he was separated from someone as famous as Shorty by only two unnamed sources, three at the most.

"Guys like Shorty don't come cheap." Norman usually went along with Ferrel but he was having trouble with this one. "You have to pay to get them here. Then you have to provide a place for them to stay, and you don't stick a guy like Shorty in just anybody's nest."

"Hello! Your losing focus here folks." Ferrel was back on the attack. "As usual you're getting bogged down in the details. First we decide if we want to take advantage of this once in a lifetime opportunity and then we work out the small stuff." Ferrel looked at the confused faces of the Committee members, wondering if this was the time to hit them with his strongest argument. He decided it was. He walked over to the meeting room window, looked out, and said as if divulging a well kept secret, "I hear the Community of Ben is thinking about signing him up."

"Where did you hear that?" Norman leaned forward, shocked by the news that another Community might snatch Shorty right out from under their collective noses.

"I can't, at this time, reveal my source but let me just say, it's reliable." Ferrel knew he had them. He had no source. He knew nothing of the plans of the Community of Ben. He had discovered that a space exists where truth ends and a lie begins and built his nest there. For him, this was just another negotiation and if you want to win you say whatever you think will work.

The motion to bring Shorty to this year's SquirrelFest passed six to one with Roscoe casting the only no vote. There was little doubt in his mind where Shorty would be staying during SquirrelFest, his nest.

Normally that would be okay, entertaining important visitors went with the job of being Chairman of the Committee, but, according to Doc, that was about the time Penny Sue would deliver their first child. They'd talked it over and wanted the moment when the baby arrived to be personal and private. They had no desire to share the experience with anyone else, especially someone he'd never met regardless of how famous he was.

Roscoe closed the meeting room door and walked down the stairs. He was trying to think of a way to get around sending the invitation to Shorty, as Chairman he had to sign it before it was mailed. He was so deep in thought he almost bumped into an upset Arlene and the small group gathered around her.

"I want to know what you're going to do about it Roscoe." She folded her arms across her chest and planted her feet suggesting she was not going to move until she got an answer.

Roscoe sighed and wished Community members with complaints would develop the habit of letting him know what they're talking about before demanding some kind of action from him. He was pretty sure her complaint had nothing to do with bringing Shorty to SquirrelFest.

"Arlene, if you will tell me your problem, perhaps I can…" is as far as he got. Leon, a friend of Arlene's stepped forward. "They practically knocked her off the feeder, that's what she's talking about."

Roscoe turned to Leon. "Did you actually see…"

"Those delinquents from seed school are always hanging around the feeder causing trouble." Leon was on a roll. Roscoe knew what was coming next. "Why back when I was their age we were taught to respect our elders," he shot a glance at Mildred, "I mean, the more mature members of the Community."

"If you'll just tell me what happened I might…" Roscoe was trapped with Arlene on one side and Leon on the other. He was getting dizzy turning his head from Arlene to Leon and back to Arlene. He felt like he'd become a victim of a tag team match, one would pummel him for awhile and then the other would take over.

"I told you it wouldn't do any good to bring it up," Arlene was addressing the group behind her. "Do you remember me saying that? It's all about youth now a days."

Roscoe heard someone at the back of the crowd ask, "What did she say?" and someone answer, "Youth."

"Arlene, I would love to help you but first you have to fill out a complaint form and after the safety team investigates the matter they will bring it to the Committee." Roscoe knew it was hopeless, she would never fill out a form and why should she? No one else did. Besides, it was easier to catch him outside the meeting room and lodge her complaint in person.

Arlene fixed Roscoe with a look. He'd seen it before and braced himself for what was coming next. "Edgar didn't require forms when he was Chairman."

Those behind her nodded they agreed.

"He didn't need a safety team running around doing his dirty work," Leon's voice grew louder. "It was just us, Edgar, and our complaint. Nothing in between. If he was still Chairman he'd go out there and whack 'um real good."

Roscoe knew it wasn't true, Edgar seldom, if ever, did anything when he was Chairman. But he gave the appearance of doing something, that was his secret. If they approached him with a problem like this, which Roscoe still didn't understand, he would have been outraged at the conduct of young squirrels today. He would shake his paw, his face would become red, and he would pace angrily back and forth in front of the one who lodged the complaint. He would agree that kids today have no respect for their elders and should be whacked regularly for no reason at all. In fact, the complainer got the impression that as soon as they finished talking, Edgar was going to lead the way to the feeder, catch the pranksters in the act and deliver the first blow.

The person with the complaint would walk away feeling that Edgar had moved their problem to the top of his to do list of and get right on it. But, Roscoe also knew Edgar would wait until they were gone, go into the meeting room, close the door, and read the latest issue of *The Abner Echo*. He'd sit back, pleased he'd dodged another situation that required action on his part. Most of the time the problem would clear up on its own so no one knew if he'd done anything about it or not.

Roscoe couldn't do that. If he said he was going to do something he did it regardless of the consequences. He made a mental note to get back with Arlene when she'd calmed down, he was sure they could work something out.

He stood at the base of his tree not sure if he had the energy to make it to his nest. Three and half days of planning for the SquirrelFest with no end in sight, had left him feeling exhausted.

Ferrel, on the other hand, thrived on meetings and seemed to gain energy the longer they dragged on. While other members of the Committee were nodding and fighting sleep, he became energized. It was only by the narrowest of margins most of his ideas were defeated. But, each one took time to explain and discuss so, since he'd become a member of the Committee, their meetings often ran late into the night.

All Roscoe wanted to do was climb in bed and get some sleep. This was his first celebration of SquirrelFest as Chairman and he had no idea it required so much work.

He walked quietly across the nest and slid in bed next to Penny Sue. He'd just closed his eyes when he heard her say, "I've been thinking about names."

Roscoe yawned. "If Ferrel is one of them, you have my permission to remove it, no questions asked." He hoped that would end the discussion of names on a light note. He'd be happy to talk about it in the morning but not tonight, he was beat.

"I've always liked Lydia." Quiet followed and he felt the bed shift as she turned and looked at him. "Roscoe, we can't put it off any longer, we need to decide on a name."

"Can this wait until morning? I'm exhausted. My mind has turned to mush." He fought to keep his eyes open.

His reply was met by an uncomfortable silence. He thought she would understand that he would be more alert and attentive if he could get some sleep first.

He heard a sigh followed by a whimper from her side of the bed. As the date for their child's arrival drew closer she'd become like this, happy one moment, in tears the next.

Roscoe sat up. "Okay," he said through a yawn and scooted closer to her, "what have you got so far?"

"Well like I said, Lydia." Any sign of hurt feelings was gone. "But then I also like Doris, which is my mother's name."

"Hold on a minute," Roscoe did his best to sound cheerful, "I haven't heard a boy's name."

"Oh dear, you're right, I just assumed it would be a girl." She thought for a moment before asking, "Do you have any boy's name's in mind?"

"Well there's always Roscoe Junior, you know, keep the old family name going, but, I've never been fond of Roscoe, there has to be a better name than that."

They stopped talking when they heard scratches on their tree and soon Darin was standing next to their bed.

"Sorry to interrupt Penny Sue but if I could talk to Roscoe for just a second." Before she could answer he continued. "I was looking at the way we have the floats lined up for the parade. I think we should move the safety team to the front, that way if there's a problem, they're not stuck in the middle like they were last year."

Roscoe shook his head. "Darin, could we talk about it in the morning? Penny Sue and I were discussing children's names even though the baby won't arrive for another two weeks." He didn't know what else to say.

"Oh, sure, no problem, it can wait I suppose. I just thought as Chairman, you…" He stopped when Edgar climbed over the side of the nest and joined Darin beside the bed.

"I heard voices and thought it might be Doc." Edgar seemed surprised to find Darin there.

Edna, Edgar's wife, entered the nest, hurried to Penny Sue's side of the bed and asked in a concerned voice, "Are you okay dear?"

Roscoe couldn't see her but he knew Penny Sue was pouting. He probably shouldn't have said the part about their child not arriving for another two weeks. "Penny Sue I'm sorry, it's just that I'm worn out. I have to get some sleep."

"If you're thinking about names, you may want to consider Edgar," Edgar said quietly, "it's been in our family for quite a while."

"Oh don't be silly," Edna cut him off, "this child is going to be special so she needs a special name. My mother's name was Lavinia, but there's no easy way to shorten it. They tried calling her Lav or Inia but it didn't catch on"

"I'm telling you Edna, she needs to be thinking about boy's names. Our side of the family has boys." Edgar felt he needed to get the name business back on track.

"I like Sarah," Darin volunteered, "but there are a lot of Sarah's in the

Community at the moment. It's funny isn't it, years go by and there's no Sarah and then boom, we've got three of them."

Another figure stepped in the nest. "Somebody said it was time. How far apart are the contractions Penny Sue?" Doc stood beside the bed and reached for her wrist to take her pulse.

"Deborah is a wonderful name." Edna was still thinking of girls names. "Our Doreen. A name that starts with D is supposed to bring good luck."

"Rubbish," Edgar grunted, "pure rubbish."

"Hey," Darin shot back, "it's worked okay for me."

"Just breath normally Penny Sue, there's no reason to be alarmed." Doc was going through his false alarm routine, trying hard not to embarrass the patient. He patted her paw and said sympathetically, "It happens in the best of families."

Roscoe left the nest and climbed to the place in his tree where three tree limbs come together. He desperately needed sleep and it was obvious the activity in his nest would go on without him. He was about to drop off when he sensed someone standing near him. He opened his eyes far enough to see Ferrel's face, inches from his.

"Ferrel if it's about the SquirrelFest, it's going to have to wait." Roscoe felt like he was drugged, he couldn't seem to get his words in order. He tried but couldn't remember what they'd been talking about.

"Whatever you say Roscoe." Ferrel sounded hurt. "I just thought you should be the first to know." He waited, debating if he should go ahead and tell him or put it off until morning when he would make the announcement to the Committee. He couldn't wait any longer and blurted out, "We got him."

"Got who?" Roscoe heard himself ask but wasn't sure why.

"Who? Who do you think? Shorty. I have the contract and he's signed, sealed, and delivered." He waved some papers in front of Roscoe's half closed eyes.

Ferrel waited for a response from Roscoe. Great would be good he thought. Super or fantastic would be a notch above great. Instead, Roscoe rolled over on his side and fell asleep.

Once the plans for SquirrelFest were finalized everyone got busy on their assigned task.

Webster and several members of his staff worked on the float for the Library. This year their entry was in the shape of a big clock with the words, *Take Time to Read*, where the numbers usually were.

Sparky was called in to solve a number of technical problems. The push to win the *Best In Parade* trophy caused competing groups to use more moving parts.

In the midst of the confusion, Arlene would show up at Roscoe's office and say loud enough for everyone to here, "Well, I see nothing has been done about the problem at the feeder, **yet.**" Or, "If Edgar was still Chairman the problem at the feeder would be over by now."

Before Roscoe could reply, she would turn on her heels and stomp out of the room.

Ferrel had volunteered to make the Committee float. When he was finished he hoped to create what he thought the White House looked like; one room, painted white, and perched on a green lawn. He'd made an opening in the front of the float where Shorty would sit and wave to the crowds. A sign on each side of the float said, *Hail to Shorty, The President's Own*.

At least, from Roscoe's point of view, conditions had improved at his nest. They'd agreed Roscoe Junior was too much of a burden to place on a youngsters shoulders, so has name was removed from the list. So was Edgar's, although they hadn't told him yet.

They were leaning toward Robert if it was a boy. It provided some options like Robbie, Bob, or Bobbie.

But, when Roscoe suggested the same thing would work for a girl, Penny Sue was outraged and said, "Roberta? Our daughter? You're kidding, right? If it weren't for Roberta I would have been the fourth cheerleader selected for the *Find the Nut* team my final year at seed school. I will not name our daughter after someone who cheats."

He decided the safest thing to do was to keep his thoughts to himself and just listen to the names she came up with. Then he would say something noncommittal like, "Interesting," or, "I would have never thought of that."

The day before SquirrelFest Roscoe found a worried Ferrel waiting on the steps to the meeting room. He asked if there was something wrong but Ferrel shook his head no and said he just stopped by to check out his float and could see it better from the platform.

He followed Roscoe inside and sat down heavily on the wooden bench beneath the small window.

After clearing his throat several times he said, "Roscoe, I hate to be the bearer of bad news but, you have a problem." Ferrel refused to look at Roscoe. Instead, he fixed his gaze on a worn place on the floor.

"Which problem is that Ferrel? Right now I have a number of them." Roscoe leafed through a stack of letters that had come in the morning mail.

"Your Shorty problem," Ferrel shot back but refused to look at him.

"My Shorty problem? How did it suddenly become my Shorty problem? You said it was taken care of? I believe your exact words were, 'he's signed, sealed, and delivered.'"

"I knew you'd twist it around to make it look like it's my fault. The Committee voted to invite him you know, it wasn't just me." Ferrel picked at something on the top of the bench.

"But your friend of a friend who knew somebody said it was a sure thing." Roscoe wasn't all that upset, he hadn't been in favor of having Shorty come in the fist place and found he was enjoying Ferrel's discomfort. "He signed a contract, he can't back out."

"Right," Ferrel hesitated. He'd considered waiting for the morning of the parade before saying anything. "I've been doing some thinking and as far as I know, nobody around knows what Shorty looks like."

"And?" Roscoe had worked with Ferrel long enough to know whatever he was thinking would straddle the line that separates fact from fiction.

"And," Ferrel hesitated, "I know this guy who looks so much like

Shorty he could be his twin brother. At a distance, you can't tell them apart."

"Forget it Ferrel. We are not going to stick some stranger out there and say he's somebody he's not. You're going to have to let this idea go." Roscoe left his desk and walked to the door.

"Did I say anything about having my friend act like he's Shorty? You must have come up with that on your own Roscoe." Ferrel stood and paced in front of Roscoe's desk. "But you know, it just might work. His name is Morty, so it wouldn't take much to change the name on our float. And, I didn't say who the presidents were or what they were presidents of."

"Ferrel, forget it. It won't work." Roscoe turned to leave. "Now, if you'll excuse me, I have to pay Arlene a long overdue visit."

"Okay, okay." Ferrel followed Roscoe out of the room. "I know this other guy who…"

Roscoe finally tracked Arlene down, she was playing cards with some of her friends at The Senior Center. He waited until she looked up. "You got that problem taken care of yet?" She asked as she smacked a card down and picked another one from a pile in the center of the table.

"That's why I'm here Mildred, I want you to tell me what's bothering you." Roscoe moved to her side of the table.

"Did you bring one of your little forms for me to fill out?" She said sarcastically as she studied her cards.

"No forms Mildred. No waiting in line. No safety committee. I've come to hear it from you." He pulled a chair over and sat down next to her.

She took a card from those in her paw and handed it to the person sitting next to her; she was torn between telling him what was wrong and staying mad. Finally she decided it would be better for everyone if she just came out with it.

"It's the kids from seed school, the boys mostly. Playing around. Running up and down the feeder pole. Showing off in front of their friends. Throwing seeds at everyone like there's no tomorrow. I mean, you get a mouth full of seeds and they zip past you so fast you can barely hold on to the feeder tube and chew at the same time."

"Tell him about their attitude," one of those at the table told her.

"Oh, right, that's another thing. Instead of waiting in line for their turn like they're supposed to, they sit on top of the feeder pole and stare at you. Sometimes I get so nervous I can't eat."

"Did she mention them running up and down the pole?" Another at the table asked.

"I think she did, yes." Her partner answered.

"And staring?"

Her partner nodded yes, she'd covered that as well.

Roscoe thought for a moment and an idea fell in place. "I may be able to come up with something but it will take a few days. So, give me a little time, okay?" Roscoe stood and put the chair back where he got it.

Arlene looked at him and smiled. "Thanks Roscoe. I'm sorry to be such a, well, you know…worry wart."

Roscoe gave her a reassuring pat on the shoulder then left The Senior Center, cut across the Clearing, and took the path that leads to seed school.

"I'm sorry to hear about trouble at the feeder but this is not the first time it's happened you know." Principal Charles told him after hearing Arlene's complaint. "It's mostly the first years. They're trying to get attention, you know how that goes, we've all been there. They've got all this energy and there's no place for it to go."

Roscoe nodded. He thought back to his fist year at seed school and had to admit he wasn't the ideal student by a long way.

Principal Charles continued. "The other thing is there's not that much for them to do. Second and third years are busy on projects or practicing with the *Find the Nut Team*. Most of the first years haven't found their place yet."

Roscoe smiled. "I have an idea that might solve that problem."

Roscoe and Principal Charles talked as they continued down the hallway to the first year classroom.

Harold Finebender, known to the Community of Abner as Seed Man, stood at the sliding glass door that opened to the small porch of his downtown condominium. He poked at an anemic looking tomato plant and poured water around its withered roots. It's no use, he told himself, to try to grow something where there's no shade and whose leaves and roots were in direct sunlight ten hours a day.

Life at the *Uplifted Arms Condominium* had been a frustrating experience for him. He found no interest in shuffle board night, or movie night, or make your own taco night; all activities planned by the condominium events coordinator, Captain Welch.

Sweetheart, on the other hand, loved every minute they'd been there. She enjoyed shopping in the stores near their condo. She ate lunch with her friends in one of the many quaint restaurants in the area known as *Old Centerline*.

Seed Man's experience had been the opposite of hers. He left for work before most in the condo had their first cup of coffee and normally didn't return until after they finished supper. Because he lived so close to work, he'd become the one to finish all the left over tasks so the other employees at *Finebruners Fine Writing Instruments* could leave early enough to beat the traffic headed to the suburbs.

It wasn't just the extra hours at the store or the failure to make friends at the condo that bothered him. At the top of his *Things To Worry About* list was the fact that their house hadn't sold. Their Realtor assured them before the ink dried on the contract they signed the first offer would roll in. "Mr. Finebender," the Realtor had told him with absolute certainty, "it's a sellers market and with the beautiful yard and the woods in back of your house, an agent still wet behind the ears could sell a place like this in a New York second."

Most of those who toured the house had been his neighbors, curious to see how they'd arranged their furniture or what they were asking for the place.

The only serious offer was made with the condition that Harold cover his garden with concrete so the purchaser could practice shuffleboard between the cruises he and his wife took.

The extended stay provision in the contract for the condo allowing the purchaser to back out of his commitment within the first three months without paying a penalty was a few days from expiring. The owner of the complex was so sure everyone would be won over by the Olympic sized swimming pool and air conditioned workout room they wouldn't consider leaving.

Harold knew if he didn't make a decision soon he'd be locked into the condo while still making payments on their house. But, whenever he brought up the idea of leaving the condo, Sweetheart would change the subject or refuse to talk about it.

He lifted the pot containing the tomato plant and checked for some sign of life but, as far as he could tell, it was dead. "And," he mumbled as he went to the kitchen and lifted the lid on the trash basket, "so am I."

He dropped the plant in the trash and tried to remember how to get to his bedroom.

Part 2: It Will Fall from the Tree

Roscoe sat up in bed and three things hit him at once. First was the sound of the SquirrelFest gong, struck at daybreak by the youngest member of the Community. The tradition of the youngest person rising early and hitting the gong had been going on for as long as he could remember.

The second thing was that someone was standing at the base of his tree and calling his name. At least it sounded like his name. "Foscoe? Or Boscoe?" Roscoe heard whoever was there holler and mumble, "I can't see a thing down here, it's too dark."

The third and final thing was the realization that Penny Sue was not in bed. That in itself was unusual because she was normally a sound sleeper.

He looked around and finally found her sitting in the rocking chair. "Penny Sue?" He whispered.

He heard a whimper.

He got out of bed and walked over to her.

He heard the voice from below call again. "Frisco? Is this your tree? Ferrel said I was supposed to look you up." Roscoe tried but couldn't recognize the voice.

He knelt beside the rocking chair. "What's going on Penny Sue?"

She squeezed his paw and answered in a shaky voice, "I'm not sure. Something...I feel...funny."

"Should I get Edna?"

TWO FEEDERS, NO WAITING

"No, no, It's just…different." She was quiet for a moment then sat straighter and said, "It's probably nothing."

Whoever had been calling from below suddenly appeared at the edge of their nest.

"Not now!" Roscoe said firmly and didn't move from his place next to Penny Sue. "Go to the Clearing. Look for Ferrel. We're busy."

"Oh, sure, sorry, I was ah…" Whoever it was said, "Sorry," again and left.

"You have a lot to do today with the SquirellFest and everything. I'll be okay." Penny Sue forced a smile.

"I'll get someone to stay with you. I don't want you to be here alone. I'll send them over." Roscoe was torn between his responsibility to the Community for making sure SquirrelFest ran smoothly and his concern for her.

He heard her moan and take several quick breaths. It sounded to Roscoe like she was in pain as she slowly exhaled. He could barely see in the early morning light but he thought he saw her nod she was okay.

"Nice going Roscoe. Of all the rude behavior I've heard this takes the nut cake. If it hadn't been for some fast talking on my part we would have lost Morty." Ferrel climbed into Roscoe's nest without being invited. He was so focused on his float and the possibility of losing Morty, he was unaware something was going on between Roscoe and Penny Sue.

"If you say another word Ferrel, I will personally throw you out of my nest." Roscoe stood and was about to take a step toward him when Penny Sue groaned. She was trying to be brave but the last pain really hurt.

Ferrel understood immediately what was going on, he had a child of his own. "Ah, no problem Roscoe. Sorry about the ah… Should I get…" He pointed in the direction of Doc's office.

Roscoe didn't bother to ask Penny Sue and nodded yes.

He heard Ferrel hurry down his tree.

He could tell from the noise coming from the Clearing those in the parade were anxious to start. The were waiting for him to strike the gong and declare this years SquirrelFest was officially underway.

He whispered, "I have to go, it won't take long." She nodded okay and gripped his paw, another pain he figured and waited until she let go. "It will only take a few minutes. Five tops. I promise."

As he hurried across the Clearing he saw the float from The Senior Center. Arlene was fluffing the paper and tucking it under the throne made from a discarded lawn chair. "*Queen For A Day,*" was printed across the front of the float and outlined with seed hulls.

"Arlene, I hate to bother you but Penny…" he stopped when he saw the silver tiara on her head. He remembered reading in *The Abner Echo* that she'd been voted queen again this year. He knew she was moments away from taking her place on the throne and receiving the cheers of an admiring Community. The float from The Senior Center was always the first one in line.

"What is it Roscoe? You look terrible." She turned from the float and studied his face. "It's Penny Sue isn't it?"

"Well she's, oh, never mind, they're beginning to move and you…" Roscoe wasn't sure what to do. Nothing in his past had prepared him for a situation like this. He'd been an only child and had chosen *Keys to Successful Nest Building* instead of *And Baby Makes Three-Adventures In Family Living* during his third year at seed school. He hated to rob Arlene of her few minutes of fame but when it came to helping expectant mothers through a successful delivery there was no one in the Community like her.

"Oh dear," she put a paw to her lips and said with certainty, "it's time." She reached beneath the throne and grabbed her purse. "Don't worry about a thing, I'll be there in less than a minute."

He watched gratefully as she hurried across the Clearing toward his nest.

"Roscoe they're waiting. You can be late for a lot of things but you never want to be late starting a parade." Edgar grabbed his elbow and pulled him past the line of floats and up the steps to the platform.

He stopped when he saw Doc hurry up the path towards Bird Man's yard.

"Now where on earth is he going? He's supposed to be at the emergency tent." Edgar started to holler and tell him he was going the wrong way but stopped when he saw him make a quick left and veer off the path toward Roscoe's tree.

TWO FEEDERS, NO WAITING

"Whoa. Hold on. Wait just a minute. Does that mean what I think it means?" Edgar was on his toes, keeping Doc in sight as long as he could. "Am I about to become…"

"What's holding things up?" Alice, the chairperson of the Women's Auxiliary asked. "I've got six first years boys from seed school over there," she nodded toward her float, "and they're getting pretty antsy. Let's get this show on the road." The float for the Women's Auxiliary was called *Equality* and showed a boy and girl working together planting a tree. The boy didn't look up, afraid if he did, his friends would recognize him and never let him forget about it.

The Women's Auxiliary had insisted, in keeping with the theme of their float, that the young person hitting the gong early this morning to announce it was the day of SquirrelFest be a female.

"She's due, Penny Sue I mean. Any minute now." Edgar spoke to Alice but kept an eye on the path to Roscoe's nest.

Alice stepped forward, took the paddle from Roscoe's hand, and hit the gong. "Parades started," she announced. "Follow me." She went back to her float and motioned for the first year students pulling her float to turn around and follow the path to Roscoe's.

Members of the safety team, marching at the head of the parade, heard the gong but missed the change of direction. They started off toward the Big Rock as they'd practiced but hadn't gone far when they heard the calls from spectators telling them to come back. They swung around, and tucked in behind the last float.

Soon all the floats were parked so close to his tree, Roscoe had trouble finding a way to get to his nest.

While he slowly moved forward he realized their plans of having a quiet, personal time when their baby arrived had been wishful thinking, it looked like every member of the Community was here.

He was walking past the *Abner Echo* float *(If You Heard It From Someone, They Probably Heard It From Us)* when he heard a squeal come from his nest. He stopped and grabbed the edge of the float for support. "It's here," he thought. "Is it okay? Is Penny Sue all right?"

His thoughts were interrupted when Doc leaned over the side of his nest. Everyone around the tree stopped talking and looked up, anxious to hear what he had to say. He didn't have to ask them to be quiet because everyone was holding their breath.

"Well, I'll tell you what," that was Doc's usual way of announcing a birth. Most of those standing beside their floats had heard it at least a dozen times. "The good news is the population of Abner has just increased by one." He waited for a moment before continuing and everyone leaned forward, afraid they'd miss what came next. "The bad news for the teachers at seed school is, they've got another boy in class."

Everyone cheered and reached out to pat Roscoe on the back or try to shake his paw.

A boy, he thought to himself, we have a boy.

Edgar moved along side of him and put a paw on his shoulder. "I told you Roscoe my side of the family has…" he stopped when he heard another squeal. Was that different from the first one? Roscoe tried to remember.

Doc appeared at the side of the nest again. "I hate to say it but I made a mistake a moment ago. That happens sometimes in my line of work. Not often mind you." He put a paw to his chin as if trying to remember the last time something like this happened. He looked at the crowd and said, "Why I remember once…" he stopped when they hollered for him to quit fooling around and get to the point.

"Let's see where was I?" Doc scratched his head. Moments like this didn't come along very often for him so when they did, he knew how to make the most of them.

The crowd cheered when Arlene appeared at the edge of the nest holding two babies, one tucked carefully in each arm. The tiara she'd put on for her ride in the parade was pushed to the back of her head.

"Oh yeah," Doc said. "There is another one isn't there?"

Everyone laughed. "Just think," they said to each other, "two boys have been added to our Community."

Doc looked at them. "Well, who said the second one was a boy? You didn't hear it from me. Because, unless my eyesight has completely failed, the one on the left, that would be your right…"

"Cut it out Doc, just tell us what we've got." Marvin hollered up to the nest and those around him roared with laughter.

"Well, if it's not a boy, it has to be?" Doc put a paw to his ear.

"A girl." The crowd exploded with joy. Everyone was laughing at Doc's performance and excited about the addition of two new members to the Community.

They froze when they heard another squeal. Edgar tightened his grip on Roscoe's shoulder.

Doc appeared at the edge of the nest. "Sorry folks, that was just me fooling around," he said without breaking a smile. "That's all there is but from my point of view, two at one time is enough for any couple." He stepped away and went back to check on Penny Sue.

Everyone laughed at the joke he'd played on them.

Edgar relaxed his grip and when Roscoe looked at him, there were tears in his eyes.

"The circle remains unbroken Roscoe," Edgar whispered not wanting to lose the importance of the moment. "Some small part of me will go on after I've…" Edgar stared at the ground, lost in thought.

"If I'm not mistaken," Roscoe spoke quietly so only Edgar could hear, "there are a couple of kids up there who are going to need your help."

Edgar blinked a few times then shook off the melancholy that had crept in and darkened his mood. His eyes were brighter and he stood straighter. "Of course," he said trying to keep the excitement out of his voice. "Someone needs to take them to the feeder for the first time. And walk them to seed school."

Roscoe had a hard time keeping up as Edgar pushed his way past the floats parked around his tree.

He was about to follow him to his nest when he heard Jules call his name. He looked up and saw him running down the path and waving his arms excitedly. After making it through the maze of floats he stopped to catch his breath.

"I'm sorry Jules, but whatever you've got to say can wait. Community business almost ruined my joining ceremony and caused our honeymoon to be cut short. I am not going to allow it to keep me from spending time with my…"

Jules nodded, agreeing with everything Roscoe said. "Right. I understand. But I thought as Chairman you should be the first to know. The second I guess, since I…"

"Jules!" Roscoe waved his paws cutting him off and letting him know whatever he had to say could wait.

He's back!" Jules blurted out before Roscoe could stop him. He hadn't been at Roscoe's when Doc announced the arrival of the twins. He'd been in such a hurry to tell Roscoe the good news he hadn't noticed the floats parked beneath his nest.

Roscoe put a paw on his tree and was ready to climb up and see his children but stopped when Jules asked, "Don't you want to know who's back?" The tone of his voice had swung from the excitement of being the first with the news to the disappointing thought that someone had beat him to the punch.

"Okay Jules but please make it quick. Who's back?"

"Seed Man." Jules was back on the emotional mountain top, knowing for sure he'd been the first to see the moving van in the driveway.

"You mean Bird Man don't you? Bird Man is back?" Sylvia had told Marvin her owner had gone on vacation.

Jules shook his head and slowly repeated the news, "Seed. Man. Is. Back."

Roscoe felt a wave of relief. If what Jules said was true, the worry of having enough seeds to make it through the winter was over. In the past, Seed Man had made sure their needs were met if he had to walk through snow or rain to do it.

He gave his friend a hug and apologized for the way he'd acted before he delivered the news.

When Roscoe finally made it to his nest he saw Edgar standing in front of Penny Sue and the babies. He held a crumpled piece of paper in his paws, slipped his glasses on, and cleared his throat.

"On this historic day," he began, "new life has come to our Community. As I reflect on my years…"

Edna stepped forward. "Put a seed in it Edgar." She took him by the arm and pulled him away to make room for Roscoe.

TWO FEEDERS, NO WAITING

"...historic, ah" Edgar fumbled with his hastily written notes. "New life to the, ah," Edna's interruption had caused him to lose his place. He tried to continue, "Bright future," but Edna kept moving him toward the edge of the nest.

"Let the two love birds spend a little time together as a family." Edna could be persuasive when she needed to. "We've had our moment Edgar, let them have theirs."

"But Edna, I stayed up all night working on this tribute." He held the paper up for her to see. "I mentioned you and when Penney Sue came to stay with us. And here's the part about her first trip to Squirrels Of Fun."

He was still talking as Edna led him down the tree and away from Roscoe's nest.

A roar went up from the crowd when they saw Edgar.

Roscoe heard Edgar say. "On this historic day new life has come to our Community." He stopped when he heard Edna clear her throat. He panicked and announced nervously, "Let SquirrelFest begin." He waited a moment before adding, "Again."

Doc quietly gathered his things. "Well, my work here is finished," he said quietly not wanting to wake the sleeping children. "Arlene, how about sharing a cup of walnut tea at The Senior Center before turning in? My treat."

Arlene nodded okay and her tiara wobbled. She patted Penny Sue on the shoulder and gave Roscoe a hug. "Congratulations," she whispered, not daring to say more. No matter how many deliveries she'd assisted Doc with, each one caused her to tear up.

Roscoe heard Doc tell the crowd to go back to the Clearing and leave the kids alone. "You'll be seeing enough of them before long."

The members of the safety team quietly directed the floats back to the Clearing.

Soon all the visitors had gone and a welcome silence descended on their nest.

Roscoe crossed the floor and knelt beside their bed. "I am so proud of you Penny Sue, they're perfect."

She smiled briefly and then her face became serious.

Roscoe started to go the edge of the nest to call for Doc to come back.

"I'm fine Roscoe." She laughed at his reaction. "Besides, Doc can't help us with this problem." She looked at him.

"Problem?" He was stunned to learn that somehow, on the best day of his life a problem had crept in. "What problem? I don't understand."

"Names silly. We picked out a boy's name and a girl's name but not a boy and girl at the same time name."

Roscoe was relieved. After dealing with the SquirrelFest Committee for the last four weeks, the thought of naming two children sounded like a walk to the feeder.

Hours later, after trying dozens of names and changing and helping feed the babies, he realized how wrong he'd been.

He sat in his chair, took his daughter in his arms, and began to rock. It had been a wonderful day. The SquirrelFest had been a success even if the floats hadn't followed the course it had taken weeks for the Committee to work out.

Jules announcement that Seed Man had returned meant the Communities seed problem was over.

Best of all, on top of all the good things that had gone on, he was now the father of twins. He didn't think anything could destroy the joy he was feeling at the moment.

He let his eyes close for a second and opened them when he became aware someone had entered his nest. He assumed it was Edgar, coming back for one last look at his grandchildren before turning in for the night.

Or maybe it was Doc stopping by on his way home to make sure everything was okay with Penny Sue.

The last person he expected to see was Ferrel.

He watched him tiptoe across the nest and crouch down next to the rocking chair. He took a deep breath before whispering, "Roscoe, you've got a problem with Morty. He wants to be paid the appearance seeds you promised before he leaves."

Roscoe started to say he'd had nothing to do with bringing Morty to the Community, it had all been Ferrel's doing.

Instead, he laughed when he realized to the list of blessings he'd received today he'd add Ferrel's name.

TWO FEEDERS, NO WAITING

Like it or not, Morty was going to have to wait because for just once, and Roscoe was sure he'd be forgiven by the Community for doing it, he was putting his family ahead of Committee business.